DATE			

HUCKLEBERRY FIEND

Also by Julie Smith

DEATH TURNS A TRICK (1982)
THE SOURDOUGH WARS (1984)
TRUE-LIFE ADVENTURE (1985)
TOURIST TRAP (1986)

HUCKLEBERRY FIEND

JULIE SMITH

THE MYSTERIOUS PRESS

New York • London

The Mysterious Press, 129 West 56th Street, New York, N.Y. 10019

Printed in the United States of America
First Printing: October 1987
10 9 8 7 6 5 4 3 2 1

Library of Congress Cataloging-in-Publication Data

Smith, Julie.
Huckleberry fiend.

I. Title.
PS3569.M537553H8 1987 813′.54 87-14053
ISBN 0-89296-237-2

For Jon Carroll, Paul's mentor

The author's sincerest thanks to Bob Hirst and Michael Frank of the Bancroft Library, to Todd Axelrod of the American Museum of Historical Documents, and to my long-suffering Virginia City companions, Brian and Aliza Rood

CHAPTER 1

Why destroy her face? Such a nice face. A freckled, wholesome face that I liked enough to look at every night. (And did most nights.) She'd been shot once in the right cheek and once in the forehead, as well as twice in the chest and once in the neck, as if the killer had gone berserk.

She'd been around six months and she was already Miss Popularity—nobody didn't like Rebecca Thaxton. But she'd opened her door to someone she must have known, someone who'd apparently followed her quietly into the living room, as if for a cup of tea, and then blown her away.

* * *

In the obvious grip of the willies, Sardis turned off the news and cracked open another beer. "It must have happened so suddenly."

"Maybe she said the wrong thing. Like, say, 'I've met someone else.'"

"Brittleness doesn't become you, dear."

"How about this? 'I'm in love with your husband.'"

"Save it for your incredibly lucrative books." She was getting sniffy.

"Please leave my personal finances out of this."

"Rebecca wasn't that kind of person."

"We don't know that." All we really knew was that she was a TV reporter with lots of vitality and intelligence, yet also with a sweetness and freshness that kept you tuning in. That's why Sardis didn't want to think ill of her. But she'd snapped at me because hunger was making her mean. We'd been unpacking boxes without a break for hours, and it was getting on towards dinnertime.

Fortunately, we couldn't have picked a better neighborhood for the ritual moving-day meal. "Let's go get a pizza," I said. "Oliveto, Guglielmo's, Zachary's, or the Buttercup?"

"What's the difference?"

I'd been briefed by a neighbor. "Zachary's is Chicago style, Guglielmo's is regular, and the Buttercup has a wood-fired brick oven—it's over the Berkeley line. But Oliveto's supposed to be the best."

"Oliveto it is then."

I placed the order on my brand-new phone while Sardis went up to her place for a quick shower—we'd made the big decision to buy a house together, but not the bigger one to live together. For us, being neighbors was a big enough step. We'd bought a duplex.

We were going to have a lot less privacy than we were used to, but at least we wouldn't have to tackle the problem of whose turn it is to do the dishes. And other messy stuff that comes up when people share a household.

The truth was, I'd sort of wanted to give it a shot, but Sardis didn't think I could handle it. Didn't think *I* could handle it! I ranted for about half an hour and then holed up to sulk for a week and she had the nerve to say she rested her case. The arrogance!

Then there was the matter of our work. I was writing my not-so-lucrative books when I could afford to, but mostly free-lancing to support my habit. Sardis was painting when she could afford to, but also free-lancing as a graphic designer. Emotional considerations aside, we genuinely weren't sure we could manage all that in the same house.

Yet we could get a much better deal if we bought one together. Sardis had been saving for years and I had insurance money. I'd actually managed to buy a miniature house once—back when I was getting union wages as a reporter for the San Francisco *Chronicle*—but I'd lost it in a fire. Now I had enough for a similar house, but my cat was sick of tripping over me.

By pooling our money, Sardis and I could get a real, adult-sized abode instead of two dollhouses, or worse yet, a couple of chintzy condos. Especially if we bought outside of San Francisco. So once we'd hit on the duplex solution, we still had to face the trauma of uprooting ourselves from the city.

Suburbia was out—either too expensive, like Marin County, or too Middle America, like Contra Costa. That left Oakland, the jewel of the mysterious East Bay. And a bitter pill to swallow. Or so we thought. A casual drive down the main street makes you think you've fetched up in Anywhere, U.S.A., only with a few porn palaces. And that was about the extent either Sardis or I knew of the place. We were pleasantly surprised to find dignified old neighborhoods, suitable for aging artistes.

And of course dear old Berkeley, transformed in twenty short years from Revolution Central to a hotbed of social rest, was just blocks away, now harboring enough wood-fired brick pizza ovens for all of Sicily and half of Calabria. That is, if Italy went in for gourmet take-out, which was the current way of life in Berkeley. I'd spent four years there as an undergrad, and could hardly recognize the place anymore. It was going to be fun to rediscover it.

Funny, when I thought about it, all those years in Berkeley and I'd ventured into Oakland only now and then, say, to buy a shirt at Capwell's or catch a movie at the Grand Lake. And here I was living just over the line in the Rockridge neighborhood, oddly familiar and foreign at the same time. The familiar part was College Avenue, which ended up right at the campus; the foreign part was the tameness, the quiet domesticity of sixty-year-old two-story single-family dwellings with nicely tended gardens. It was nothing like San Francisco and nothing like the East Bay I was used to. It would probably be a great place to write if I could get used to the quiet.

It was certainly a great place for an evening stroll to the neighborhood pizza joint. On the way, we picked up a bottle of cheap and delicious California red at Eddie's Liquors and an Arnold Schwarzenegger movie at Home Video. The future was showing a lot of promise: we'd eat, drink, rot our brains with Arnold, make love, and sleep the sleep of those exhausted in a good cause. In our very own house that we didn't even have to live together in.

"Oh, no. Not pizza!" The voice came from our brand-new porch, where no one had a right to be passing judgment on our dinner choice. Where, in fact, no one had a right to be. Sure enough, it was a burglar.

I'd met Booker Kessler on a story, back when I worked for the *Chronicle*—a yarn about how a kid from the right side of the tracks got into burglary. Booker was in analysis to get the big picture, but he was pretty sure it had something to do with the fact that his mother had left his dad for another woman when he was in junior high. We had a few things in common, Booker and I—he'd also been an English-lit major at Cal and was one of the few people who'd indulge me in pedantic conversations about books. But I hadn't found that out until we'd known each other a while. We'd become friends, I think, because I was frankly fascinated by his career choice and he was flattered by that. Also because I was one of the few people with whom he could be himself. He told most people he was in real estate so naturally they thought he dealt dope.

"Why stand on ceremony?" I said. "Why didn't you just pick the lock?"

"I wouldn't do that." He looked hurt. "I brought housewarming gifts."

"In that case, come in for some wine—since pizza isn't good enough for you."

"It's not that. I just wouldn't want to get pizza gunk on what I brought."

"The presents?"

"Something else. I'll show you after we eat." We agreed, but only because we were starved. Booker's whole body was in perpetual motion. He kind of swayed his shoulders and tapped his foot and bobbed his head, as if he were coked to the gills. He was excited about something and I didn't think it was our new digs.

He went to his car for the gifts while Sardis and I set up. I brought out my interim Cost Plus plates, and set my round oak table—the one nice piece of furniture I'd bought since the fire. Sardis dripped wax onto a saucer to serve as a candleholder.

"You may want to reconsider that," said the returning Booker. He spoke to Sardis, but handed me a package. In it were a pair of antique pewter candlesticks, perfect for my table and a most curiously sensitive gift for a burglar to give a member of the Private Eye Writers of America. He had an eye, that Booker, no doubt the result of all the nice homes he saw in his work. "For romantic dinners with Sardis," he said. "And by the way, I actually bought them."

Sardis leaned over to kiss him for the sentiment, but he waved her away. "After dinner. When I give you yours."

We went through the pizza like the Cleveland Wrecking Company. After a couple of glasses of wine, the moving aches were beginning to leave my back and legs. If I'd resented Booker's intrusion on the evening, I didn't any more. Pretty much anything was okay with me now.

Booker said, "Time for show and tell. Let's clean up and put the wine away."

He'd hit on just about the only two things that weren't okay. "Give me a break."

"Okay, okay. We don't have to clean up. Let's just leave our glasses here and go in the living room a minute."

"What on earth is so precious we can't even have wine in the same room with it?"

"Trust me."

He took two ordinary shoeboxes out of a paper bag and

opened the top box with such ceremony I half expected a toy snake to pop out, or maybe a live frog. But there was nothing the least bit unruly in the box. Just a pile of what appeared to be old letters. The paper was half-sheet size, covered with a clear, expansive handwriting, a handsome script that emphasized roundnesses and fullnesses. Leaning over my shoulder, Sardis read the first couple of lines, "You don't know me, without you have read a book by the name of 'The Adventures of Tom Sawyer,' but that ain't no matter. The book was made by Mr. Mark Twain, and he told the truth, mainly . . ."

I got instant goose bumps. It began to occur to me that the pages were far too uniform and there were far too many to be letters; also that I saw no salutation. And finally, that the first two lines of *Huckleberry Finn* were a damned funny thing to put in a letter. In fact, there seemed only one appropriate place for them. And Booker was a rabid Mark Twain fan who was also a burglar. I was suddenly horrified at what he might have done. "What the bloody hell is this?" I blurted in a tone that accused, tried, and convicted.

"Hold on," he said. "I didn't steal it. That is, I did, but only sort of accidentally. I don't *know* what it is, dammit! What does it look like to you?"

I spoke cautiously: "Like an old handwritten copy of *Huckleberry Finn*."

"It's not the whole thing—less than half, in fact. But what makes you think it's a copy?"

"It *couldn't* be the real thing. Could it?" The words came out sounding scratchy. Could I possibly have Mark Twain's original manuscript in my house?

"I wish I knew." He sounded defeated. "I was up staring at it half the night—just the first page, sort of—I didn't dare paw the thing." He spoke with reverence, then rue: "Much as I wanted to. Finally I remembered about you."

I hadn't a clue what he meant by that, but first things first. "Where did you get this thing?"

"You know I'm in analysis."

We nodded.

"I'm trying, you know, but there's still a few dumb childish things I can't seem to quit doing."

When neither of us mentioned the obvious, he kept talking: "After Mom left, Dad spent a few years in mourning, and then he lived with a nice woman for a while, when I was in college. But lately, he's been chasing young stuff. He goes out with all these women my age. Younger even, sometimes. How do you think that makes me feel?"

"I should think you'd be happy for him."

"Some people might. But you've gotta remember, I'm fucked up."

Sardis gave it a go: "It must make you feel left out. And sad probably."

I had a better idea: "And kind of like burgling, I'll bet."

He looked sheepish. "He's been dating this Japanese stew named . . ."

"Sukiyaki?"

". . . this Nisei flight attendant—Isami Nakamura. Nice girl about twenty-three; two years of college, probably; no intellectual pretensions. But nice, like I said." He shrugged. "I don't know; something came over me. I hit her last night."

"You mean you broke into her house—and found *this?*"

"Yes. But I don't think it's hers. It was in her roommate's closet—another stew named Beverly Alexander."

Sardis said, "Flying's a good job for smuggling. What's the airline?"

"Trans-America. A new no-frills one that only flies to New York."

"Oh."

I just couldn't take it in. The original Huck Finn in a flight attendant's closet? I said: "It must be a fake. Or maybe just a copy."

"Who'd copy it? It can't be that. Now, it *could* be a forgery . . . but I'll tell you something. That thing gives me goose bumps."

I knew what he meant.

"Suppose it *is* the real thing—then what was Beverly Alexander doing with it? I'll tell you what—almost certainly something criminal. Maybe she stole it from some collector—

somebody it really meant a lot to. Or listen, maybe it belongs to a university. Maybe even Cal. They've got a huge Mark Twain collection."

"But if something this important had been stolen, wouldn't it be news?"

"Maybe not. If you stole it, maybe what you'd do is, you'd hold it for ransom. The insurance company would quietly pay off—some sum less than it would cost them if the manuscript were lost—and the police would never come into it."

"Wait a minute, Booker—are you thinking of collecting some ransom money yourself? Or maybe just making a simple sale?"

"I can't believe you said that."

"Said what?"

"I just can't believe you don't know me well enough to think a thing like that. In the first place, if I had any original Mark Twain manuscript—not even Huck Finn, which must be worth hundreds of thousands—I would never sell it. Never, never, never. I'd keep it and cherish it, and love it . . ."

"And honor and obey it."

"Oh, can it, McDonald—you know how much I love my paintings? I'd trade all of them for that. If it's real." Booker had a spectacular art collection—probably not worth hundreds of thousands, but he did dote on it. "The thing is, it's not right, don't you understand? Just because I'm a burglar, do you think I don't have any morals? If that's a genuine Mark Twain manuscript, I personally feel it should be in a university library, where everyone can see it. But if it belongs to a private collector, I figure it's someone who knows how to appreciate it. And I want it returned."

"You want it returned." I'd been a bit slow on the uptake, but there's no predicting the twists and turns in people's private codes of ethics. I, for one, could never understand why Sam Spade felt he had to avenge the partner whose wife he was happily boffing. Booker's position made a damned sight more sense than that; I just hadn't seen it coming.

"I do," said Booker. "And I'll pay you to do it for me."

"Why not do it yourself?"

"I'd rather not be associated with it—due to my eccentric line of work."

"What if it's authentic, and Beverly's the rightful owner?"

He shrugged. "Then give it back. For all I know, she's a Mark Twain scholar who saved up for it by high-altitude hash-slinging. I wouldn't deprive her."

"But why me?"

"You know why you. You're an investigative reporter—of sorts, when you get off your ass. And you've got the time. And you need the money."

"How much?"

"What do you charge for free-lancing?"

"Forty-five dollars an hour."

"I'll make it fifty-five, with a five-hundred-dollar minimum. I mean, say the thing turns out to be worthless, and you find out in half an hour, and then mail it to Bev. You'll still get the five hundred. But if you need a month to work on it, take it."

"Done."

Sardis said, "Okay. Now where's my present?"

"Already installed," said Booker. "But don't worry, I didn't force the lock." He held up a fistful of keys and picks.

CHAPTER 2

If Booker ever quit burgling, he had a great career as a decorator. Sardis's gift was a small tree (*ficus benjamina,* according to the proud owner) and it made all the difference in her living room.

Having climbed the stairs to see it, we had no strength left for the Schwarzenegger movie, and barely enough to make it to the bedroom, where we collapsed in a pitiful heap. I dreamed blissfully of life on the Mississippi, and found you feel mighty free and easy and comfortable on a raft. I was smoking my corncob pipe, trailing toes in the water and feeling all warm from the sun when the idyll turned into a horrible nightmare. A hideous harpy suddenly swooped from the sky and tore the very pipe from my mouth. Soaring again, she opened her talons flat-out, showing each gleaming claw in the light and dropping the pipe in a gesture of utmost contempt. Then she dive-bombed, beating me with her wings, soaring again to reconnoiter. She laughed the laugh of the Wicked Witch of the West and shrieked in the voice of Margaret Hamilton: "I'll civilize you, young man!" And I knowed, as Huck would say, who she was; not to mention who she warn't: not the witch and not the Widow Douglas and not Aunt Sally nor Aunt Polly nor Miss Watson. She was Sardis.

Fully awake and staring at the ceiling, I wondered what on earth I'd have dreamed if we *had* moved in together. Something told me Sardis had been right not to push things. I lit out for the Territory.

My own personal territory, downstairs. But certainly not because of that thoroughly silly and childish dream. I can't imagine what my unconscious was thinking of and hasten to say it in no way reflected the views of the management.

I left because I couldn't get back to sleep and didn't want to wake Sardis with my tosses and turns. I made myself a cup of hot chocolate and repaired to my living room-cum-everything-else to sip it. And there before me, reposing in a couple of common shoeboxes on my ugly coffee table, lay the mystery manuscript.

Booker had had the forbearance not to touch it through an endless night of longing and staring. And he had actually forbidden wine in the same room with it. Surely only a hooligan and a Philistine would finger it with a cup of hot chocolate at hand. But I was like a teen-ager pumping hormones—absolutely unable to keep my mitts off.

What a beautiful hand it was written in. The very definition of "flowing." It seemed to have a kind of motion of its own, as if the author were writing and thinking at the same felicitous rate. Flipping through, I saw hardly any changes. Here and there a word or a paragraph crossed out; that was all. Could anyone write so well in first draft? Still, Mark Twain had been a journalist. I knew from experience one chance was all you got in that life. Maybe he'd just gotten used to it.

I settled back with the first shoebox. I'd come to a decision and I only regretted it wasn't as properly respectful as Booker's had been. On the off chance that I actually had in my hand what I considered America's greatest novel, penned by the actual hand of America's greatest novelist, humorist, and possibly journalist (if you didn't care much for facts), I was going to damn well read it. Perhaps a bit of genius would fleck off.

Mumbling "Damn the torpedoes!" I poured brandy into my hot chocolate. By sun-up, I'd been through both shoeboxes, about four hundred of the little half-sheets, and I was in a perfect haze of delight. Sleepy and sated. Thinking, "God, that last scene was great!"

It was the one where Huck goes into town to put up handbills for the king and the duke and old Boggs rides in, "drunk and weaving about in his saddle," sassin' and cussin'. "I wisht old Boggs'd threaten me," says one of the rustics, "cuz then I'd know I warn't gwyne to die for a thousan' year." Old Boggs, alas, doesn't live out the hour—he's shot dead for his insults by the arrogant Colonel Sherburn.

So sad when Boggs's sixteen-year-old daughter throws herself on her dead father. So funny when people start elbowing for a peek at the corpse: " 'Taint right and 'taint fair, for you to stay thar all the time, and never give nobody a chance; other folks has their rights as well as you."

So thoroughly satisfying.

And so was the two-hour nap I grabbed before it was time to go over to the Cal library and ask some questions. Drinking coffee, I pondered. I had to think up a whopper for the scholars and it had to be plausible. I could say I was doing my dissertation, but I'd be unmasked as a Twain ignoramus in seven seconds. Or was it Clemens ignoramus? I didn't even know how scholars referred to the great man. Ah, but then it came to me—there was one kind of researcher with a license to know nothing. I hunted up my old press card.

By ten o'clock I was at the library, following the fourth-floor signs that said "Mark Twain Papers." I knew what was there: a $22-million collection of notebooks, correspondence, and other treasures, most of them given to the university by Clemens's daughter, on the condition that it publish them all. I was glad when I came to a door that would have foiled the Barrow gang—scholars could be so careless.

The one inside wasn't opening up to just anybody. She sang out (as Huck would say): "Who is it? Do you have an appointment?"

"Paul McDonald from the *Chronicle*. I was just taking a chance I could talk to someone."

"Sorry. The general editor's on vacation."

"I'm not picky. How about a specific one?"

"Could I ask what this is about, please?"

"I don't think I ought to yell it through the door. What about if I go downstairs and call you on a pay phone?"

"Oh, never mind." She opened the door and stepped out. "I'm Linda McCormick. May I see your press card?"

I showed it to her. "Are you the one?"

"I beg your pardon?"

"The specific editor."

She laughed uneasily, as if not sure I was joking. "I'm the best you're going to get, at any rate. What can I do for you?"

"I'm doing a story about manuscript collecting."

"God. Have you come to the right place." She stepped aside and let me in, leading the way down a hall lined with pictures of Mark or Sam. To tell the truth, I preferred looking at her.

Though she wore a rather shapeless and loosely belted dress, I could see movement inside. I liked her face even better. She was thirty-five perhaps, had dark curly hair and looked a little sleepy. Sleepy-looking women always inspire me to picture them on a pillow. Picturing Linda, I was actually a little overwhelmed at how impressed I was.

When she sat me down across from her, I saw that her eyes were a lovely hazel and rather smeary, which was probably what caused the sleepy effect. One of the endearing things about academic women is that they never quite seem to learn their way around a makeup kit.

"I gather from your response that a lot of people collect Twain. Or should I say Clemens?"

"Anthony Burgess said, 'T.S. is the only Eliot and George Eliot is an unabbreviable pseudonym, like Mark Twain.' That more or less reflects the views of the senior generation. Around here, we tend to say Clemens, but we don't think 'Twain' is terrible, the way our forefathers did. As a matter of fact, the old boy even signed some letters 'Mark.'"

"If you can't trust the man himself—"

"But then he stopped. Perhaps the recipients didn't much

care for it." I could have sworn the way she looked at me was the least bit flirtatious. She blushed a little, too, but perhaps that meant she was embarrassed about losing her train of thought. "I'm sorry," she said, "you asked about collecting. It's kind of a hot thing, actually. The letters alone sell for a thousand dollars a page. Actually, that might even be a little low."

"And the manuscripts?"

She gave me an intimate look. "Megabucks."

"How about the biggie?"

"Huck?"

I nodded.

"A sad story about that one. Part of it's lost. The Buffalo Public Library has the rest."

"What part is known to exist?"

"Oh, about the last three-fifths. Except that's not quite right, because some of the material is from the front of the book. He wrote the first two-fifths mostly in 1876—up to about the middle of Chapter 12, and including most of Chapters 15 and 16. The part they have at Buffalo is the middle of Chapter 12 through 14, and from Chapter 22 through to the end."

"He went back and put some stuff in later?"

She nodded. "The Walter Scott Episode and the King Solomon Debate."

I couldn't remember either from earlier readings, and certainly hadn't read them the night before. I was getting goose bumps again. "He wrote in longhand?" I asked.

"Oh, yes. But being extremely modern, he did have his books typed for the printer. The printer's typescript is missing as well."

"So what they have in Buffalo is a holograph."

"Yes. By the way, there's a published facsimile of it."

I tried not to jump off my chair.

"Do you have it, by any chance?"

"Can you cure warts with spunk-water?"

I must have looked blank, because she flushed again. "A little joke. From *Tom Sawyer*."

"It's coming back to me. I prefer the dead-cat method."

She smiled. "I can send the facsimile to the reading room if you'd like to see it."

"I'd love to. I think I'm getting a hook for my story."

"Oh?"

"I think I'll build it around the lost part of the Huck Finn manuscript, and what would happen if it turned up."

"Ah." I was beginning to figure her out. She said hardly anything except on the subject of Twain, and plenty when she got on that.

"What do you think *would* happen?"

"Everyone would want it, of course."

"How much would it be worth?"

She shrugged. "If you figure it at the going rate of letters, you'd have to say conservatively a thousand dollars a page."

"It would probably be about four hundred pages, wouldn't you think?"

"Maybe five hundred." (I knew better, of course.)

"So maybe half a million dollars?"

"Well, it might depend. A partial manuscript is worth a great deal less than a complete one. Unless the Buffalo Library wanted to sell—and that seems *very* unlikely—there'd be no chance of completing it. So in the end, maybe it wouldn't fetch more than $250,000."

"That sounds fairly low, considering."

She nodded. "Absolutely. After all, we're talking about *Huckleberry Finn*."

"'All modern American literature,'" I quoted, "'comes from one book by Mark Twain called *Huckleberry Finn*. . . . There was nothing before. There has been nothing as good since.'"

She nodded again to show she knew the quote. "Hemingway wasn't the only one who thought so. I could show you people who'd probably kill to own a thing like that."

"Veritable Huckleberry fiends."

"Oh. You know about us."

"I beg your pardon?"

Once more she flushed in that appealing way she had. "Nothing. I was just surprised you used that phrase. The point is, you just can't imagine the amount of reverence and hero-worship and *cultism* that's grown up around this man. I could introduce you to people who'd give ten years of their lives if they could just spend an evening with him."

"But what would they give for the long-missing Huck Finn holograph?"

"Who knows? But I think $250,000 is cautious. Certainly that much. Maybe as much as a million."

"How would you get such a thing authenticated?"

"If you were smart, you'd come to us—that's what the best dealers do. But a lot of people just don't bother."

"What! Why wouldn't they?"

She put up her palms in simultaneous frustration and puzzlement. "I guess they just don't want to know. A dealer once said to me, 'Put it this way, Miss McCormick—if you found a nugget that weighed a ton, would you want to know it was fool's gold?' "

"He must have read *Roughing It*."

"That's mostly about silver." She spoke automatically, her heart not really in it. I could see she was feeling downcast about the authentication problem.

She pushed over two copies of letters from Mark Twain—the same words, but different dates. One was written on letterhead from the Bohemian Club in San Francisco. "Look at the date," said Linda.

"Eighteen eighty-three."

"He left San Francisco in 1866, returned briefly in '68, and never went back after that."

"Maybe he had some leftover stationery."

She shook her head. "Look at the blue lines."

She had drawn diagonal lines from the left-hand margin to the right-hand one, a few inches down the page. "Compare the two documents," she said, "and note that the lines cross the same letter of the same word in each one. The one dated 1875 is genuine. It's possible Clemens copied it later on Bohemian Club stationery, but not with every letter lined up exactly as it was before. That's far too precise to be real. This one's a forgery. But it's one of the few times a collector's bothered to check. Unfortunately, he did it as an afterthought."

"So he's out of luck."

"Not necessarily. If he wanted to, he could probably unload it for what he paid or more."

"It's that bad, is it?"

She shrugged. "People are stupid."

"What kind of paper did Mark Twain write on?"

"Half-sheets, usually. Why don't I send you a sample of the real thing along with the facsimile? I know—'1002.' "

"What's that?"

She smiled a scholarly and secretive smile. "Probably the worst story Clemens ever wrote. But he finished it about the time he finished Huck, so the paper and handwriting ought to be similar."

I left Linda with reluctance, but that's the way things are done at the Bancroft Library, the noncirculating collection of which the Mark Twain Papers are a part. You may examine documents or books only in the reading room, and before you go in, you must check your belongings in a locker, bringing in only a pencil or typewriter. Absolutely no pens. I liked that about the place—it made me feel as if the collection were being well taken care of. I also liked the idea that anyone over eighteen could use the library, not only Cal students and graduates. Anyone off the street could walk in and examine a rare, important manuscript. But of course hardly anyone wanted to.

I did, though. It surprised me how much I looked forward to holding papers that this time I knew, without a doubt, Mark Twain had written with his own hand.

When the facsimile and the story finally came down, I was so excited I couldn't decide which to look at first. I settled, finally, on the story, and almost fell on the floor when I saw it. The cream-colored paper was the same thickness, size, and color as that of the manuscript I had at home. The clear, expansive handwriting was unmistakable.

Just to be sure, I pulled out the one-page Xerox I'd brought. Booker's manuscript couldn't—just couldn't—be other than the real thing. There was simply no way. I knew instantly why collectors didn't bother to have documents authenticated. You just *knew.*

I turned to the facsimile, placing my Xerox over the first page—exactly the same size! I started to read: "Well, it being away in the night, & stormy, & all so mysterious-like . . ." That didn't sound right. It should have picked up after Colonel Sherburn shot old Boggs. This seemed to have to do with finding a wrecked steamboat. But then, out of some dusty corner of memory, I remembered the name of the steamboat—*Walter Scott*. It was the insert. Clemens had numbered it "81 A-1," the "A," I supposed, meaning exactly what it does now—"add" or "addition." The add ran sixty of those tiny pages, and the next numbered page was 160. The first sentence began like this: "They swarmed up the street towards Sherburn's house . . ."

Before I went home, I tried to read the story, but, frankly, I was too excited. Its whole name was "1002: An Oriental Tale," and it purported to be Scheherazade's version of a lost manuscript. A good idea, but I honestly can't say whether I agree with Linda that it's the worst thing the great man wrote. I wondered if, up in the Mark Twain Project, new editors had to take a few months to inure themselves to handling such things. It had been different in my own living room when I didn't really know what I had. Here, I just couldn't calm down.

I managed to read enough pages—and also to look at enough of the facsimile—to give me an idea. On these, as on the pages I had at home, the author had changed very little. On the typescript of the Oriental Tale, which Linda had also sent, he had changed a lot more.

After turning in the materials, I gave Linda a call. "Paul!" Her voice was pleased, no doubt about it. "I enjoyed our talk."

"Me too. You were nice to give me so much time."

"Nonsense. I felt badly it couldn't have been longer. Maybe we could continue later."

I realized with surprise that this had suddenly become a full-blown flirtation. And why not? I wasn't a bad-looking guy, for a bearded and bespectacled bear. And I suppose I *had* been looking at her in rather an interested manner. "I'd like that," I said. "Maybe we could have coffee. Meanwhile, though, I've got another question. Did Twain make a lot of revisions on the printer's typescript?"

"Absolutely. That's why the typescripts are so important to scholars."

"So the hypothetical Huck Finn holograph ought to be slightly different from the book as we know it."

"Oh, yes."

All I had to do was compare—but my copy of the book had burned with my house. "Say, Linda," I said. "I need a new copy of Huck. Which edition should I get?"

"Ours, of course."

"The new one, you mean. But aren't there several other UC Press editions?"

"There *is* no other edition." She spoke severely.

"What about the 100th Anniversary Edition?" This was quite a famous one, launched with much fanfare.

She made a noise that sounded oddly like a snort. "Little-known fact: They left the last line off."

Heading for the bookstore, it occurred to me I was learning lots of little-known facts. I couldn't even imagine how a university press had managed to leave the last line off of any book. Yet there it was. The Mark Twain Library edition (the one Linda called "ours") had it, the other one didn't: "The End, Yours Truly Huck Finn." Sold.

Comparing book with manuscript, I was rewarded on the very first page, where Huck tells part of the plot of *Tom Sawyer* and then says: "Now the way the book winds up, is this: Tom and me found the money the robbers hid in the cave, and it made us rich."

In manuscript, the sentence read like this: "The way the book ends up is this: Tom and me found the gold the robbers hid in the cave, and it made us rich." The author had added the "now," changed "ends" to "winds," and "gold" to "money."

I read on. And found many more discrepancies. And was convinced: If this wasn't the real thing, I was the King's Camelopard.

CHAPTER 3

I started to understand the appeal of collecting. What a thrill to have these papers in my house, knowing that the great man's thoughts had come out of his head and down his arm and out of his pen and spilled onto them!

I was consumed suddenly by the same compulsion Booker had felt—to get this thing back to where it belonged. Unfortunately there was only one person I knew about who was likely to know where that was—Beverly Alexander. But perhaps not so unfortunately—just because I had property stolen from her bedroom didn't mean I couldn't talk to her. Perhaps I could say I was from the Bancroft Library and I'd heard she had the manuscript; if she were legitimate, that ought to prod her into sobbing out her tale of woe. If she weren't, I'd be able to tell from her reaction.

I liked it. Since she would have no idea who I really was, I wouldn't be putting myself in any danger. She wouldn't know where to find me, but if I needed to, I could investigate *her* to my heart's content. To make it work, though, I'd probably need a disguise. Nothing too elaborate—maybe I'd wet my hair and slick it down, take off my glasses, stick a pillow under my jacket. Ah—and put something in my cheeks to fill them out. That would alter the shape of my head, face, and body, so that, from a distance, anyway, I probably wouldn't be recognized right away.

I felt it absolutely necessary to call on her—she might sob out a tale of woe on the phone, but I was never going to get any idea of what she was like if I didn't meet her. And I confess to an overwhelming curiosity about what sort of flight attendant would keep a priceless manuscript in her closet. So I wet down my hair and stuck a pillow in my jacket, though, in the end, I couldn't bring myself to wear cheek fillers.

Like Sardis and me, Isami and Beverly shared a duplex—only they shared it with the upstairs tenants as well. It was a square stucco building in the Noe Valley, painted a depressing aqua that had caught and held the dirt of ten or a dozen years. I whipped off my glasses as I mounted the stairs, transforming myself into Langhorne Langdon of the Bancroft Library's Mark Twain Project. (If Bev were a Twain scholar, the name would give me away as a fraud, but that was part of my master plan—she'd grow increasingly upset and give *herself* away as she caught on that I'd combined Clemens's middle name with his wife's maiden name.)

A female voice answered my knock: "Who is it?"

"I'm looking for Beverly Alexander."

The door opened instantly. Behind it stood a very pretty, very scared looking young Japanese woman. And behind her stood the last person in the world I'd expected to see, or wanted to see, or for that matter, could in any way tolerate seeing. "Paul McDonald. Do come in," said Inspector Howard Blick of the San Francisco Police Department. "Got a pillow in your jacket?"

Damn Blick! The most irritating thing about him was that I never understood his insults. Was he accusing me of being fat or letting me know I wasn't exactly a master of disguise? The former, I thought, and had half a mind to fling open my jacket, letting the pillow fall zanily at his feet. But the thing was that Blick was a homicide inspector; his presence indicated this was no time for hilarity. I said: "Howard. What a surprise."

"Get your butt in here." The next most irritating thing about Blick was that he was unnecessarily bossy, but the worst thing about him—going far beyond mere irritation—was that he had the brains of a ball-peen hammer. I'd known him since my days on the police beat, when I could incur his orangutan-like wrath merely by using words he didn't know in my stories. Arcane stuff like "the" and "as."

Not wanting to even a little bit, but knowing better than to try to flee, I got my butt into the hallway. "You a friend of Beverly's?"

"A friend of a friend."

"You still goin' out with the gorgeous Kincannon thing?"

Kincannon thing? I wanted to hit him, which was the idea, I guess. Due to an unfortunate matter occurring some months earlier, he knew Sardis and he knew a lot better than to call her a "thing." Especially to me. But I just shrugged noncommittally, proud of myself for not taking the bait. "I mean," said Blick, "here you are at Bev's and everything." He turned quickly to the woman. "Do you know him, Miss Nakamura?"

He spoke so sharply she winced. A headshake was all she could manage. He turned back to me. "Beverly's dead, dildo. Somebody offed her last night."

"Don't call me dildo, shithead."

"I said she's dead, asshole."

"No need to swear about it, fuckface." I was walking a very fine line here. Probably if I called him one more name Blick was going to start reading me my rights, but I figured I could get that last one in. "Impolite to the lady."

"McDonald, what the fuck are you doing here?"

I said: "Miss Nakamura, you'll have to forgive him. He's under stress." She jumped as if I'd sneaked up behind her.

"You know her? McDonald, how do you know these ladies?"

How indeed? It was the very question I was struggling with. Ah, but I remembered something. "We haven't met, but you mentioned her name yourself, Inspector." I turned to Isami. "Miss Nakamura? Paul McDonald. I'm very sorry to hear about your—about Beverly." I was playing for time, trying to think up some plausible story, and it was finally starting to come to me.

"McDonald," said Blick, "I'm runnin' out of patience."

"Okay, okay. I got a message on my machine. It said, 'This is Beverly Alexander. You don't know me, but I'm a friend of a friend.' Something like that."

"What friend?"

"The lady didn't say."

"Go on."

"She gave me this address and asked me to meet her here this afternoon about a possible story for the *Chronicle*."

"Yeah? What story?"

"She didn't say."

"She didn't say? McDonald, you so poor you come to somebody's house you don't know on the off chance of making fifty, a hundred bucks?" He looked totally disgusted. "How's your book sellin', huh? Finally got one published after all these years. Hollywood called yet?"

I stared at him with unadulterated hatred. This was my weak spot, this business of never knowing where Spot's next can of Kitty Queen was coming from.

Blick made his voice even lower and nastier. "Even you ain't hard-up enough to do a crazy thing like that."

The whole thing was pissing me off—he was right, even I wasn't. But he had me in the position of having to pretend I was even more embarrassingly poverty-stricken than I actually was. Meaning he got the best of me whether I told the truth or I lied. I lied, of course: "I was curious."

"When did she call, dildo?"

"Yesterday. She was killed last night, right?"

"How the fuck do you know that?"

"Howard, I'm really afraid I'm going to have to ask you to watch your language. Miss Nakamura—"

"Answer the fucking question!"

"You said so. A minute ago."

"Oh, hell. Get your ass out of here, McDonald."

I was history, as the young people say, almost before he'd

finished speaking. And on my way to the chic Russian Hill digs of Booker Kessler, boy burglar. If I knew Booker, I was pretty sure he wouldn't be alone—in the event he was home at all—but I was too shaken up to care.

It was a good five minutes before he answered the door, and when he did, he was wearing only a pair of blue jeans, obviously just pulled on, which meant I could see and marvel at his skinny, freckled chest with its five or so scraggly hairs. His reddish head hair was mussed, and he looked approximately seventeen and a half. In fact, the little runt was at least twenty-six, and the scourge of San Francisco's singles bars. Considering his thorough and phenomenal success with women, it was amazing the twerp hadn't had a crimp put in his enthusiasm by some jealous husband or swain. In fact, the whole thing was amazing; I wished he'd answered the door naked so I could have seen whether he was hung like a Clydesdale, which would have explained things.

"Paul, I didn't expect you." He was trying his best to be welcoming. "Would you like to come in?" His tone said he'd prefer I turned into a frog.

"Afraid I have to, buddy. Beverly Alexander's dead."

He looked alarmed.

"Murdered."

"Excuse me a minute." He started to walk out of the room, and then apparently remembered something drummed into him by his mom in her pre-lesbian days. "Sit down, okay? Have a beer."

The beer seemed a fine idea, if it was the only alcoholic beverage he was offering; a belt of something stronger would have been even more to the point. But who knew where it was, so I made for the fridge. It held eight or ten premium imported brands, along with equally impressive selections of mustards and ice-cream toppings. On nearby counters there were canisters of teas, and others of coffees. The kitchenware was Le Creuset. The gadgets were the best and the latest. Booker's kitchen was a microcosm of his whole house—the finest of everything, and lots of it.

I went back to the living room, where I could have spent

hours looking at the famous art collection, or browsing the record library, which covered nearly a whole wall, with several shelves containing only compact discs. Need I mention that the audio equipment was state-of-the-art? The furniture was covered in leather, the surfaces were glass, the colors were black and white—the better, said the owner, to show off his art. Pretty opulent for a runty kid—a runty kid who was even now showing to the door the source of his interrupted afternoon delight, a tall and gorgeous drink of water in black leather skirt and three-colored hair. She and Booker proceeded to kiss for a good part of the afternoon. I was thinking of clearing my throat when I heard her whisper, "Tomorrow?"

"I'll call you," said Booker, and the door snicked shut.

"How do you do it?" I blurted.

He looked puzzled. "How do I—? Oh, women. Easy. I work at it."

"Doesn't everyone?"

"McDonald, please. Begging your pardon, but I am a pro. Have I ever shown you my wardrobe? I know exactly what to wear to every joint on which night. I know what crowd is going to be where, and when they're going to get tired of that and move on. I can smell a new joint before the ink's dry on the lease, and I can tell you what kind of women it's going to draw."

"Don't you ever meet women at—you know—art exhibits or anything?"

"What's the point? If I brought someone nice here, she'd just think I was a dope dealer, like the rest of them do."

"You mean you can never have a meaningful relationship?"

"I'm trying, McDonald, okay? Am I in analysis or not?" He spoke with such heat that I couldn't help hearing the hurt underneath. I supposed being wealthy at twenty-six had its drawbacks, and I hoped I'd remember that next time I became envious of Booker and tempted to learn my way around a 'loid.

"Sorry," I said.

"It's okay. Tell me about Beverly. Is Isami okay?"

"No worse than you'd be if you'd spent the afternoon with Howard Blick. I don't know if she's a suspect or not. I don't know anything—I just wanted to tell you she's dead. It happened last night," I added, watching him carefully.

He didn't react at all. I hoped it had happened sometime between seven and ten, when Booker was with Sardis and me, but nothing in his expression told me he was thinking of that at all. "How'd she die?"

"Don't know yet. Except that she was murdered."

He was quiet a while. "I can't get it out of my mind," he said at last. "She must have been killed for the thing."

"The manuscript?"

He nodded. "Maybe she was supposed to deliver it, and couldn't, because I took it. Or maybe someone knew about it and tried to steal it. Only they couldn't, once again because it wasn't there. So they killed her, trying to make her talk."

"Hey, you shouldn't think like that." But my heart wasn't in it. It was the way I was thinking.

"McDonald, I'm responsible for that woman's death."

"You know that's—"

"There's no two ways about it; I might as well have pulled the trigger myself."

"How do you know she was shot?"

I was getting goose bumps again, like I had when I'd first seen the manuscript. But Booker seemed unaware that, so far as I was concerned, he had just seriously incriminated himself. "Figure of speech," he said, waving a hand so dismissive I came close to believing him. But there was still some nagging going on in the back of my mind.

"It's too much of a coincidence," he continued, "that she was killed the night after I burglarized her."

I agreed with him, but held my tongue about it.

"We've got to get the murderer. It's no longer enough just to return the manuscript."

He sounded as if he were thinking aloud. I wondered if I could sneak out before he came out of his reverie.

"Paul, I don't care how much it costs. Get him."

"Get him?"

"Get her, if that's the case."

"Booker, this is big. Don't you think you'd better go to a pro?"

"A private eye? Don't be absurd; I have to have somebody I can tell the truth to. Besides, you used to work for a private eye and you used to be an investigative reporter. That's good enough for me."

"I appreciate the vote of confidence." Actually, I was scared silly. "By the way, I feel funny about hanging on to the manuscript, now that we're pretty sure it's valuable. Have you got a wall safe or something?"

He waved dismissively again—premature wealth had made him imperious. "Put it in a safe-deposit box."

CHAPTER 4

The problem was, the banks were closed for the day. Very well; I knew what I'd do with it.

I pointed my Toyota eastward, looking forward to getting home and half-wishing I'd find Sardis in the kitchen, filling a chicken, perhaps, with her very fine sage stuffing. But I knew I wouldn't. It was I, as a matter of fact, who'd balked at exchanging keys. If Sardis felt I was too immature to live with her, then I was going to make damned sure she wasn't going to get the benefits of living with me. Maybe she'd be a little inconvenienced every now and then by not having my key, and maybe, I reasoned, that would make her think twice. (Though actually reason had little to do with it—it was pure pigheadedness and I knew it as well as Sardis did. But I'd been pigheaded all my life and I wasn't going to stop now. No matter how much I inconvenienced myself.)

And to tell the truth, the inconvenience was just about all mine. Sardis's apartment, furnished with her artist's eye and her hedonist's love of textures, was completely inviting and mine was more than a bit on the bare side. We each had the same number of rooms—living room, dining room, kitchen, bedroom for sleeping, and second bedroom for office or studio. In my case, though, I wouldn't be using either of the bedrooms until I could afford to furnish them. My burned-up furniture was insured, of course, but I'd put all the money into the house, which was a considerable step up from the old one.

So far I'd bought only five big things—my nice dining-room table, a VCR, a stereo, some unfinished bookshelves, and a painting. I'd lost a painting I loved in the fire, and I'd needed the small Mary Robertson river scene to console myself.

There was one other nice thing in the place—another painting, the one Sardis had given me as a housewarming gift. I thought it was the best example of her work that I'd seen and I was proud to have it. It was a very powerful stylized depiction of a fire, an image that had several layers of meaning for both of us, beginning with the way I lost my house and the way Sardis had taken me in afterward and the things that had happened not only between us, but also around us in the ensuing weeks.

The few other things I had were other people's discards—an old bed, which doubled as a sofa, a TV, chest of drawers, old plastic-covered, chrome-legged chairs that were monstrous with the oak table, and an unbelievably heavy, ugly coffee table. The thing consisted of glass on top of an elaborately and hideously machine-turned stand, so that you could look down and see every tasteless curlicue.

That was the dump to which I was depriving Sardis of free access—more or less an indoor junkyard. This was only my second day there, but it certainly didn't feel like home. Still, it would get there—my bookshelves were already overflowing and now I had Booker's candlesticks. With the money he was paying me, I might just be able to get some decent dining room chairs and a new coffee table.

When I pulled up, Spot was lying on the porch, a medium-sized ball of black fur, which unrolled and stretched at my approach. Well, it *was* home. Sardis or no Sardis, Spot was there.

The manuscript was lying on the egregious coffee table. Now that I was pretty sure it was real, that offended me on aesthetic grounds. And now that I believed Beverly had been killed for it, it terrified me as well. The purloined-letter approach was the only hope of hiding it—and God knows I had the manuscripts to pull it off. Five of my unpublished masterpieces had been in the hands of indifferent (and eventually rejecting) editors at the time of the fire. One was at a potential agent's and a copy of my current one had been at a friend's. So one thing I hadn't lost was my life's work. I had plenty of worthless manuscripts in which to bury Mr. Clemens's. I took the first chapter of *Vandal in Bohemia,* plunked it on top of Huck Finn, labeled it like all my other ones, and thrust it near the bottom of the pile.

Next, I went up to fill Sardis in, hoping for a dinner invitation, which was not forthcoming. Instead, I started some tuna pasta and, waiting for the water to boil, put in a call to Debbie Hofer at the *Chronicle*: "Sweetbuns, it's Paul."

"Lovebomb! When are you going to leave your blonde and come home to Deb?" Debbie is near retirement age, quite fond of Sardis, and would give me no end of motherly lectures if I broke up with her.

"I'm downstairs with my suitcase."

"Stop teasing old Deb. How's the new place?"

"The place is great, Deb. I have this interesting little job that might even enable me to furnish it." Because Debbie is like a favorite aunt—and completely in my confidence—I hadn't the slightest hesitation about telling her the whole story, not even omitting Booker's name; she knew him from my long-ago news story, so why pretend? Her reaction was typical: "Honey, you've got to write it! Best yarn I've heard all year."

"Yeah, but I've got one hell of a conflict, wouldn't you say?"

"Well, if it's a simple choice between money and glory—"

"It's not, actually. Booker's a friend, remember?"

"Details."

"And anyway, I'd choose the money. The only thing is, I need a little help."

"I figured. You want me to call the cop shop." And she rang off without waiting for an answer.

I was polishing off the last of the pasta when the phone

rang. "Sweetums, it isn't pretty. Somebody choked poor Beverly, and beat her head against the floor."

"Oof. But at least she wasn't shot."

"Beg pardon?"

"Never mind. When did it happen?"

"Lateish. Between nine and eleven."

Not so good for Booker.

"But more like nine, they think. Because someone tried to call her at nine-thirty and got a busy. It turned out the phone was off the hook, which was the way her roommate found it when she returned the next morning."

Better for Booker—he'd been with us at nine.

"The police think your buddy did it."

"Excuse me?"

"Bev and Isami reported the burglary, of course. The cops think the burglar came back."

"Why would he do that?"

"He didn't get Beverly's jewelry. As a matter of fact, so far as the cops know, he got nothing of Bev's; she certainly didn't report the loss of a priceless manuscript. They figure he'd just hit Isami's room and something scared him away before he could get to Bev's. So he came back the next night. She surprised him by being there, and he gave her the good-bye look."

"That's the theory, is it?"

"Not bad if you ask me. Who's going to believe in a neurotic burglar getting back at daddy dear?"

"Tell me something, Deb—was she sexually assaulted?"

"Apparently not. Just strangled and knocked around."

"Thanks, darlin'. Let me know when I can return the favor."

"Sure will, hon. Glad to do it."

Good old Deb. She'd done me so many favors I'd lost count—even lent me money—and never asked for a thing in return. She talked tough—as befitted a tough newshen—but if anyone ever had a heart of gold, it was Debbie Hofer, and I would gladly have married her if she'd have had me. Which she would not.

She'd made that perfectly clear. And Sardis wouldn't even live with me.

Very well then. I would have to depend on one of the world's great humorists for company. I opened a bottle of Glen Ellen Proprietor's Reserve Red, my current favorite jug wine, and picked up my new copy of Huck Finn. After all, I'd started it the night before—why not finish? But after a while I had a brainstorm and got on the phone again. "Isami Nakamura? This is Ben McGonagil of the *Examiner*. I'm doing an obituary on your roommate, and I was wondering if I could ask you a few questions?"

"Actually, I was just on my way out. I'm staying somewhere else for a while and just stopped by to pick up some clothes."

"Oh. Then maybe you could tell me who else to call—her parents, perhaps?"

"Mr. and Mrs. George Alexander. In Hillsborough. But I'm confused about something, Mr. McGonagil—why didn't you ask me about this earlier. When you interviewed me about the murder?"

"One thing at a time, I always say."

Interesting that she'd talked to McGonagil. He was a star. If he was on the yarn, that meant the *Ex* was going to do it up big. I called Hillsborough, already assuming a post-McGonagil identity: "Hello. Blick of the *Progress*."

George Alexander couldn't keep the distaste out of his voice: "Any relation to Blick the homicide inspector?"

"Oh, him. Heavens, no. Very common name where I come from."

"What can I do for you, Mr. Blick?"

"I'm writing an obituary on your daughter and I wonder if I could ask you a little about her?"

"Plenty of reporters already have. Why not you?"

"How old was she, sir?"

"Thirty-four."

"Excuse me. Did you say twenty-four?"

"Thirty-four."

"How long had she been flying?"

"Ten years. Quit graduate school to see the world. Guess she liked it. Never went back."

"Where was she studying?"

"University of Michigan. History. She got her B.A. at Bryn Mawr. Also in history."

"I guess you get so you can anticipate what a person's going to ask next."

"She's survived by her mother and me and one brother."

"You've been very helpful, sir. Thanks very much."

I hung up, rather regretting that it's impolite to ask a bereaved parent if his daughter had a criminal record, but nonetheless feeling it had been a most profitable phone call. Beverly Alexander was no trifling bit of fluff. Or if she was, she was at least a well-educated one of a certain age. Obviously she was a bit underemployed, but maybe there was a reason for it. Maybe she was an alcoholic or a druggie. Or just lazy. At any rate, a more complicated woman than I'd expected. On impulse, I dialed her dad a second time: "Mr. Alexander? Blick again. I might do a larger story about Beverly, and I'm trying to find out what she was like as a person. I wonder—do you know who her favorite author was?"

"Albert Camus."

"I mean—actually—her favorite American author."

"Mr. Blick, are you sure you're not related to that homicide fellow?"

Crusty old buzzard; no wonder his daughter wanted to fly away. I went back to Huck, Jim, and Glen Ellen—better company altogether.

But I was irritated at the way McGonagil and Blick had gotten to people before I had. True, they'd learned about Beverly's death before I had—because it was part of their jobs—but I'd had that odd sort of forgetful moment when there were still bits of the job to be done. If I were going to be worth the big bucks Booker was paying me, I'd better look sharp. The next day I was standing at the library door when it opened.

The lovely Linda was looking fresh as the morning itself, yet once again endearingly smeary-eyed. She flushed when she saw me—another plus. "Ah. Paul McDonald."

"Linda, I want to ask you a weird thing."

"Splendid."

"The lost part of Huck Finn—what if it weren't lost after all?"

"I thought we covered that—we'd want it badly."

"No, no—let me rephrase. Are there any stories about it? I mean, like Clemens gave it to his daughter for safekeeping and she sold it to an unknown buyer. Or maybe it's in someone's very private collection; a particular person's even. The sort of thing everyone knows, but no one can prove—like the rumors about stolen artworks."

"You mean folklore. Like ghost stories or UFO sightings."

"Exactly."

"There was a sighting once. But only one that I know of—there's not a complex mythology or anything."

"Who made the sighting?"

"As a matter of fact, I can tell you exactly who, because I took the phone call. It was"—she squinched up her eyes—"back in '78, maybe? No, '77. Or maybe it was the fall before. No, it was winter. I remember because—"

"Ten years ago more or less?"

"About that. If you'll just give me a minute—"

"That's okay." I hoped she'd take the hint and get on with it. "Who was it?"

She squinched up again—her makeup was looking worse every second. "Edwin . . . Apple. No, Lemon. Edwin Lemon."

"Is he someone you know?"

"Oh, gosh no, he just called up and said, 'This is A-id-win Limmon fromm Foo-all-ton Miss'ippi.'"

"Foolton?"

"Fulton, I think."

"And what did he say?"

"Come to think of it, he asked me the same kinds of questions you did the other day—were the whereabouts of the manuscript known? What part was missing? And like that. Then he said he thought he had the rest of it."

"You're joking."

"No, he did. Just like that. Only time it's ever happened. He said he'd bring it in right away for us to look at."

"And?"

She shrugged. "That's the last we heard of him."

"You didn't try to follow up on it."

"I figured he was a nut."

"Do you have a U.S. map around here?"

"I could probably find one. Why?"

"I want to look up Foo-all-ton."

Fifteen minutes later I was on the phone to Booker, who was railing. "Get your ass on a plane, McDonald. What do you think—I'm a piker? I want the job done and I want it done right. Go anywhere you want, I don't care what it costs. And go now! I'm nervous about this shit."

"Well, actually, I could get a plane to Memphis in an hour and a half."

"Do it."

"To tell you the truth, the Visa folks are still mad." (When they closed my account for nonpayment, I cut my card into little pieces, smeared it with cat food, and sent it back. I kept trying to tell them I'd since grown up, but they saw through me.)

"Come by and I'll give you an advance."

I dashed home, threw some things in a bag, and was just locking the door when I remembered the manuscript. I'd planned to take it to the nearest bank as soon as it opened. There was no time now. Should I take it with me? No. Way too much margin for error. I'd have to get Sardis to take it to a bank. But there wasn't even time to go up and speak to her. Oh, well—I had to ask her to feed Spot as well; I could call from the airport. I stuck the key under the mat and hit the road.

What with dropping by Booker's I walked on the plane with about thirty seconds to spare. So I didn't call till we touched down in Memphis and by then the ungrateful wench had stepped out on some selfish errand of her own. Too bad she'd have to hear my newly acquired accent secondhand. "This is your Huckleberry free-and," I told her machine, "calling from Mimphis, on my way to Foo-all-ton, Miss'ippi. I'm trackin' down the provenance of a l'il ol' manuscript." Sardis herself was from Mississippi and I knew she'd be pleased I'd learned her language.

CHAPTER 5

Fulton was just out of Tupelo, birthplace of a great American hero, and such a thriving metropolis I wasn't sure I'd be able to find Elvis Presley Park to pay my respects. But that was one thing I vowed to do before I left town.

First I found the Natchez Trace Inn, checked in, and pored over the phone book for awhile. There weren't any Edwin Lemon, but there were five others. Two never heard of Edwin, the third was out, and the fourth thought Edwin might be related to her husband's third cousin once removed, Veerelle Lemon, over in Ballardsville. Veerelle was the fifth. Her voice was listless. "Edwin? Edwin hasn't lived here in ten years. Since '77, I b'leeve. Or was '78 the year he left? I declare, I can hardly remember any more."

If, in sizzling Itawamba County, anyone's blood has ever run cold, mine did at that moment. "He was your husband?"

"My son. Best boy there ever was too. Wadn't anything he wouldn't do for me."

"And where is he now?"

"Haven't heard from him in ten years, just about."

"Mrs. Lemon, I'm a private investigator from California. I wonder if I could see you for a few minutes?"

"You know somethin' about Edwin?"

"Maybe. I'm trying to find out, anyway."

"I wish you'd come on over, then. First thing in the mornin', you hear?"

Going to Ballardsville was like going back in time, almost to Huck and Tom's day. There were no sidewalks and no street lights. The roads were paved and there were plenty of cars on them, and tractors in the fields, but you could tune that part out. The farmhouses had wide front porches with swings on them. Some had ponds that had really been dug to be stocked with catfish, but that looked like good swimming holes. Sharecroppers' children played barefoot, brown legs covered with red dust.

Instead of one of the charming old ones, Veerelle's house was a low-ceilinged and badly built modern one. She'd apparently furnished it with the hand-me-downs of a dozen Lemon families whose taste ran to early American, with plenty of Naugahyde recliners thrown in. Somewhere in the family tree were a knitter of afghans and a crocheter of antimacassars.

As for Veerelle, she was as nice a lady as you'd ever want to meet. Primly permed salt-and-pepper hair, pleasant summer dress, bucket of beans in lap. ("You don't mind if I string my beans for supper, do you?") She seemed very much like someone's mother.

"I can't tell you who my client is," I began, "but I've been asked to look into a matter that may concern your son."

Her eyes brimmed. "You're not gon' tell me there's a chance he might be alive?" They overflowed.

"I'm sorry to upset you, ma'am. But, honestly, I haven't any idea. I was given his name at a university library where he'd made some inquiries."

"A library? Why, Edwin worked in a library. Over at Itawamba Junior College."

"He was a college librarian?"

"Sure was. Ole Miss graduate, but he came home to work. Built me this house, too, after his daddy died. 'Course, he lived over in Fulton himself. In a tiny little place."

"Was he married?"

"No. Always said wives were too expensive. Didn't like to spend money—except on me. Didn't want a thing for himself, but couldn't do enough for his mama."

"He doesn't sound the sort who wouldn't get in touch for ten years."

"Well, he wasn't."

"You sound pretty much as if you've given up hope."

Now that she apparently felt I hadn't brought her any false hope, she had herself under control. "I've known for a long time that Edwin's dead."

"How's that, Mrs. Lemon?"

"I just know it. I know it in my heart. If he were safe, he'd have found some way to let me know."

"I wonder if you could tell me how he happened to leave."

"Don't know whether I should or not. Still don't know what you're here for."

"I think something happened ten years ago that concerns my client, and also concerned your son. I may be able to find out what happened to him."

"I'm not sure I want to know."

"You think he was involved in something that—how shall I put this? Something that—" Something criminal, I meant, but I couldn't bring myself to say it to poor, innocent-seeming Veerelle in her awful little brick house that she probably considered the finest in the neighborhood.

"Edwin had a side to him that I don't like to think about sometimes."

"Mrs. Lemon, I don't mean to pry, but it could be very helpful if you could tell me what you mean by that."

She snapped the bean she was working on with two loud cracks that let me know it was standing in for my right arm. "Not going to. But I've made up my mind to tell you how he left. Maybe I do want to know what happened to him. Maybe—" She was losing control again. "Just maybe—" She got up without a word, left the room, and returned clutching a tissue. She sat down, put her bowl of beans carefully on an end table, and gave me her full attention. "Edwin came over one day and said, 'Come for a ride in my new car.' Law, you could have knocked me over with a feather. Edwin never bought anything for himself. His car was ten years old, and he swore there was plenty of life left in it. Mind you, he bought *me* a new car, but that's the way Edwin was. Didn't ever treat himself to anything. But that day, he came ridin' over in a pretty little bright-yellow Datsun. I made some remark about the color and he said, 'Why, Mama, that's *Lemon* yellow.'

"He took me for a ride and we came in together and had some coffee and he said, 'Mama, I'm takin' a little vacation.' Well, I wadn't sure I heard right because here it was October—and Edwin a school librarian. I said, 'Edwin, what on earth are you talkin' about?' And he said he was takin' a one-month leave of absence. Said, 'Wanda Kimbrough's gon' fill in for me. She was glad to get the work and they'll prob'ly be glad to get her.' Well, can you imagine how that made me feel? I said, 'Son, you talk like you're not comin' back.' He said, 'I'll be back. I'll be back for sure and when I do I just might have a little surprise for you. I just might be about to come into some money.' And the next day he left in that Lemon-yellow Datsun."

"He didn't say any more about the money?"

"Didn't matter how hard I tried to make him, he wouldn't say a word. Just kept sayin' he wadn't sure yet and he didn't want to get my hopes up."

"Did he say where he was going?"

"He did." She set her lips in a thin hard line. "San Francisco."

"Was that all he told you? He didn't mention anything about a book? Or a manuscript maybe?"

Suddenly, for the first time in the interview, she smiled. "Why, no. Was he workin' on a book? Was that it?"

"I beg your pardon?"

"Edwin wrote a book! So that's what this was all about. And I see now why he left so suddenly—I bet he'd sent it off to someone who was gon' publish it."

"Ma'am, could I ask you something? I just have a hunch and I want to try it out on you. I'm wondering—who was Edwin's favorite author?"

"Favorite author?" She looked confused. "Wait! I know. That nigra man."

"Excuse me?"

"You know." She pulled a worn paperback from a nearby bookcase and turned the cover towards me: *Giovanni's Room*.

"Oh. James Baldwin."

"Is that who you thought it'd be?"

I shook my head. "I thought it might be Faulkner."

She smiled for the second time: "We don't think much of *him* around here."

"I thought I might talk to some of Edwin's friends while I'm in town."

"I'd start with Wanda Kimbrough if I were you. She's still workin' over there."

Meaning still the librarian at Itawamba Junior College, where she'd gone to fill in for a month ten years ago. I wondered momentarily if the job were good enough to kill for.

If it were, though, I couldn't see Wanda as a suspect, maybe just because I didn't want to. She was big and friendly, which I liked; and she would say anything that came into her head, which I find the most compelling of human attributes.

"Tell me something," she started out. "Is your client gay?"

"I gather Edwin was."

"You gather right. But Veerelle's a Bible-thumpin' Baptist and a bloodsuckin' old tyrant to boot. I'm happy for Eddie. Always have been. Because I guaran-damn-tee you what happened—he found all the dicks he ever wanted to suck in San Francisco and that was it for Fulton, Miss'ippi. See, Eddie never could really be himself here, with his mama lookin' over his shoulder, and he felt so guilty about being gay he spent every penny he ever made on her and never had a goddam thing for himself. And you know what? I think Veerelle knew. I think she knew all the time. And she never would give him the ease of sayin' she knew and that it was okay. She just took everything he had and made him wait on her hand and foot."

"She didn't seem so bad to me."

"Oh, I guess she's no worse than any other old hypocrite in these parts. The woods are full of 'em. But the plain fact was, she was making Eddie's life a living hell and he had to get out."

"How did you and Eddie know each other?"

She picked up some books from a cart, shelving them as we talked, handling them with the sensuous pleasure of the true bibliophile. "Met at Ole Miss. We were English majors."

"That reminds me—who's your favorite author?"

"What? Are you nuts?"

"Quick. Who is it?"

"Faulkner. What's it to you?"

"Next favorite?"

"Eudora Welty."

"Who was Eddie's favorite?"

She made a face. "James Baldwin, of course. Why the hell did you ask?"

I decided to try one more bit of amateur psychology: "I wanted to see if you'd say Mark Twain."

She looked utterly bewildered. Maybe she was a good actress, but I didn't think she knew doodley-squat about the manuscript. As they say in Miss'ippi. I said: "Because your friend called a university library and made some inquiries about him. Right before he disappeared."

"So what's this all about?"

"I can't really tell you that. But I'll tell you one thing. It was the library at the University of California."

"You mean Berkeley?"

I nodded, forbearing to tell her the true institutional nickname. "He said he'd be there in a few days to do some research, but he never showed up."

She gasped. "So maybe he didn't get there."

"It's certainly possible."

"And all these years I've imagined him in hard-on heaven."

I shrugged. "He might have decided to do his research elsewhere. The point is, I think he knew something important to the case I'm working on. What can you tell me about the way he left?"

"He just told me he was going to San Francisco to check out the Castro District. Said if he liked it, he might move there."

"But he went awfully suddenly, didn't he? It seems odd to pick the beginning of the school year when he could just as well have gone the previous summer."

"He never told me this for sure, but I think he had the hots for a guy from San Francisco who was here that summer. Visiting a friend, quote unquote. Eddie didn't have a lover here and I think he went all warm and gooey for Tad—Tad Ludwig, his name was. Hunky blond, if you like that type. But Tad was already taken. Or so it would seem."

"You think he and Eddie had something going on the side?"

"Let's put it this way. I came upon the two of them in the parking lot one night. I wouldn't want to convict on circumstantial evidence, but Eddie was on his knees."

"So you think Eddie got a sudden, uncontrollable yen for Tad."

"Either that or a phone call from him."

"Tell me something. Veerelle said Sonny had a side to him that she didn't like to think about. What do you think she meant by that?"

"That he was gay, I guess."

"Just off the top of your head—do you think Eddie was honest?"

She laughed, or rather more or less bellowed. "Eddie? He taught me how to shoplift when we were eighteen."

"Is that all?"

"Darlin', all I can say is, it's a good thing Edwin Lemon had no ambition whatsoever. Because if he did he would have screwed ol' Veerelle herself to get what he wanted."

Besides herself, Wanda told me, Edwin had had only one other close friend who still lived in the greater Tupelo area: Tad Ludwig's friend, Duncan Jones. Dunc taught English and had an office almost within shouting distance of the library. He was getting on now, and probably wasn't currently attracting too many of Wanda's hunky blonds. He had lank hair and glasses, but offsetting both, a warm, open face that looked honest and probably wasn't.

After ten years, he seemed still not to have forgiven Edwin for something: "He never told me he was going anywhere. One day he just wasn't in the library and Wanda was."

"Do you have any ideas about why he left?"

"Only what Wanda said he told her."

"You don't sound as if you believe it."

"I've got enough sense to take Wanda with a grain of salt."

"Did Edwin seem like an honest person to you?"

"Completely. Why—did Wanda say he wasn't?" He snorted. "*Wanda* has the morals of a tree toad."

"Oh. Well, who's your favorite author?"

"Mark Twain. Why?"

I wasn't ready for that. But I thought fast and hit him with a *non sequitur* he couldn't ignore: "Did you know Edwin had a thing with your friend Tad Ludwig?"

"That cunt!"

"Tad or Edwin?"

"Wanda. Minefield-mouth."

"Meaning she talks too much or she lies?"

"Both."

This was going nowhere. Time to segué home: "Did you and Edwin ever discuss Mark Twain?"

"Not that I can recall. Why?"

"Think carefully. *Huckleberry Finn*, in particular."

He wrinkled up his brow. "No. I'm sure of it. But would you mind telling me why?"

"I would, I'm afraid."

But I figured he'd find out from Wanda, since they were such good friends.

One more errand before I could do what I really wanted. At the office of the *Journal*, I penned the following: "I may have something that belongs to you. It was written by Mr. Mark Twain, who told the truth, mainly. Please call collect."

Then I wrote another ad, asking for information about the whereabouts of Edwin Lemon. After inserting both, I set out, as any real American would, to seek deep spiritual experience at the birthplace of Elvis Presley.

There was something there that made me downright sentimental. Some clever architect, in constructing the Elvis Presley Memorial Chapel, had lined it up on a direct axis with the hallowed spot. Thus if you happened to be getting married in the chapel, you'd be looking out at the tiny house that spawned the King himself. Momentarily, I wondered if Sardis would consider a proposal.

CHAPTER 6

By being out when I phoned, that young lady missed a great opportunity, as the fit may never come over me again. But no matter, she'd get another—to welcome the prodigal home—in a few measly hours.

I was in San Francisco by one P.M. the next day, and entering Oakland about two, full of plans. I would simply find Edwin Lemon through Tad Ludwig and everything would fall into place. Maybe one or both of them was actually listed in the phone book. I was singing loudly: "It's a treat to beat your feet in the Mississippi mud." I was enjoying the sunny but coolish weather, delightful after the racking heat of Tupelo. I was being greeted by my faithful cat Spot on my own front porch. And then I was in my living room, staring at ankle-deep carnage: papers, papers everywhere. All over the dining room floor. Empty manuscript boxes and their contents willy-nilly. The living room itself was as neat as ever except for one foreign object: The key I'd left for Sardis was lying on my awful coffee table.

With leaden chest, I went to confirm what I already knew:

Huck Finn had escaped from my care just as surely as he had from his Pap's.

I bellowed, "Sardis!" She was downstairs in a minute, tearing through the door in a pair of khaki cutoffs. I liked seeing her legs and I liked the way she neither minced nor wasted words. She could have said, "Hi, Paul. Omigod, what happened?" But the simple and eloquent "Shit!" she pronounced said it all.

"I guess," I said, "I should have just given you the damn key."

She ignored that. "They got the manuscript?"

"Uh-huh."

"I feel awful—if only I'd . . ."

"What? Broken in yourself and got it first?"

"You left Spot out or I would have. I just kept him with me and hoped for the best about Huck. Did you forget the key or what?"

"No. I put it under the mat. Someone just got there before you did. What time did you get home yesterday?"

"About five, I guess. I was shopping for new-apartment stuff. When I got your message I came down right away, but the key was already gone."

"For all I know, someone watched me put it there, and had Huck on their own raft five minutes later."

"Should we call the cops?"

"No." Instead, I got Booker on the phone. "Bad news, buddy. While I was away, someone stole the manuscript."

"You just got home?"

"Yes."

"Don't touch anything. I'll be right over."

While I made the call, Sardis made herself useful. She was waiting in the living room with a couple of open beers and a slightly belated hello kiss. "So, Paul. Exactly what was going on in Foo-all-ton Miss'ippi?"

"I heard about a fellow—"

"Which by the way is pronounced Fulton. It's you people who go in for extra syllables, not us. For instance, no Mississippian would ever say 'schoo-ul,' which every Californian does with an air of great superiority. It's school."

"Right. Schoo."

"You can hear the 'l' if you listen. And now you may get a word in edgewise."

"You would have been proud of me, babe. I said 'ma'am' for the first time in my life."

"To whom?"

"To Veerelle Lemon, mother of Edwin, and thereon hangs a tale." Quickly, I told it, getting Sardis so excited she went upstairs to find the San Francisco phone book she'd brought clear to the East Bay. Alas, however, neither Tad Ludwig nor Edwin Lemon was listed.

I was on my second beer and pondering whether to let bygones be bygones and get an extra key for Sardis when Booker got there. He took one look at the mess and curled his lip. "Amateur hour. Pathetic."

"How can you tell?"

"Shouldn't have made the mess in the first place, but certainly should have cleaned it up. This guy had a terrible case of nerves. Real bad nerves. Sweaty armpits, sweaty palms. I just hope he didn't sweat on the goods."

"Why should he have cleaned up the mess?"

"The idea, McDonald, is to give the illusion nothing has happened. That way it could be days before the crime is discovered, giving the pro plenty of time to find a fence. Besides, there's professional pride—if you did a job and left your office looking like that, could you feel good about it?"

"I guess not."

"Let's see the point of entry."

I pointed. "The front door, I guess. I left the key under the mat for Sardis, but when she got home it wasn't there, so she assumed I'd forgotten it."

"I may have to revise my opinion. A pro would definitely look under the mat."

"Booker, if I may say so, it hardly matters, does it? Whoever it was wanted the manuscript. They obviously headed right for the papers and went through them until they found the right box."

"By the way, how come you didn't hide it any better than that?"

"You won't believe me, but at the time, I thought it was a terribly clever hiding place."

Booker looked disgusted and I couldn't say I blamed him.

"Look, if you want me off the case . . ."

He gave me his familiar wave of the hand. "It could have happened to anybody. Besides, I made you get on the plane before you had time to get to the bank."

"The thing is, I wasn't all that nervous about it because I didn't think anyone knew I had it."

"Except Sardis and me. Sardis, did you tell anybody?"

She shook her head.

"Neither did I. You, McDonald?"

"No."

"So either someone followed me here on Saturday night or someone guessed. No one knew I had it, so why would they follow me? That leaves guessing."

I was getting a nasty inkling. "Isami!"

Booker tried not to look too pleased. "Why Isami?"

"Suppose she knows the manuscript is missing—in other words, knows Beverly had it, and was in cahoots with her, somehow or another. The manuscript disappears, Beverly gets killed, then the next day I turn up with a cock-and-bull story about Beverly wanting me to meet her for a possible *Chronicle* story. What could that mean to Isami? Maybe she thinks Bev was about to double-cross her and give the whole story out. Or maybe she gets the idea Bev already had. So she comes looking for my notes and accidentally finds the manuscript. Or maybe it isn't that. Maybe she figures I've got the manuscript and came around to hold it for ransom or something." I turned up my palms. "I don't know. All I know is she's the only possibility I can think of."

"I guess we'll have to take a look."

Sardis put her face in her hand: "Oh, no."

"You mean," I said, "burglarize her again?"

Booker nodded. "I don't see what else to do. Do you?"

"Excuse me," said Sardis. "I don't think I want to hear the rest of this." She walked out on tanned and luscious legs.

A part of me wanted to get out too. But another part felt guilty about losing the manuscript and yet another was frankly excited at the possibility of participating in a burglary.

With Booker's help, I'd burgled before, but that was out of desperation. This time no one's survival was on the line, but the manuscript *was* important—and there wouldn't really be a victim. It wasn't, after all, as if we were going to steal anything from Isami; we were merely going to look for something she wouldn't have if she were a law-abiding citizen, and then we were going to walk away, leaving the place exactly the way we found it. Unless she actually had the manuscript—in which case we'd take it—she wouldn't even know we'd been there.

There was that argument and then there was the other, the product of almost forty years of socialization. We *would* have been there. We would have invaded her privacy and her home, whether she knew it or not. It wasn't right.

But the thing was, Booker was going to do it whether I helped him or not. What difference would it make if I went along for the ride? I reminded myself that I'd done a few illegal things—and certainly lied—in my reportorial days and thought it perfectly permissible in the interests of getting a story. Meaning permissible because it had society's sanction—or at least that of an important publishing corporation. Surely an irreplaceable literary treasure was as important as a newspaper story. So couldn't I act on my own?

That didn't get me anywhere because I knew I wasn't going to be acting on my own and wouldn't in any case. Without Booker, there was simply no possibility that I would break into Isami Nakamura's house for any reason.

The question was a thicket of thorns and I decided not to pursue it a millimeter further. The plain fact was that since I didn't think anyone could get hurt and some good might actually be done in the long run, I could justify the burglary to myself in a dim way. Barely. And so I was going to do it.

Why did I want to? For the same reason I'd been a reporter, probably. Sardis liked to call me an experience junkie and I guess I was, in a way. I would do just about anything once if it wasn't dangerous, illegal, or immoral. And some things, apparently, that were all three.

Booker gave Isami a call. "Damn answering machines. With people screening their calls, it's hell to case jobs any more." He sighed. "But she doesn't answer, so let's go on over."

"Should I wear anything special?"

"You mean like jeans, black sweater, and stocking mask? I don't usually, but it can't hurt. Don't forget gloves, though."

I certainly wasn't going to trouble Sardis for a stocking, so that settled that.

Not even a porch light was on when we arrived. Perhaps Isami was still staying with a friend. Booker gave me the OK sign, but walked around the house anyway, listening for tiny noises. We'd stopped for a bite and it was now about nine-thirty, so I figured if she was out for the evening, she wouldn't be back for a while. Booker was a little nervous—people sometimes came home right after dinner, he said. But he thought she'd have left a light or two on if she planned to.

He'd gotten in a half-open bathroom window Friday night. By now, he figured, she'd have burglar-proofed—people usually did that after a break-in. But no problem—his collection of keys would get us in the back door in a trice. While he worked, I held a penlight.

"What do you do," I whispered, "when I'm not here?"

"Teeth," he said. "Or sometimes nothing. I've got a pretty good sense of touch."

When the lock finally moved, he sighed deeply and sensuously, like someone tasting honey and nectar. We closed the door behind us and cased the rooms quickly, making double sure no one was home. The curtains hadn't been closed and there was enough light to see the living room. It was furnished in the makeshift way of people who aren't home much and don't care to be. The sofa was old, looked secondhand, and hadn't been very nice to begin with. There were a couple of overstuffed chairs in a similar condition and one rattan one that didn't go with anything else. A few *Cosmos* and *Vogues* had been tossed into a basket, but there wasn't a sign of a book, and there was hardly any place to hide anything. Quickly Booker looked under the cushions and moved on.

I wanted to stop and go through the bathroom cabinets, but he nudged me towards Isami's room. "The plan is to get in and out fast," he said. "You know how long the average burglary takes? Forty seconds. But of course that's just the hit-and-run grab-the-stereo kind. We could be here as long as ten minutes." He turned his penlight on as we reached a bedroom threshold. "Get this."

The curtains were pink-checked and so was the bedspread. On the bed was an extensive teddy bear collection. The furniture was painted white, except for an old trunk, the sort in which college kids send off their clothes. It had been painted pink. "My dad's girlfriend's room," said Booker. "I wonder what it's like to make love in a bed with a dozen teddy bears."

"Your dad's a psychologist, isn't he?"

"Not exactly. Psych professor."

"She's probably doing him a lot of good. You ought to have a more open mind."

Booker started opening her dresser drawers and going through them with the utmost care, even, I thought, caressing certain intimate garments rather more tenderly than necessary. I was starting to worry, but watching him later—going through towels, papers, even kitchen utensils—I realized that was just the way he worked. With utmost care.

Because he wanted to get the job done fast, he condescended to let me take the trunk, though I'm sure my ham-handed touch must have driven him nearly mad. As it happened, the trunk was Isami's laundry hamper; thus there was no need in the world for a delicate approach. Next I looked under the bed and in the closet. Booker carefully checked under the pillows and under the mattress. If Isami had the manuscript, it wasn't in her room.

Next we went through the bathroom and the kitchen. Finally, we entered Beverly's room. A chamber more different from Isami's it would have been difficult to imagine. One wall held her books, others, traditional art she'd probably picked up traveling—African tribal masks, Balinese paintings, Japanese scrolls. A good collection, both eclectic and extensive. The bed was covered with a simple white down comforter, and the other furniture was white wicker. The overall effect was rather tropical, certainly very individual. Briefly, I wondered why I hadn't seen her taste anywhere else in the apartment. Then I saw a cluster of pictures of herself that she'd arranged on her dresser and I thought I knew.

She was the female equivalent of Wanda Kimbrough's hunky blond—a gorgeous blonde in a sporty, wind-blown, conventional sort of way. In the pictures she wore tennis togs, safari clothes, jeans, and fancy dresses, everything looking made for her—and not more than ten minutes earlier, either. Something about her was just a little too sleek, reminding one more of a panther than a cat. There was a smugness there, and a lot of vanity, and a no-holds-barred acquisitiveness.

All that I got from a few photographs in near-darkness. With that kind of imagination, it's no accident I write fiction, probably, but in that moment I felt I had a real sense of Beverly Alexander. I thought the reason she'd holed up in here, rather than actually spread herself throughout the apartment, was simply that the idea would never have occurred to her. She was older, better educated, far worldlier than Isami Nakamura and didn't, in her own eyes, really live with Isami, I was sure. Just a little on the shorts and passing through till something better came along.

"You take the dresser," said Booker and, happily, I plunged in. Quite truthfully, I was enjoying myself. There was something evilly satisfying about going through someone else's things. I thought I could understand Booker's pleasurable sigh when we came in.

There were scarves in the first drawer, and a jewelry box. There was really no need to look in the box, but, frankly, I was carried away. I found a long rope of pearls, gold bracelets, ivory bracelets, and every kind of earrings—sapphire, ruby, emerald, diamond. Just studs, to be sure, but here was a woman who liked her gems. I imagined I heard her voice. "Paul, darling, how did you know?" as she ripped off the wrapping paper. And then I heard it echoing and echoing, again and again.

On to the underwear, which I'm afraid I handled quite as tenderly as Booker had handled Isami's. It was silk and filmy and after all, how often did a man have a chance to touch women's underwear? If you wanted to feel your girlfriend's (without her in it) she'd think you were a pervert. Yet women were permitted to handle and caress these dainty things any time they wanted to. I thought of touching my cheek with one of those camisoles, just to see what it would feel like, but worried that Booker might see. I wondered if he did that sort of thing when he burgled alone and felt a shiver up the spine. These forbidden pleasures were getting a little creepy.

"McDonald, aren't you done yet? Let me finish."

Dreamily, in a kind of pleasant trance, the way women get when they're shopping, I abandoned the dresser and opened Beverly's closet. Shoeboxes were piled from the floor to the hems of dresses packed in tighter than tissues in a box. On the shelves above were more shoeboxes and some that looked like hatboxes. "I've gone through those," said Booker.

I'd seen him check the pillows and mattress too. Wondering what was left for me to do, I sat for a moment on the bed, next to a small table with a white phone on it. Idly, I opened the table's little drawer. If there had been a personal phone book, the police had undoubtedly taken it. I was just rummaging. The drawer was full of bills and bank statements, photos, rubber bands and hair clips. There were also a couple of books that Bev had apparently dipped into at bedtime. One was Barbara Tuchman's *March of Folly*, the other a trashy best-seller. Considering Beverly's history background, the Tuchman book wasn't surprising, nor would *Diamonds*, the Pamela Temby potboiler, have been odd on its own. But the wild diversity of the two caught my attention. I couldn't imagine what there could possibly be about *Diamonds* to interest a woman who was also reading *March of Folly*. In fact, was so puzzled I opened it to the bookmark. Attached to the middle of the page was a yellow

Post-It with six names on it. Or rather, three, and three variations of another. Sarah Williams, at the top, was underlined. Then three were listed, followed by phone numbers: Herb Wolf, Russell Kittrell, and Pamela Temby. Off to the side, more or less doodles, were Sarah M. Williams and Sarah Mary Williams.

I'd never heard of either of the men, but Temby was a huge celebrity, possibly the best-selling author (if you could call her that) in the country. Still, that wasn't the name I found most eye-catching. Sarah Williams was. I peeled off the Post-It and turned to Booker. He was frozen, like a dog watching a bug crawl. "Somebody's home," he said, even his whisper cracked with terror.

No lights were on, so all that really had to be done was close the two drawers we'd been investigating and slink out the back door. Stealthily, we made for the kitchen, Booker a basket case and me, for some reason, cucumber cool. Probably because my professional pride wasn't at stake.

Booker was just reaching a surgically gloved hand toward a doorknob when a man's voice shouted, maybe two feet from us: "Kitty? Kitty, kitty, kitty? Isami, she's back here. Come around, okay? Maybe she'll come to you."

"That's my dad," mouthed Booker, significantly paler, even in the dark.

Apparently the thought of being caught by his old man had immobilized him. It was up to me to get us out of there. Waving him after me, I headed toward the front, thinking Booker the prideful professional must be a wreck indeed if this simple but effective strategy hadn't even occurred to him. He shook his head, rooted to the spot.

"Luna! Come to Mommy," cooed Mommy. "Oh, you big pretty Looney Tunesey, that's a good kitty."

There was absolutely no time to waste. Grabbing Booker by the elbow, I began to march him to freedom. It took nearly all my strength to budge him, but right was on my side. He had momentarily lost his mind, and I was leading him to safety. "Paul, listen, it won't work. Paul!" He was whispering these and other nonsense syllables, but I simply paid him no mind. He scuttled along beside me, there being precious little else he could do.

Finally in the living room I opened the front door with a flourish. Or what would have been a flourish if the door had opened. I actually spoke out loud: "What in hell . . ." And that seemed to rouse Booker from his trance. First he shushed me, then pointed at the double deadbolt. Too late, I remembered this was the second time he'd been here, and even if it were the first, he would have been thorough. On that occasion, he would have searched to see if there were a key around, in case of fire. And judging from his reactions of the past few seconds, there wasn't. But now he was functioning again. "Isami's room," he mouthed, as a key clicked in the back door lock.

Without argument, I followed him to teddy bear heaven. It was there or nowhere—a guinea pig couldn't have wedged itself into Beverly's closet. Without the slightest hesitation, Booker took the trunk, leaving me no option but the closet. It was probably better that way, I thought. He was smaller, and we might have to spend the night there. Squeezing myself into a corner, the horror of it hit me: Spend the night there! Standing up, trying not to breathe too loud, or sneeze.

I tried to steel myself. Human beings had gone through worse, though usually only in wartime. I thought of some of the tiny cars I'd slept in on cross-country trips in my student days. I'd been a lot thinner then, but even so, my recollections were of a particularly virulent hell. Oh, well. Maybe I should think of the Warsaw Ghetto.

Light steps and heavy ones came into the room. "Oh, Looney, Mommy's bitty kitty. Itty bitty bad kitty, staying out like that."

"Ohhh, Isami Wommy's daddy's little bad girl, said the Papa Bear." I practiced deep breathing, mostly to keep my gorge down, but partly to calm myself down—I figured there was about a ninety-percent chance Booker was going to rise up screaming, a maverick pair of Isami's undies perched rakishly on his head.

Instead, there was only a long pause, with heavy breathing. Then the Papa Bear spoke again. "Wouldn't Isami Wommy like to get out of these troublesome old clothes?"

"Papa Bear first."

"Isami first."

They were speaking in the most nauseating baby voices. But suddenly Isami turned into a human being again. "Catch me!" she said, all full of fun and good cheer. She exited, pursued by a bear. She must have been fast. There was a great trampling and thumping that seemed to go on for hours. I took advantage of the noise to stretch a little. There wasn't a peep out of the trunk. Finally I whispered: "Booker?"

Nothing. I figured he'd gone catatonic.

Then the two merry chasers clattered back into the room. There was a great whumpf and squeak, as Isami jumped on the bed and Booker's dad jumped on her. Dear God, I thought, please don't let him say he's going to eat her all up. But magically, the Papa Bear had metamorphosed into a pirate. "Arrrrh," he said. "Now the Gypsy girl will do the captain's bidding."

"Noooo!" shrieked Isami. I could hear her struggling.

"Yes! Yes. Now!"

"Nooo!"

"Yes!"

"No, Jack. I can't." She was sobbing. This was for real. They weren't playing games any longer. Was Booker's dad going to rape her? Would his only son and the son's loyal companion have to save the fair damsel? Not a cheering prospect so far as I was concerned, but I thought Booker would rather relish it. What a splendid castrating revenge! He might never burgle again.

However, now we had neither Papa Bear nor pirate, but concerned swain. "Isami, what is it, darling?"

"Not here."

"But you have to come home sometime. You can't stay with me forever."

"I know. I'll be fine when we get back from Hawaii—I just need a few days away from here."

"Honey, I need to talk to you seriously. Like a psychologist, okay? The longer you stay away from here, the scarier it'll be to come back. I agree you need a few days away. That's why I'm taking you, isn't it? But, please. Let's stay here tonight."

Big bully! I thought. You just don't want to be stuck with her. All you ever think about is yourself. If only I were telepathic. Get out of here! Not tonight, Isami Wommy. Pretty please.

She said: "You really think we should?"

"It's best for you, honey. When we leave tomorrow, you'll feel much better about yourself, and your house will be yours again. You won't have to dread coming back all the time we're in Hawaii."

She laughed.

"What's so funny?"

"I've been dreading going to Hawaii. Because I've been worried that I'll just worry all the time we're there. About coming back."

"You see? Is Papa Bear right?"

"Um-hmm." There was a rustle, as of a large bear enfolding Goldilocks in his masculine embrace. Then there were squeaks and things. Then someone walked a few steps and the room went dark.

And then passed several eventful centuries, during which every muscle I owned put up a protest that made the anti-Vietnam movement seem insignificant. After that, light breathing and heavy snoring.

Looking at it logically, Booker's father was well into his fifties and therefore surely wasn't capable of making love for more than a couple of hours maximum. That meant there were still five or six hours till dawn and no telling how long before Isami and Papa Bear would get up to catch their plane. I simply was not going to make it. If I woke them up trying to leave, at least they'd be distracted and maybe Booker could get away. I'd save him from the horror of getting caught spying on his father's leisure-time activities. I was a pal when you thought about it. Holding my breath, I reached for the closet door. It wasn't there.

CHAPTER 7

A hand grabbed mine and Booker whispered, "Paul, it's me." By the time I'd stifled the automatic gasp, he was already padding soundlessly toward the kitchen. I followed, thanking God for professional help. I had no idea if I could have gotten the door open without a telltale snick. As it was, I rustled a few of Isami's frocks, but she and Kessler Senior were apparently too exhausted to stir. Getting out of the pitch-dark bedroom was the worst, but once in the hall, I turned on my pen-light and was out of there in two shakes, through the open back door, stopping only to close it. By the time I got to the car, Booker was already warming it up.

I had to drive, though. A more unnerved human being I have rarely seen than the scrawny, sweat-soaked redhead who beckoned me into the driver's seat and seemed to need all his remaining strength to slide over the gear shift to shotgun. Neither of us spoke for a few blocks. Finally I ventured, "You okay?"

"Uh-huh."

"Shall I drop you at Langley-Porter?" (As this was the local mental hospital, I was making a feeble joke.)

"Take me to Perry's."

"Listen, buddy, I know you need a drink, but Perry's is too damn noisy."

"I've got to get laid."

"You mean you were excited by what we—uh—witnessed?" But that wasn't it—I could tell by the look of him. He wanted human warmth and comfort.

"Back off, McDonald."

"Sorry. But—"

"Shut up, will you? Just take me to goddam Perry's!"

Very well then. He could just wait till morning to find out that the mission hadn't failed after all. If he was going to talk to me like that, I certainly wasn't going to bother trying to cheer him up.

"Your trouble," said Sardis later, "is you get your feelings hurt too easily."

"Hurt, hell! I was mad."

"Same thing."

"It certainly isn't."

"Not for everybody. For you it is. Some people just go lick their wounds—you attack."

"That is far and away the most unfair thing I ever heard in my life. I most assuredly did not attack."

"Not directly, maybe."

"Oh, go shrink your head." I stalked out of her apartment, seething. There might have been something in what she said, though. I felt less like a raging bull than one pierced by picadors. As soon as that thought entered my head another one did: *Goddam,* she makes me mad!

Well, the hell with her. I stepped in the shower.

And because I still hadn't given her the damn key, had to get out when she came down and knocked on the door.

She'd changed into a caftan sort of thing—kind of azure and mesmerizing—and she had a bottle of wine. "Go dry off and I'll open this."

I hate being easy. But I confess that a sudden desire for a couple of drinks and a talk overwhelmed all inner resolution to get back at her by withdrawing my incredibly sterling self.

Anyway, it wouldn't have worked. Sardis just laughed when I got tough with her.

"So tell me," she said, as if nothing had happened, "what was the big deal about the Post-It?"

Striving for maximum drama, I'd told her the whole yarn except for that. I produced the yellow note: "Just have a look at it."

"Pamela Temby. You could get saccharin poisoning just from the name."

"Look at the other names. Carefully."

"I never heard of Wolf and Kittrell. Sarah Mary Williams could be anybody."

"Listen to this." I got my new copy of Huck and turned to the relevant passage.

* * *

"What did you say your name was, honey?"

"M-Mary Williams."

Somehow it didn't seem to me I said it was Mary before, so I didn't look up; seemed to me I said it was Sarah; so I felt sort of cornered, and was afeared maybe I was looking it, too. I wished the woman would say something more; the longer she set still, the uneasier I was. But now she says:

"Honey, I thought you said it was Sarah when you first come in?"

"Oh, yes'm, I did. Sarah Mary Williams. Some calls me Sarah, some calls me Mary."

* * *

It sent Sardis to Memory Lane. "That's when he disguises himself as a girl," she said. "But then he gives himself away because he can't thread a needle, right?"

"Or throw or catch like a girl."

"So, really, when you get right down to it, it's another name for Huckleberry Finn. Like a code name."

"That's what I think. Beverly wasn't any fluffbrain—or if she was, at least she was one who'd almost certainly read a major work like Huck. I think she picked the name to appeal to Twain collectors. Look here." I pointed to the way she'd repeated variations of it on the Post-It. "I think she was doodling while she made her phone calls, trying to figure out which version would go down better."

"Ah. And you think the people on the list are collectors—potential buyers for the manuscript."

"That's right."

"But—*Pamela Temby?*"

I shrugged. "Just because she can't write doesn't mean she can't read. Anyway, I shouldn't say she can't write. I've never read a word of hers."

"Lifestyles," said Sardis, making a face, "of the rich, famous, dissolute, and revolting. But anyway—assuming she's a collector—what about the other two? Have you ever heard of them?"

"No, but I'm an ace reporter, remember?"

"Just for the sake of interest—how does an ace reporter track down a name out of the blue?"

"Easy. Gets someone else to do it."

The someone I had in mind was Debbie Hofer, who really was an ace, and more important, was currently employed, with access to clips. If Wolf and Kittrell were rich enough to buy the Huck Finn holograph, they'd probably made news at one time or another. I had a lot more confidence that I'd find them than that I'd find the manuscript.

Sardis was still with me when Blick turned up the next morning. It would have been a good excuse not to invite him in, but she threw on her caftan and fled. Stepping over my threshold, Blick let his potato face take on a sneer. "Nice place."

Dammit, it was a nice place, but the words didn't go with the sneer. Was he actually trying to be polite (and failing), or was he being sarcastic about my furniture? "Can I make you some coffee, Howard?"

"You can tell me what you know about Beverly Alexander."

"I already told you. Nothing and zero. Zip and doodley-squat."

"What's this?" He picked up the Post-It from the coffee table.

"None of your damn business."

"Pretty fast company you're keeping. Pamela Temby a friend of yours?"

"Howard, would you mind stating your business? I've got things to do."

"Yeah? Like knocking out one of those blockbusters? I guess your public's waiting, huh?"

"Did I ever tell you you look like a potato?"

"Somebody hit Isami Nakamura last night."

"Excuse me?" For a minute I thought he meant Isami'd been in an accident. But that couldn't be because I'd left her asleep. If he was trying to gauge my reactions, it was a good thing I was slow on the uptake.

"A burglar hit her—for the third time this week." (Technically the second, but I didn't feel like correcting him.)

I said, "That seems like too many coincidences."

"There's another interesting little coincidence." Blick walked into the dining room, got himself a chair, brought it back, and sat down.

"Make yourself at home, dildo." I sat on the rumpled bed.

"Listen up, douchebag. Miss Nakamura thought she heard a noise. When she got up to investigate, she found her back door unlocked. Nobody was in the house, but she had this weird feeling somebody had been. See, she could especially remember locking the door—on account of the two other burglaries, one of which, if you'll recall, resulted in the murder of her roommate. And she happened to remember something—know what that was, jerkoff?"

"Haven't the foggiest."

"When she came in last night, she saw a light-colored Toyota parked down the street. She couldn't help noticing it was just like yours."

"Mine? But how could she know mine?"

"That little call you paid on her. Don't you remember how you parked across the street? She and I were talking in the living room at the time—and she happened to look out the window and notice you getting out and walking up to her door."

"Howard, for Christ's sake! How many light-colored Toyotas are there in the world?"

"It's kind of coincidental, don't you think? This mysterious stranger shows up for no explainable reason, with a pillow in his jacket, like some kind of half-assed disguise, and a few days later she sees his car and she gets burglarized."

Now he had me going. Not because there was any chance in hell he could connect me with the burglary, but because he'd said "mysterious stranger." Surely that couldn't be a coincidence. "Did you know," I said, "that Mark Twain wrote a story named that?"

He looked as confused as a potato can. "Named what, asshole?"

"'The Mysterious Stranger.' Several stories, actually. Don't you think it's kind of coincidental you should use that phrase?"

"McDonald, you want to spend a few hours at the Hall?"

"Just pointing out that life is full of coincidences." (He didn't, I was now convinced, know the half of it.)

"You want to tell me how you know Beverly Alexander?"

I did. The hell of it was, I was dying to. As little faith as I had in Blick as an investigator, I had the sense to know I was concealing evidence. But I couldn't incriminate Booker and, anyway, I had no manuscript to support the story. True, I had the Post-It . . . my eyes strayed to the coffee table. It had mysteriously disappeared.

"How I know her is, she left a message on my machine. Do you want to tell me why you're so eager to get Pamela Temby's unlisted number?"

He turned red, though not, I'm sure, with embarrassment. He was mad. "What are you talking about?"

"You want my list of phone numbers, you get a search warrant." I held out my hand, but Blick stood up and flung the thing on the floor.

"Fuck off, asshole!" He left in what you might call a huff. Things had gone so swimmingly I didn't even give him a "dildo" back for his "asshole."

I was in such a good mood I called Booker, who castigated me for being careless and also for waking him up. News of the list, however, picked him up a bit. "Why didn't you tell me last night?"

"You told me to shut up."

"I guess I was upset."

"I guess I don't blame you."

"One thing, McDonald—you make any Papa Bear jokes, I'll burgle every friend and relative you ever had."

Next I called Debbie Hofer to ask for the clips on Wolf, Kittrell, and, just for good measure, Temby. While she was looking them up, I made one other call. Isami Wommy hadn't yet left for what our man Mark would have called the Sandwich Islands. She sounded very upset: "Jack, is it you?"

"Miss Williams?"

"What?"

"May I speak to Sarah Williams, please?"

With a noise like a sob, she rang off, but what that meant I didn't know—maybe just that she was upset about the burglary.

It was an hour before Deb got back to me, but when she did she had good stuff. "Did you know Temby's your neighbor?"

"Pamela Temby in Oakland? I'd sooner believe Liz Taylor lives in Lodi."

"Not exactly Oakland. Piedmont."

"That's different." Piedmont was a bubble of affluence that had the misfortune to be surrounded by déclassé Oakland. I didn't know how its well-heeled citizens could stand to drive through the one to get to the other. They held their noses, I suppose.

"What else do you have on her?"

"Just the usual author interviews and sightings at parties."

"How about Kittrell?"

"He's a case. Another local—lives in San Francisco. Telegraph Hill to be exact, in quite a grand apartment, I'm told."

"What does he do?"

"Goes to parties, you'd think from the clips. I asked the society editor, and she confirmed it. Quite the aging social butterfly. He comes from old money, but he's gone through most of it by now. Never worked a day in his life that anyone knows of. Married four times, not currently hitched. But, curiously, he's said to be quite erudite. One of these elegant, sophisticated, bitchy wits that everyone loves."

"The Truman Capote of Telegraph Hill."

"The same type," she said, "but don't imagine he's ever

written a word in his life—except scholarly pieces for literary journals."

"You're kidding!"

"Not a bit of it. Guess what his hobby is?"

"Collecting rare books and manuscripts, by any chance?"

"Bingo. You're obviously on the right track."

"What about Wolf?"

"That one's a little dicier. I've got stuff on a Herb Wolf, but I don't know if he's your boy. He's a second-rate movie producer, from the looks of things."

"What things?"

"Oh, stuff like 'The Robot Who Ate Rhode Island.' That was a comedy, I think. However, the drive-in critic gave 'City of Vampires' a ten on the vomit meter."

"He doesn't sound like an intellectual."

"He's the best I can do."

"You did great, Deb. Thanks a mil."

Looking at the Post-It again, I saw that our Herb Wolf had a Los Angeles area code. It could be the same guy.

Full of my news, I went up to tell Sardis, hoping to chew it all over over a cup of coffee. She answered the door in shorts and paint-spattered T-shirt. "Oh. Paul. I'm painting."

"You certainly ducked out at the right moment."

"You know what the tough do."

"You left too soon. Blick was putty in my hands."

"Listen, could you tell me about it tonight? I'll make dinner."

"Oh. Okay. Sure." She must have seen I was a little nonplussed, because she softened up and gave me a little smile.

"What are you doing today?"

"I thought I'd go over to the Bancroft Library and see Linda McCormick again."

"The specific editor?"

"Yeah. I could just call, but—"

"You kind of like her, don't you?"

"Well, sure. She's—"

"You know what? It kind of pisses me off." She gave me a quick kiss and closed the door. Well, hell, I thought; it was nice of her to say she was jealous—even if she didn't mean it.

Okay, if Sardis wouldn't have coffee with me, maybe Linda would. I did call her. And made a date for twenty minutes hence, at the espresso joint known to Cal students as Café Depresso.

She was wearing pants today, and a slightly wrinkled silk blouse. Her eye makeup was blue, to match the blouse, and had been applied every-which-way. I certainly hoped she was never tempted to undergo one of those "beauty makeovers" you hear about.

"Linda, I have a confession to make."

She nodded, dabbing discreetly at a cappuccino moustache.

"The story I'm working on isn't just a feature. I think it's developing into something bigger than that."

She nodded again.

"I'm afraid I can't tell you what it is, but I need to ask you a few more questions. Is that okay?"

"Sure."

"I've been given the names of three collectors, and I'm wondering if you know them."

Silence. Just a nice, big encouraging smile. This Linda didn't waste words, but she was eloquent in her own way.

"Pamela Temby, Russell Kittrell, and Herb Wolf."

"I know Temby. She bought a letter once, and was nice enough to let us see it. The others I never heard of, but that doesn't mean they aren't collectors—even big collectors. Some of them collect just so they'll have something no one else has. And some carry it even farther—they don't even want you to know what they have."

"But why?"

She shrugged. "I guess it makes them feel important."

"God. Can you imagine what Mark Twain would have thought of that?"

"He was a doer." She smiled shyly. "Like you. Some people don't do anything."

I was a little embarrassed at being compared with Mark Twain. "I don't do much."

"You wrote a good book."

"You know about that?"

"Sure. I looked you up in the card catalogue. You don't work for the *Chronicle* either. I tried to call you there."

"Oh. I don't know what to say." Things had gone so well with Blick and now this specific editor had me speechless.

She smiled invitingly. "Just tell me what you want."

"That wouldn't be polite." God! I was flirting again. Well, Sardis had driven me to it. "But here's what I need. Scuttlebutt. Gossip. I need to know who's in the scholarly Mark Twain community, if there is such a thing—and who'd be interested in buying an important manuscript."

She answered quickly. "We would. You have something to sell? You know, you can get a big tax break just by donating."

"I'm not the seller. I think—" I hesitated, not sure how much I dared tell her.

Her eyes looked wide and interested, even encouraging.

I plunged ahead: "I'm pretty sure a stolen manuscript is about to go on the market. I'm trying to recover it for the rightful owner."

"How did you get involved?"

"I can't tell you that." I'd probably already told her far too much—especially in view of my earlier questions about the Huck Finn holograph.

"Okay." She shrugged, apparently deciding I had an honest face. "First, see Rick Debay in San Francisco. He's the biggest dealer around, and he specializes in Mark Twain. Second—" She blushed. "—are you free this evening?"

"Sure." (After dinner with Sardis, anyway.)

"I could take you to a meeting of the Huckleberry Fiends."

"I beg your pardon?"

"You're familiar with Sherlockians, aren't you?"

"Sure."

"And fan conventions in various genres?"

"Yes."

"Well, why shouldn't Mark Twain have a fan club too?"

"Holy mother of mackinoli—that's what it is?"

"Listen, I've got to run. Meet me at seven, okay? At the library."

So much for dinner with Sardis.

CHAPTER 8

Richard Debay, Rare Books and Manuscripts (Specializing in Mark Twain) was listed in the phone book, on Sutter Street. If I hurried, I might be able to get there before Rick went to lunch.

It was a bibliophile's Disneyland. It smelled of books—old musty, delicious books, many in leather bindings, some beautifully preserved, some in stages of decay that only made them seem even more enticing, as if they'd been through a lot. It was a tiny store, lined with hundreds of volumes, and there was a circular stairway up to a second level. There were also plenty of library ladders and a warm crimson carpet on the floor. On the very few feet of wall space that weren't covered by bookshelves were framed letters signed by authors or other important people, like Abraham Lincoln.

And behind the counter was one of San Francisco's leading literary lights. "Hello," I said. "You're Jenny Swensen, aren't you?"

She was a small, dark, nervous-looking woman about forty-five, with a sour expression that dissipated instantly on being recognized. "Yes, I am."

"I've read all your books."

"All three," she said, looking miffed, as if mad at herself for not producing more.

"Short stories too."

"One of them *is* short stories."

"*Dark Nights*. It's my favorite." I was lying a little—it was actually the one I disliked least—but I didn't feel even a little bit guilty about it. If ever a woman needed a boost, it was clearly Jenny. She was published routinely in the *New Yorker* and despite her meager output contrived to be the very darling of the *New York Times Book Review*. Yet she seemed so unsure of herself she couldn't even take a compliment until it was offered several times in a variety of forms. I seemed to have gotten through to her at last.

"Thanks," she said finally. "What can I do for you?"

"I'm looking for Richard Debay."

She picked up a phone, pushed a button and asked while it rang: "What name shall I give him?"

"Paul McDonald. From the *Chronicle*."

The nervous look came back. "Oh. The *Chronicle*. Rick doesn't really—" but Rick must have come on the line then. She spoke too low for me to hear, then hung up and said he'd be right down.

"He doesn't like reporters?" I asked.

She smiled. "Maybe he'll like you."

Rick came down the ladder and extended his hand, the perfect preppie from central casting—blond, tanned (just a little, as if he sailed on weekends), khaki pants, open-necked white shirt, even Top-Siders. He was in his early thirties or damned well-preserved.

"I thought," I said, "you'd be a bespectacled old man."

"That was my dad."

I waved an arm. "I should have known this wasn't built in a day."

Debay moved behind the counter, maybe to put a little distance between us. Jenny Swensen, one of America's most touted authors, busied herself with the mundane business of dusting. "What can I do for you, Mr. McDonald?"

"I'm working on a story about manuscript collecting."

He narrowed his eyes. "Odd sort of news story."

"Yes, well, that's what attracted me to it. No one cares about books anymore. Have you noticed?"

"Not at all."

"You're fortunate. Out in the concrete jungles—" I turned around to point to the outside, but I found myself flustered. I'd been about to speak of the Philistines abounding in the lanes and hedgerows when I realized Debay was making it clear he thought me one of them. "In the age of TV, I wanted to write about some people who really care about books—care passionately, I mean."

"And how may I help you?"

"I thought that, since the university has just published that wonderful new edition of *Huckleberry Finn*, I'd write about Mark Twain collectors. The people at the Bancroft Library say there are lots of them, and they're quite colorful. I've even heard Pamela Temby is a collector."

"Have you?" His expression said he smelled rotten eggs, but I couldn't tell whether it was aimed at me or Temby.

I shrugged, hoping I seemed casual and worldly-wise. "I haven't confirmed it yet. At any rate, the folks at the Bancroft sent me to you."

He looked as if I were speaking Bulgarian. "Whatever for?"

"I'd like to interview some collectors. They thought you might be able to give me the names of some of the big ones."

Now I'd done it. I'd obviously made a request on a par with drinking the blood of his firstborn. I knew it before he spoke. "I'm afraid I couldn't possibly violate the privacy of my clients."

"Sorry. I didn't realize privacy was involved." But I should have, after Linda's remark about collectors not wanting people to know what they had. Debay's extraordinary standoffishness added another dimension to this urgent need for privacy—combined with the fact that dealers didn't like to have documents authenticated, it had started to smell a little on the piscine side. "Without giving names of specific collectors," I said, "can you tell me how I might go about meeting some?"

More eggs seemed to be rotting. "There's some kind of

organization called the Huckleberry Fiends. But I'm afraid I really can't tell you much about it."

"I'll check it out. Thanks for your time, Mr. Debay."

I more or less staggered out, still reeling from one of the most thorough bum's rushes I'd ever been treated to—and for an ex-reporter, that's saying something. For a while I just stood on the sidewalk, staring into space and trying to get my bearings; and then I turned around and stared in the window. Jenny Swensen was putting on her coat, probably getting ready for lunch, and it occurred to me she might have a thing or two to say about working conditions in a rare bookstore.

She came out looking purposeful. "Miss Swensen." I tried to look nonthreatening. "I thought you might like to have lunch."

"No, thanks. I don't think so."

"I'd consider it a very great pleasure. I'd love to treat a literary star."

"I only have half an hour—"

"We'll find a deli."

She knew one, of course—it was her turf. When we were seated over sandwiches, I said, "It must be hard trying to write and work at the same time."

I'd spoken out of firsthand knowledge of publishing poverty, and I couldn't have hit on a better subject if I'd been psychic.

"To write and work and raise two children? It's hell. But Rick spells me for a couple hours a day so I can write in a back room. He thinks it's classy to have me around."

"I didn't think the pay could be very good."

"It's shit—but a little better than I could make anywhere else. I have no marketable skills—not even typing."

"You write in longhand?"

"Yes. And then pay to get my stuff typed." She spoke bitterly.

I shook my head in genuine sympathy. "A writer of your caliber ought to be able to make a living from her writing."

"Literary merit doesn't sell. They want you to write what they call 'big books.' Swill like family sagas and mysteries."

Didn't I know it, but she'd got it garbled about the mysteries—no books were "smaller."

"Know how long I've been writing? Twenty-five years. A quarter of a century and I still can't support myself." I was thunderstruck—only three books in twenty-five years, and one of them a short-story collection! But they did read as if she took forever over them—they were squeezed out and stingy; dark, depressing and bitter. Revengeful and hateful. Worst of all, oblique and elliptical—they asked the reader to fill in a lot of blanks and when he did, to my mind there still wasn't much there. I couldn't stand them, but I was beginning to understand the shadowy cave they came out of. Jenny Swensen wasn't what you'd call a cockeyed optimist.

She was still talking. "I started writing in college. My first story was published in a 'little magazine'—infinitesimal, almost—and so was my check. Twenty dollars they paid me. Twenty big ones and I had writer friends a generation older who said that's what they were paid for their first stories. Then I got married and used to get up at five A.M. to write when the kids were in diapers. And then"—she threw open her arms and let her eyes fill with tears—"my husband left me and I had to work full time."

"I'll bet you kept writing even then."

"I tried, but I couldn't turn out more than about a short story a year."

"It must have been tough."

"Dear God! They talk about movie rights and foreign rights and paperback rights and hard-soft deals—spare me! Do you want to know what my dearest ambition is? To support myself. That's all. Just to be able to support myself by my writing and to quit working for that miserable little—" She stopped, apparently remembering she didn't know me from Noah.

I gave her an encouraging smile. "It's okay. I didn't care much for him either. He seemed needlessly closemouthed. Almost suspiciously so."

She looked over her shoulder, as if worried about being overheard. "I guess he has good reason."

"Do I detect something rotten in the collectors' market?"

"Tell me, Mr. McDonald—"

"Paul."

"Of course. And you call me Jenny." She was actually quite pretty when she smiled—very white skin against stark, straight black hair, and red, red lips. Not my kind of face at all—much too sad, too melodramatic—but she was striking if you could bring yourself to concentrate on the features instead of the sour expression. "Tell me," she said, "is that what your piece is really about? An exposé of some sort?"

Though the piece was the merest fabrication, I almost laughed to think how little the reading public would care about chicanery in such a rarefied atmosphere. Instead I said, "No. But I suppose if I found out something—"

"Oh, please, no. I wasn't suggesting that. I don't want to lose my job."

"No fear of that. I'm doing a perfectly harmless story—just like I told Debay."

"You know why he wouldn't give you any names?"

"I'm beginning to suspect. Does he deal in forgeries or something?"

"I wouldn't put it past him."

"But you don't know for sure."

She shrugged. "Not exactly."

"Wait a minute. Not forgeries. Hot stuff."

This time she lifted an eyebrow.

"You mean the guy's a fence?"

"Oh, hell, I don't know. Let's put it this way—I've heard some pretty questionable conversations in there."

"Can I ask you something? Why are you telling me all this?"

Fear leaped into her eyes. "You said—"

"I know. I said I was harmless. But still—why tell a perfect stranger?"

She stared past me, out towards another galaxy, and she looked for a moment as if her youngest child had been had for breakfast by a pack of wild dogs. I thought I saw a way out of her financial pickle—she could rake in big bucks modeling for tragedy masks. And then fury replaced the misery.

"Because it's all I can think about! That's why I told you. Frankly, I've gotten to the point that I tell anyone who'll listen to me—I can't stop myself. I buttonhole strangers at parties and pour it out to them. Goddammit, I can't even afford a shrink to tell things to! Do you know what it's like for me to work there? For that man? To hear the things I hear and keep my mouth shut? Shut to keep from spitting on Mr. Stanford Business School? I'm a writer, do you hear me?"

How many times had I wanted to shout out that last sentence myself? World, I'm a writer, goddammit! Treat me better! I wanted to say something sympathetic, but I felt too raw, too naked; so I said nothing.

"I'm sorry," she said.

"You should write about that." I thought it as eloquent a statement of case as I'd ever heard.

She looked pleased. "I am. That's what I'm doing now—a nonfiction book on how hard it is to write if you're poor and a woman. I think it'll be my breakthrough book."

"I hope so," I said, and also hoped she had the strength for another disappointment. I figured the audience for it was about a thousand writers so poor they'd have to get it from the library. "Could I ask you something else about Debay?"

"After all that, I don't see why not."

"Does he do business with Pamela Temby?"

"I don't know. I've never seen her around, though."

"How about a guy named Russell Kittrell?"

"Not that I know of."

"Herb Wolf?"

"Doesn't ring a bell. But who knows? I don't know all his clients."

"Doesn't it strike you as a little pretentious to call them clients?"

She laughed and I deemed the lunch a success—if you could make this one laugh, you'd done your good deed for the day.

CHAPTER 9

Driving home, I reassessed the problem. My original assignment had been to find the owner of the manuscript. But my current one was to assuage Booker's guilt by finding out who killed Beverly. The murderer, as I saw it, was one of four people—the original owner or one of the three potential buyers. At least I knew where to look for the last three. And until I met the Huckleberry Fiends, I'd made about all the polite inquiries I could. Now it was time for more direct action.

I went inside, fed Spot and petted him awhile, getting up my nerve. Finally I called Sardis. "How's the painting going?"

"Great. I'm taking a break. Have you had lunch?"

"Uh-huh. With a literary dark—as opposed to light. I need some help. Could you make a phone call for me?"

"Your dialing finger's broken?"

"I need a woman's touch."

"Come on up."

I did, and told her my plan—to have her phone Pamela Temby as Sarah Williams, crooked manuscript dealer. After she identified herself, the conversation—as reported—went like this:

"Wonderful, dear. Are you ready to talk now?"
"I think it's time."
"Splendid. One thousand Alpine Glen. I'll be home till four-thirty."

"And then," said Sardis, "she hung up without even asking if it's convenient. Which it isn't."

"Gosh. Who knew she'd do that?"

"I certainly didn't, or I'd have never made the call. But no matter, it's not your fault. You'll go with me, won't you?"

"Are you kidding? She might be a murderer."

"Does that mean no or yes?"

I didn't dignify that with an answer.

I might not have cared much for Jenny Swensen's work, but I had a feeling I'd care even less for Pamela's. Yet hundreds of thousands of book-buyers put me in the wrong. She was on top of the heap, and, fittingly, lived on top of the East Bay, on about an acre of land in something resembling an English stately home. I made a mental note to read one of her ten-pound opuscules—maybe I'd pick up some tips.

The front door was a football field away, and every blade of grass appeared to have been hand-clipped. Yet smack in the middle of what might otherwise have been a croquet court was a mean-looking Harley under the loving attendance of a scruffy human. The grease monkey was tall, lanky, filthy, crowned with a spiky shock of purple hair, and female. She stood and put up a hand against the afternoon sun. "Welcome to Miniseries Manor. Is one of you Sarah Williams?"

"I am," said Sardis.

"Mummy's waiting." She stuck out a tentative hand but, noting the condition of it, used her better judgment and plunged it into her shorts pocket. Her voice was husky and her manner masculine. "I'm Rosamund Temby, by the way." Despite her punky hair and get-back vehicle, there was something about her that said, "Like me, like me." She was oddly appealing.

She led us into a parquet foyer roughly the size of my living room. "Mummy's in the library." We went through a living room that *Architectural Digest* would have doted on into a library out of the Musée de Cluny. Sun streamed through leaded-glass windows and French doors. Deep chairs, an antique desk, and more books than Rick Debay had contrived an ecclesiastical effect, rather like that of a reading room in a Catholic college. Pamela Temby stood in Titian-haired splendor on an Oriental rug she could have traded for a Mercedes if money got tight. She was in her fifties, tall like her daughter, well-padded, and handsome. Her red-gold hair was parted on the side, falling fetchingly over the right side of her face in a long, languid shoulder-length wave. Caftans, I'd thought, were regulation wear for writers of high-gloss tales of love and money, but Temby made do with baggy white pants and billowy shirt. No cat or Pekingese nestled in the crook of her arm, but the way Rosamund looked at her, she didn't need another pet.

She gave Sardis a relentlessly manicured hand. "Miss Williams."

"This is Joe Harper," said Sardis, "my business associate."

"Joe. How's the ransoming going?"

She knew her Huck Finn. We'd picked a name out of Tom Sawyer's Gang, which specialized in ransoming. "Tolerable slow," I said. "It was more fun being a pirate."

"Ah, but that was another book." (*Tom Sawyer*, if memory served.) "Darling," she said to Rosamund, "could you excuse us now? And do get cleaned up—we're taking Sukie to dinner."

"Nice girl," said Sardis, "is she home for the summer?"

"Rosamund? Heavens, no. She's twenty-seven. But we don't age quickly in our family—except those who become writers." She positively smirked.

"It must be a pretty stressful life," I said, glad Jenny Swensen wasn't there to bat her about the room. Truth to tell, I was feeling a little violent myself.

"I'm so glad," she said to Sardis, "to have finally gotten

you in my house. I've so much wanted to show you some of my things. I collect all the great American authors, you see. I draw inspiration from them."

I was speechless, but Sardis was more amused than Mark Twain aboard the *Quaker City*. "I can see that in your work," she said. I hoped she had the grace to cross her fingers.

"You can? How nice of you to say so."

"You know, I once heard a dealer say that one day your letters will be worth as much as Twain's."

"Oh, I doubt it." She brushed hair out of her eyes, showing a face making little success of looking modest. (And I'd thought Sardis had gone too far.)

For the next hour we were treated to the collection—shelves of first editions, cabinets of manuscripts and letters. Everyone of any importance in American literature was represented, from Cotton Mather to Dashiell Hammett to Bellow, Mailer, and Joyce Carol Oates. Truly a wonderful collection, with lots of Mark Twain papers, not only the one letter the Bancroft folks had seen. Then there were the clips and letters of appreciation—she'd donated generously to libraries and universities; she'd invited distinguished scholars to use her papers and they'd accepted gratefully. Though the newspaper stories had run mostly in small university towns, they outnumbered her author interviews and reviews, a fact on which Sardis unkindly remarked in the guise of congratulations on Temby's generosity.

Again, the hand brushed the hair, and Temby shrugged. "It gets sort of old-hat, you know—just another best-seller by Pamela Temby. Anyway, *I'm* not the point; Mark Twain is. I think you may possibly understand how seriously I take my little hobby."

"I think we're beginning to."

"Tell me. Have you brought the holograph?"

"Not today, actually. It's in a safe-deposit box. However, I do have copies of a couple of pages." I produced some I'd made. A moment before I could have sworn I'd seen naked greed in her eyes; now there was no mistaking a pair of real tears.

"It's authentic! There's no question about it." Her hands

shook as she reached for one of her own Mark Twain letters to compare the handwriting. But she did it almost absently, having already made up her mind. "I'm *so* glad you got back to me. The condition is good?"

"Mint."

"I want to withdraw my original offer—" She paused for effect. "I think now it was much too low. I want to go up another $250,000."

"That's very generous," said Sardis.

"But of course," I noted, "there's other interest."

"I understand. I just hope you . . . fathom how much this would mean to me." The pair of tears did an encore.

She showed us out herself, not even calling a servant or Rosamund. She pumped Sardis's hand: "*So* nice to meet you in person, my dear. And you too, Mr. Harper. You're so very *sympatico*—the sort of people who truly love and appreciate books."

By now, Rosamund had put her Harley away, leaving the yard as pristine as a mountain meadow. "I wish," said Sardis, "she'd taken us for a turn around the grounds."

"Maybe she didn't think we truly love and appreciate flowers."

"Hey, something's funny about the car."

I bent down. "You're not kidding. Two flats on this side."

Sardis walked to the other. "And two over here."

"Oh, God. If it were a dark and stormy night, I'd be awfully nervous."

"Even then we could just call AAA."

"We couldn't, actually."

"You're not a member?"

"Canceled for nonpayment."

"Damn! Why didn't we bring my car? I've got one of those little compressors you plug into your cigarette lighter."

"Maybe Rosamund has one—she looks the handy type. Or we could just call a cab."

"Let's fling ourselves on the duchess's mercy."

This time the door was opened by a uniformed maid—unfortunately one who spoke no English. After much sign language, we wrote our names—Williams and Harper—for her to show to the chatelaine. Once again, we were ushered into the library. Pamela was sitting at her desk, now wearing a pair of pink-tinted aviator glasses. In front of her, open to the picture on the back flap, was a copy of *Vandal in Bohemia* by Paul McDonald.

"Miss Williams and Mr. Harper. I didn't expect you again so soon." She looked pointedly from the picture to me.

"Really? You seem to have taken pains to keep us here."

"I beg your pardon?"

"We're easy—you could have just offered tea. You didn't have to have your daughter let the air out of our tires."

"Rosamund? Rosamund did what?"

"Rosamund or someone let the air out of our tires."

"How awful! I assure you it isn't my doing. I *am* glad you're back, though. Perhaps you'll sign my book."

"Just what are you up to, Mrs. Temby?"

"Nothing! How could I be? We were together all the time—I could scarcely have given any orders, could I? These things happen in a city. Why are you so suspicious of me?"

"You knew who I was."

"I didn't at first, exactly. I just thought you looked familiar. And then it began to dawn on me. I have an excellent memory for faces, you see—particularly those I like." She took off the glasses. "Actually, I've been perishing to look at the picture for the last half-hour. I must say, Mr. McDonald—"

"Paul."

"When I was a struggling author, I did typing to make ends meet. But you seem to have come up with a more innovative solution. I hope you were careful making those copies, incidentally. You can damage the delicate pages that way."

"This isn't actually my show. I'm here because Miss Williams wanted company this afternoon."

"It's still Miss Williams, is it?"

"Sarah," said Sardis.

"Sarah." She crossed her legs slowly and elegantly. "You

wanted company, did you? Did you think I'd bite you, my dear?"

Sardis smiled. "I'm representing someone who's trying to sell a property worth a small fortune. People get nasty over things like that."

Temby raised a perfectly shaped and colored eyebrow. "I thought you told me you were acting alone."

Panic flickered briefly on Sardis's face. The real Sarah Williams—Beverly—had contacted Temby, and we had no way of knowing what she'd told her. But Sardis composed herself quickly. "Did I say that? I guess I forgot."

"Do you know what I think, my dear? I don't think you're Sarah Williams at all. I remember voices almost as well as faces."

"One can't be recognized on the telephone. For her own reasons, she didn't want to come in person."

"It's someone I know, then."

"Perhaps."

"Tell me—is there something illegal about all this?"

"Do you care?" Sardis spoke with the practiced cool of a master criminal. I wondered briefly if she'd been leading a double life.

Temby considered. "Not really," she said after a time, "so long as the manuscript itself is authentic."

"We're satisfied that it is."

"I'll have to have a look at the whole thing, of course."

"When the time comes."

"I think we understand each other."

I was getting more insight into Linda's remark about collectors who didn't bother having documents authenticated. For one thing, it was obvious Temby considered herself perfectly competent to do the authenticating. For another, in a questionable deal (like this one) it could be dangerous to take possibly stolen documents to legitimate dealers or scholars who might know their provenance. In fact, this deal was dicey indeed, since the manuscript was a major find. Absolutely no one could be trusted to keep his mouth shut about it. So if Temby had convinced herself the thing was real (and I wouldn't blame her—I'd convinced myself), by showing no one she'd be able both to avoid the risk of discovery and to keep her expensive dream intact. I wondered just how expensive. Something over $250,000 was all we knew, but I figured she was negotiating in quarter-million-dollar increments.

"I think we should call the police," I said. "About the tires."

"Of course. Would you like to phone AAA as well?"

"We thought Rosamund might have one of those little lighter compressors."

"I'll check. Sit down, won't you?"

She left in a cloud of perfume, returning with Rosamund, now in jeans and neat black T-shirt, hair wet from the shower. She was trailed, in turn, by a pillowy young woman whose hair was also wet. "I've called the police," said Temby, "but Rosamund doesn't seem to have the gizmo."

Rosamund smiled and ran a hand through her wet hair. She had a charmingly coltish look about her. "Not the way Mummy's explained it, anyway. Something about a hand pump for tires?"

"A compressor," said Sardis. "It works on a car's cigarette lighter. I've got one, but it's at home."

Rosamund laughed, probably at the notion of such a daintily amateur item. "Sorry. Haven't got; I'll be glad to run you home, though."

"Thanks, but we have to wait for the cops."

She laughed again. "You don't know Piedmont. They'll be here before we can drink our sherry—you will have one, won't you?"

"Personally," said Sardis, "I'd like one in each hand."

"Good. This is my friend, Sukie. Sarah Williams and—sorry . . ."

"Paul McDonald."

"Darling," said the elder Temby. "Mr. McDonald's a wonderful new author." She held up my book.

"*Vandal in Bohemia*—how marvelous."

"It takes place at the Bohemian Grove," said her mother. "Jeffrey Pebbles recommended it. He's a Bohemian, you know. Anyway, Paul, I'm such a fan—" She walked over to a large section of shelves. "—see all my mysteries? I think you're simply splendid. In lots of ways." She stared, locking my eyes with hers. There was no mistaking her meaning.

"Oh, Mummy, you're so bawdy!"

"How about you, dear? You and Sukie with your wet hair."

Sukie blushed, sinking into a chair as if to hide in it. "But this is a honeymoon," cried Rosamund, pouring sherry all round. "You see," she said to Sardis and me, "Sukie and I just met. We've been together for seventy-two whole hours now." She took Sukie a glass, and bent to kiss her.

The cops came then, providing a welcome distraction—to one person at least. Poor Sukie looked like a person pursued by the Hound of the Baskervilles.

CHAPTER 10

All the way home—in Pamela Temby's white Rolls-Royce—Sukie spoke not a word, while Rosamund kept up a running stream of chatter, mostly about the joys of owning a Harley. "Sukie's never been on one, but not to worry. We'll make a diesel dyke of you yet—won't we, dear?"

Sukie's mortification notwithstanding, I couldn't help liking Rosamund, admiring her exuberance. The truth is, I was a fan. "I suppose you think all she needs," said Sardis later, "is a good man to straighten her out."

"Couldn't hurt."

But she wouldn't be baited. "Pah! She's Mummyfied. As who wouldn't be?"

"Easy on the old babe—she thinks I'm 'simply splendid.'"

"Babe, hell! Mae West without the hourglass."

It wasn't the time, I figured, to tell her about the Huckleberry Fiends, so I waited till we'd retrieved my car. But luck went against me again. "Oh, hell," said Sardis, looking at her watch, "the afternoon's shot. Want to come up for a pre-dinner nap? Euphemistically speaking, I mean."

"Uh, listen—I don't think I can make dinner, after all."

"You don't *think* you can? What's this think, McDonald? I thought we had a date."

"Well, Linda McCormick—"

"Linda McCormick!"

"Hold on, hold on, it's business. She invited me to a meeting of a Mark Twain fan club."

"That certainly sounds important."

"I'm hoping I might meet somebody—"

"It sounds as if you've already met her." She started up the stairs.

"Sardis, come on. This is important."

"You listen to me, Paul McDonald—next time you decide to waste my entire afternoon, you tell me in advance that you also intend to stand me up for dinner." She continued the climb. At the top of the stairs she turned around and lifted an eloquent finger. "Huck you!" she shouted grandly.

I suppose that meant she thought I was a Huckleberry hound. The hell of it was, I could see her point—it would have been more honest to mention the Fiends first, not to mention better strategically. I'd have to make it up to her later. At the moment, though, I was wondering whether the Fiends would feed me.

Linda was waiting outside when I arrived at seven. "My car or yours?"

"Mine. I'm parked illegally. Where are we going?"

She gave me an address in North Berkeley. "We always meet in someone's house."

"What happens at these things, anyway?"

"Oh, there's a buffet and social hour. Then someone gives a talk."

"Who's speaking tonight?"

"Me."

"How great! What's the subject?"

"The biggie."

"I beg your pardon?"

"Can't you guess what it is?"

"No. I mean—it couldn't be. Could it?"

"I don't know. Try me."

"The missing manuscript?"

"What missing manuscript?"

"I guess that's not it."

"Why don't you mull it awhile. Maybe it'll come to you. By the way, how do you want to be introduced?"

"I've thought about that. Joe Harper, maybe? Ben Rogers?"

"Come on."

"Say, have you ever heard of a woman called Sarah Williams?"

"Who?"

"Sarah Mary Williams."

"It sounds familiar, but I can't quite place it."

I guess even scholars have lapses. I said, going back to her question, "I think I'd better be myself. That's the advice my mother used to give me."

"Do you want to stand up and make a pitch for information? Or just talk to people?"

"I think I'd like to go about it informally, but I'll let you know if I change my mind."

We ended up at the home of one of her fellow editors, a typical Berkeley apartment full of the ubiquitous white sofas, Dhurri rugs, tasteful plants, and Japanese prints that replaced India-print bedspreads and pillows on the floor when hip yielded to yup.

Instead of the spaghetti and jug wine of old, there was goat cheese, sun-dried tomatoes, charcoal-grilled vegetables, pasta salad, marinated string beans, salmon mousse, mussels on the half shell, Cajun popcorn, and, specially chosen for summer sipping, an elegant selection of blush wines. Smoking, needless to say, would have been an unpardonable breach of decorum.

Some of the Fiends, however, hadn't kept up with the times. There was one man in a ponytail and two or three wore scraggly beards and jeans. One of the women actually had long, straight, center-parted hair. But I supposed these people were mostly grad students, professors, erudite carpenters or longshoremen, and maverick psychologists. One couldn't expect such folk, no matter what other fads they followed, to have the fashion sense of hairdressers, hot-tub salesmen, and chefs from chic restaurants.

Over the crayfish, I fell easily into conversation with the longhair. His ponytail was graying and a little greasy, his shoulders stooped, his spectacles mended with tape. Automatically, I checked his pocket for a nerd-pack, and my instincts weren't far off. He was Dan Dupart, software designer. I told him I was Paul McDonald, mystery writer and friend of Linda McCormick.

"Oh, man," he said, "Twain must be one of your idols, then."

"Because of Linda?"

"No, because he was such a great mystery writer."

"You think so?"

"Oh, sure. *Tom Sawyer, Detective, Double-Barrelled Detective Story,* and, of course, my personal favorite, *The Stolen White Elephant*."

I was uncomfortable. "I like *Pudd'nhead Wilson,* myself."

"But that's not really a mystery."

"It's got more crime per paragraph than anything Hammett ever wrote, probably including *Red Harvest*. And it's got fingerprints—maybe the first use of fingerprints in an American story." (I had no idea whether this was true, but anything to throw him off the track.) "Then there's 'The Man That Corrupted Hadleyburg.' What an evil, evil little story."

"But it's not—"

"It's certainly suspense. I'd be glad to see it in any criminous anthology. And *Tom Sawyer* itself—that's got a murder in it."

"But what about the detective stories? Is Inspector Blunt the greatest or what?"

"Well—I—uh—" I was nearly choking on my mousse. But manfully, I spat it out: "I never cared much for him actually."

"What? You don't like *The Stolen White Elephant*? I thought I'd die." He fell forward laughing at the mere thought.

"I just didn't find it a very good parody."

That sobered him. "You didn't?"

What was this? Had I criticized Mark Twain and got away

with it? Anyway, lightning hadn't struck me, and Dan Dupart hadn't kicked my teeth in. "Not really," I ventured.

"Maybe that's what he meant."

"Who?"

"Justin Kaplan. You know, Twain criticized Conan Doyle for what he called 'cheap and ineffectual ingenuities.' And Kaplan said he was envious."

Vindication of sorts! And from no less a scholar than Twain's biographer. I relaxed a little, even venturing to drift into a conversation about Olivia Langdon, Clemens's wife, his "dear little gravity," who had censored and emasculated him, transforming him from adventurer to petit bourgeois. The only problem was, I was way out of my depth, according to Professor Marcia Dunlap, a hundred-and-one pounds of fun who seemed to have packed several libraries under the brandy-colored mop on her head.

"Perhaps you recall," she prompted, "that Clemens fell in love with her image—a picture he saw six months before he ever met her. That's the important thing to remember about the relationship."

"He didn't *marry* a picture."

"But it's hardly as if he fell under the spell of *la belle dame sans merci*. On the contrary, he camped on her doorstep till she gave in."

"Still, she made him take the temperance pledge and become a Christian."

"Thereby setting himself up beautifully to spend the rest of his life playing the role of the henpecked husband. He enjoyed it, Paul, don't you see? It was another way of saying, 'It didn't happen on my shift.' Despite his carryings-on, he actually had most things his way. In fact, Livy ended up drinking beer every night and becoming an unbeliever. While he not only never became a Christian in any true sense, but continued drinking most enthusiastically."

"You can't get around the fact that she censored his work."

"If ever a man begged to be 'censored,' it was our Mr. Clemens. At his behest, Bret Harte 'censored' him, and so did William Dean Howells and so did Mary Fairbanks before he even met Livy. Later on, so did his publisher, so did Paine (who did considerably more than edit) and so did De Voto. Charles Neider's my favorite. He simply took it upon himself to reorganize Twain's *Autobiography*, after casually dismissing the author's notion of stream-of-consciousness as 'an extraordinary idea.' For that matter, any editor 'censors' any writer."

Cheered by her mention of Bernard De Voto, who was no admirer of Livy's, I remembered another scholar, Van Wyck Brooks, who agreed with De Voto on Mrs. Clemens but on virtually nothing else. "Oh, come now, Marcia—about the only thing most Twain scholars actually *agree* on is the stifling influence of her Victorian ideas."

"I'm afraid, Paul, you're a little out of date. Today, we're taking Twain's own portrayal of Livy—as suppressor of his artistic genius—for the self-serving drivel it was. As a humorist, he himself was extremely careful to choose 'safe' subjects that wouldn't offend—from the pious pilgrims of *The Innocents Abroad* to slavery in *Huckleberry Finn*. Yet he persisted in portraying himself as the sensitive and suppressed artist. Perhaps you recall what he told Paine on his seventy-third birthday."

"I can't say that I do."

"He said his best book was *Joan of Arc*."

"I beg your pardon?"

"*Joan of Arc*."

This was embarrassing. "I didn't even know he wrote a book by that title."

Dunlap folded her arms and lowered her chin in a gesture of utter complacency. "I rest my case."

"Well, you might fill me in on what it is."

"There's a reason you never heard of *Joan of Arc*. It has about as much life to it as the telephone book. The point being that Twain was a terrible judge of his own work. After Livy died, he published the books she'd forbidden. Maybe you remember *What Is Man?*"

"Afraid not."

"How about *Extract from Captain Stormfield's Visit to Heaven*?"

"Vaguely, maybe."

"In the preface to *What Is Man?* he said the ideas in it had been thought by millions who never dared to express them, and that he himself hadn't dared up till then."

"My God, what's it about?"

She shrugged. "Nothing very exciting. Man's helpless position, I guess—pretty straightforward determinism. That was the great censored material."

"Please, Marcia." I wasn't going to be daunted by a mere dazzling display. "He read to Livy every night. She 'edited' as they went."

"Did you know that the idea for *The Gilded Age* came from Livy and Susan Warner? It's certainly no genteel work of self-congratulatory Christianity."

Ha! Now I could give her back some of her own. "It's not exactly Twain's best book, either."

"As Huck would say, you are the *beatin'est* man! Very well, then." She now had the look of a boxer beginning to circle. "After Livy, Howells, Livy's mother, and Livy's aunt all had read *Tom Sawyer*, Clemens wasn't satisfied. When Huck complained about life at the Widow Douglas's, he remarked, if you recall, 'They comb me all to thunder.'"

I didn't, but I nodded, anyway. "Sounds like Huck."

"Well, Clemens originally wrote, 'all to hell.' He changed it himself."

I was a broken man. Feebly, I summoned the tiny bit of breath I still had. "Professor," I gasped, "as the old man himself might have said, you're too many for me." I made my way towards the genteel and self-congratulatory blush wine.

Whew! I remembered Linda's description of the talk she was going to give—the biggie. Did that mean the Livy Question? Was I going to have to listen to the whole thing all over again? It had been a long time since my Cal days, but I felt suddenly thrown back to the old life of faculty parties and discussions like the one-sided one I had just had with Professor Dunlap. As I recalled, I'd been able to hold my own a little better, but perhaps I was misremembering. I figured I'd better keep my opinions about "The Mysterious Stranger" to myself. In truth, I liked Paine's pastiche better than Twain's "No. 44," but wild horses couldn't have dragged it out of me.

I tried to figure out the best way of doing what I'd come there for, but after a few half-hearted attempts finally gave up trying to meet and question everyone there. Not only was Dunlap too many for me, so were the Fiends—there must have been twenty-five of them, and I hadn't a prayer. I'd have to make a general appeal. I barely had time to find Linda and tell her I'd changed my mind before someone rapped for order.

It was a sixtyish woman, the lady of the house and apparently the head Fiend. "Our speaker tonight is Linda McCormick, on a topic that so far all of us have managed to avoid. It's a brave person who would take on such a task, but she has graciously agreed to tackle it—it being, of course, The Ending."

Whistles, catcalls, loud applause. You'd have thought she was about to perform The Royal Nonesuch. I cursed myself for an idiot—the biggie, of course, was the controversial ending of *Huckleberry Finn*.

Linda looked nonplussed. "Really, I don't deserve all that. Let me just say up front that I don't have the answer. I'm just going to run through a few thoughts on the subject. Actually, it's kind of a grim joke around the office. Whenever anyone says 'Ending,' we've gotten so we cringe. After you've heard fifty thousand explanations, they tend to cancel each other out. But I'm going to talk about it, and also about the last ten chapters, when the book turns from so-called serious intent to burlesque.

"To begin with, even so great an admirer of Huck as Ernest Hemingway said, 'If you read it you must stop where the Nigger Jim is stolen from the boys. That is the real end. The rest is just cheating.' The plain fact is that it reads as if Twain simply wrote himself into a corner. As Huck himself asked, Why would a runaway slave run South? Twain was an improviser. And so he found himself in a situation where he had a comic setup, but he needed a serious ending. However, given the political and social circumstances of the day, there was no reasonable way for Jim, having run South, to get free. Thus the author relied on the ancient and, some would say, cheap device of a *deus ex machina*: It was simple; Jim was free all along. And to get to that point, Twain chose to introduce Tom Sawyer and to descend into what De Voto called 'a trivial extravaganza on a theme he had exhausted years before. In the whole history of the English novel,' De Voto said, 'there is no more chilling descent.'

"In his boyish quest for what he calls 'adventure,' Tom is horribly cruel to Jim, making him wait weeks for his freedom, in the prison of a cabin infested with the rats, snakes, caterpillars, frogs, and spiders Tom insists are essential in a good escape story. Huck stands by and lets it happen, not only abdicating responsibility, but disapproving of Tom for what he believes to be a compromise of his character in doing so antisocial a thing as freeing a slave."

She paused a moment, lapsing into a more conversational tone. "Most professors seem to find that about fifty percent of their students aren't offended. After all, Huck is used to cruelty. He's seen lots of it by this point in the book and has even noted, when the King and Duke are ridden out of town on a rail, 'Human beings can be awful cruel to each other.' These students remember, I think, that Huck has always deferred to Tom. They may remember as well that both books—meaning *Tom Sawyer* and *Huckleberry Finn*—are full of childish superstition. If Huck can believe a dead cat will cure warts, why shouldn't he believe that, to make a successful escape, a prisoner has to have snakes, frogs, and a rope ladder? It's enough for these readers that when Huck says, 'All right, then, I'll *go* to hell!' his sound heart, as Mark Twain called it, has triumphed over his deformed conscience.

"Yet for many readers—obviously De Voto among them—the ending is tremendously disappointing. I think myself that its success has been underestimated. No one has yet proposed a more successful one. Bear with me for a moment while I read you a passage from the book." Her smeary eyes were mischievous. "Can you stand that?" (Mock boos and hisses—she knew her audience.)

"'There was a nigger there, from Ohio; a mulatter, most as white as a white man. He had the whitest shirt on you ever see, too, and the shiniest hat; and there ain't a man in that town that's got as fine clothes as what he had. . . . And what do you think? they said he was a p'fessor in a college, and could talk all kinds of languages, and knowed everything. And that ain't the wust. They said he could *vote*, when he was at home. . . . It was 'lection day and I was just about to go and vote, myself, if I warn't too drunk to get there; but when they told me there was a State in this country where they'd let that nigger vote, I drawed out. I says I'll never vote again. . . . And to see the cool way of that nigger—why, he wouldn't give me the road if I hadn't shoved him out of the way. I says to the people, why ain't this nigger put up at auction and sold?—that's what I want to know.'" She closed her book. "Does anyone know who the speaker is?"

"Pap," someone piped.

"Exactly. Huck's pap. It's a mistake to forget that Huck is, after all, the son of Pap. No wonder he had a deformed conscience! Frankly, I think the reason people become so disappointed is that they expect too much of him. They want him to be a hero, to rise above his roots. In a way, he *is* a hero, of course—he believes he's given up his immortal soul to save Jim from slavery. That's pretty heroic, I think. But what Huck certainly isn't is a little Berkeley liberal, and you can't make him into one no matter how hard you try. He's simply a person of sound heart.

"But perhaps we make too much of all this. In our work at the university, we have a rule of thumb—if Mark Twain says something happened, or is based on fact, it probably is. We usually take the tack that if we think it didn't, we're wrong. When we begin to go off into flights of fancy about the author's intent—as we imagine it—or get angry at him for not writing a better book, or, worst of all, start thinking of ways *we* could have made it better, it's probably best if we remember these words." She picked up her copy of the book once again and turned to the notice at the front. "'Persons attempting to find a motive in this narrative will be prosecuted; persons attempting to find a moral in it will be banished; persons attempting to find a plot in it will be shot.'" (Thunderous applause.) But Linda had one more thing to say before she sat down: "The Huck stops here." (Boos and hisses.)

When the tumult had died, Linda introduced me and turned over the floor. I said: "I'm doing some research on collectors and I'd like to ask for your help. Maybe there are some of you here tonight, or perhaps you know of some. But I'm not looking for your average collector. I'm looking for someone whose fanaticism surpasses even yours—not a mere Fiend, more like a Hound of Huck. The sort of person whose whole life is Mark Twain, who identifies with him so thoroughly he almost has no other identity and no other interests."

"Pamela Temby," said Dan Dupart, "would kill to get her hands on a manuscript she wanted."

"Yes," said the straight-haired woman, "but would she sell her mother down the river?" Full-scale hilarity broke out again—why, I had no idea. I was reminded of the story about the prisoners who got tired of telling the same jokes all the time, so they assigned them numbers that cracked everyone up on utterance. (Later, I realized the remark had been an allusion to an incident in *Pudd'nhead Wilson*.)

When order was restored, and I'd thanked Dan for his lead, an old man spoke up, a bald old man with a cane and a spot on his tie—retired high-school teacher was my guess. "Tom Sawyer's who you want."

Was he senile?

But then there was a chorus of finger-snappings and "of courses." And once again I was in the dark.

"Tom Sayers, he used to be. Had his name legally changed. One of our founding members, left here about ten years ago. Before that he worked over at the Berkeley Public Library. Lived, slept, and ate Mark Twain. Uncle died or something, left him pots and pots of money, and you know what he did? Bought up every Twain document he could get his hands on and moved to Virginia City to open a museum."

"A Mark Twain museum in Virginia City—there's a novel idea." Laughter again, and again that left-out feeling.

But no matter. A man who had had his name legally changed to Tom Sawyer! I was still reeling from that. "He certainly sounds likely. Is anyone in touch with him? Is he still collecting?"

Marcia Dunlap spoke up. "Oh, yes. I'm a collector and I've corresponded with him from time to time. He's fanatical."

"So I gather. I don't know how you can top that, but are there any other biggies I should know about?"

The bald old man tapped his cane on the floor. "Tom Sawyer's your man."

Linda wanted to go for a drink, but I didn't trust myself. The time had arrived to come clean. "Sorry. I've got to get home. I'm expected."

"You're married? I should have known."

"Just involved. But—"

"Stop! You're about to say it."

"About to say what?"

"Arrgh. 'Let's be friends.'"

I was taken aback. "You mean we can't? I thought you liked me for myself."

"Oh, sure we can—I do like you. I'm sick of those three words, that's all. I wish just once someone would come along and say, 'Let's run away together.'"

There's a lot of free-floating passion in the academic world—probably because of all those healthy young bodies.

It was too bad about Linda, but I really didn't want to blow things with Sardis. I'd gone through more personal anguish for her than I ever had for any woman—at least, I called it anguish; her name for it was "growing up"—and so far we were only co–property owners. I had too big an investment to split my attention now. She was a terrific woman and I was going to concentrate on her. Period.

I was so moved by my own resolve and virtue that I popped into the all-night Safeway to get her some flowers. Home again, I saw her car parked in front and her lights on, but due to circumstances completely within my control, I didn't have a key to the damned door, so I was forced to phone first. Her machine answered. That meant she didn't want to be disturbed, of course, but I couldn't see how it could possibly apply to me. Nothing to do but ring the doorbell.

She was dressed as if to go out, in white pants and one of those fancy women's T-shirts that cost fifty bucks or so. Her makeup was fresh and her hair newly blow-dried. I dropped to one knee and proffered the flowers. "Want to go out for a drink?"

"How sweet. They're lovely. But, listen, I can't go, I—oh, there he is now."

Feeling like the first jerk of June, I got to my feet.

"Hi, Steve. Paul, I—this is my . . ."

I'd left my own door open and I ducked into it, fast, not waiting around for any goddam introductions. In case you've never thought about how it feels to be kneeling to a damsel when her date shows up, try it now. Go ahead. And please send your secret if you can do it without the sure and certain feeling that the top of your head is about to go speeding into the ozone.

Actually, five minutes and a glass of wine later, I was calm as a Yogi. Due to Linda and the flowers and all, I'd just overreacted. I realized I should have shaken hands like a gent. The realization sent me back to the depths.

CHAPTER 11

I can act pretty childish sometimes, but this was a new low. Maybe another glass of wine.

The more I drank and sat the more I felt the same way—insecure about Sardis. That was new, too. I used to worry about her crowding me. This business about the separate apartments must have gotten me more than I'd thought. She was right about the matter of the Fiends—it had been taking her for granted to stand her up when she'd asked me to dinner. When you got down to it, it had been downright churlish. I'd have to buy her some flowers to make up for it.

But then I remembered I already had. So what to do now? My sorrows wouldn't drown; indeed, they seemed to thrive on Glen Ellen red. Work. That was it. What next on the Huck hunt? Well, simple. See Tom Sawyer. It was a long drive, but . . .

I had a brainstorm. You could probably get to Carson City in an hour if you flew, and I had a friend who lived for flying the way Sawyer apparently lived for Mark Twain. I got Crusher Wilcox on the phone.

"Crusher? Paul. I have to go to Virginia City on business. Feel like flying to Carson tomorrow?"

"That's funny. Virginia was still a ghost town, last I heard."

"Not your kind of business." Crusher, who works for a multinational corporation, thinks Geneva is the sort of place you go on business. "I've got to interview a guy."

"Why didn't you say so? I've got a meeting at three—can we be back by then?"

"Why not?"

"See you at seven."

That was how easy it was to get Crusher to take you anywhere a Cessna could go. I was sorry I couldn't offer him a scarifying storm or a hair-raising landing opportunity—that would have really got his juices flowing—but it didn't matter, in the end. He was a wild-blue-yonder junkie and didn't care where he went so long as he didn't do it on land. He'd once told me his nickname had something to do with his driving record, but I wasn't sure how much that had to do with anything. All I knew was, he was obsessed.

So obsessed, in fact, that flying was his only adventure. Whenever I asked to be flown somewhere, he'd let me off at the airport and pick me up at some appointed time, pursuing aerial amusement in the meanwhile.

Before we landed in Carson, we flew over Virginia, which, in Mark Twain's words, "roosted royally midway up the steep side of Mount Davidson, seven thousand two hundred feet above the level of the sea, and in the clear Nevada atmosphere was visible from a distance of fifty miles."

I was up on all that because, fretting over Sardis, I hadn't been able to sleep the night before and had ended up boning up with *Roughing It*. Seeing Virginia hours later, I almost convinced myself I'd seen a photograph of it, so vividly had the master described it: "The mountain side was so steep that the entire town had a slant to it like a roof. Each street was a terrace, and from each to the next street below the descent was forty or fifty feet. . . . From Virginia's airy situation one could look over a vast, far-reaching panorama of mountain ranges and deserts. . . . Over your head

Mount Davidson lifted its gray dome and before and below you a rugged canyon clove the battlemented hills, making a sombre gateway through which a soft-tinted desert was glimpsed . . ."

How eloquently he had written of Virginia's heyday, the "flush times," as he called them. In truth, I could see how a person like Tom Sawyer would pick the romantic old place as his home. It was synonymous with Mark Twain at his most adventurous, and it was also important for another reason—it was the first place he'd ever used his celebrated pseudonym, in a real sense the birthplace of Mark Twain the writer.

He'd gone there at a low point in his seven-year sojourn in the West, but not, for once, in the outright search for metallic riches. Though the opulent Comstock lode was producing ton upon ton of rich silver ore, he'd been invited to work on that most colorful of frontier papers, the *Territorial Enterprise,* for twenty-five dollars a week. The job came about after he'd amused himself writing letters to the *Enterprise*, professing later always to have been surprised when they were printed. "My good opinion of the editors," he wrote modestly, "had steadily declined" as a result.

What he found on arrival was as merry a carnival as this country has ever seen. "The sidewalks swarmed with people. . . . The streets themselves were just as crowded. . . . So great was the pack that buggies frequently had to wait half an hour for an opportunity to cross the principal street. . . . Joy sat on every countenance and there was a glad, almost fierce, intensity in every eye, that told of the money-getting schemes that were seething in every brain and the high hope that held sway in every heart. Money was as plentiful as dust and a melancholy countenance was nowhere to be seen."

Then came a list of what was available in the seething city of 18,000 people or so—"brass bands, banks, hotels, theatres, 'hurdy-gurdy houses,' wide-open gambling palaces, political pow-wows, civic processions, street fights, murders, inquests, riots, a whisky mill every fifteen steps," etc., etc., etc., etc., "and some talk of building a church."

It must have been as much fun as the Haight-Ashbury in the sixties (though in a different way): "Every man owned 'feet' in fifty different wild cat mines and considered his fortune made. Think of a city with not one solitary poor man in it! . . . Money was wonderfully plenty. The trouble was, not how to get it—but how to spend it, how to lavish it, get rid of it, squander it."

How, one might ask, did all this apply to a humble reporter on a $25 salary? It was simple—the currency of the day was mining stock and the denizens, if Twain is to be believed (and Linda McCormick says he is, mainly), were as generous as they were rich. First, there was the custom of giving stock to reporters in order to have one's claim "noticed." And then there was another curious social more: "If you are coming up the street with a couple of baskets of apples in your hands, and you meet a friend, you naturally invite him to take a few. That describes the condition of things in Virginia in the 'flush times.' Every man had his pockets full of stock, and it was the actual custom of the country to part with small quantities of it to friends without the asking." Thus, "we received presents of 'feet' every day. If we needed a hundred dollars or so, we sold some; if not, we hoarded it away, satisfied that it would ultimately be worth a thousand dollars a foot."

In such a freewheeling atmosphere, it was no wonder that Clemens learned journalism rather informally. Upon inquiring how to do the job, he was told to go all over town, ask questions, make notes, and write them up. After five hours of following instructions, he found out that no one knew anything, and once again returned for instructions. "Are there no hay wagons in from Truckee?" asked his boss.

The young cub proved a quick study. "I canvassed the city again," he wrote, "and found one wretched old hay truck dragging in from the country. But I made affluent use of it. I multiplied it by sixteen, brought it into town from sixteen different directions, made sixteen separate items out of it, and got up such another sweat about hay as Virginia City had never seen in the world before."

The reporter's temperament, so much abhorred by non-newsfolk, came easy to him. After the hay extravaganza, he found things dull till a desperado killed someone and "joy returned once more . . . I wrote up the murder with a hungry attention to details, and when it was finished experienced but one regret—namely that they had not hanged my benefactor on the spot, so that I could work him up too."

Finding he still had a column to fill, he heard of some emigrant wagons that had recently come through hostile Indian territory. Clemens felt he could make the story much more interesting if only reporters from other papers weren't on it as well (a feeling I'd often had at press conferences). But, by exercising what I can only think of as territorial enterprise, he managed to find a wagon that was about to leave and whose proprietor, therefore, "would not be in the city the next day to make trouble. . . . Having more scope here, I put this wagon through an Indian fight that to this day has no parallel in history.

"My two columns were filled. When I read them over in the morning I felt that I had found my legitimate occupation at last."

I feel I should mention here that the Indian-fight story, if indeed he really wrote it, didn't survive, though I fully expect Booker to turn it up in a burglary someday. Clemens did rather specialize in hoaxes, though, sometimes as vehicles to get back at his enemies. Two of the most famous were the "Petrified Man" and "Massacre at Dutch Nick's," a gorier tale than Poe ever dreamed of. Clemens said he meant them as satires, but found an unappreciative audience received them "in innocent good faith."

Nonetheless, in the course of his first writing job, he succeeded in making enough of a name for himself that when he left, the paper ran an editorial noting that he had "abdicated the local column of the *Enterprise*, where by the grace of Cheek, he so long reigned Monarch of Mining Items, Detailer of Events, Prince of Platitudes, Chief of Biographers, Expounder of Unwritten Law, Puffer of Wild-cat, Profaner of Divinity, Detractor of Merit, Flatterer of Power, Recorder of Stage Arrivals, Pack Trains, Hay Wagons, and Things in General."

He made a name for himself in another sense too. On

January 31, 1863, he wrote a dispatch from Carson City and signed it "Mark Twain." For scholars, that was the real importance of his stay in Virginia City. I figured Tom Sawyer had taken it to heart in a big way.

I rented a car in Carson City, promising to meet Crusher at one o'clock, and headed for the hills. The countryside around Virginia seemed like the middle of nowhere—and was. Most authorities say the population during the flush time eventually reached 30,000 or so, but it had dwindled over the years to about 750. Though billed as a ghost town, it isn't, really. It's both the Storey County seat and a thriving tourist spot. Supposedly, many of the permanent residents are artists, writers, and musicians, but a recent incident that had put the old burg back in the news indicated a more conservative Comstock vein. The incident, appropriately enough, involved none other than the *Territorial Enterprise*, which was bought by city slickers who attempted to restore its former satirical glory. Unfortunately, they made such mistakes as attacking God and deer-hunting, employing such Twainian devices as having a theologian expound the theory that man is descended from the dough of an anchovy pizza, and "interviewing" twenty-five deer. The argument that the paper was merely harking back to the days of freewheeling frontier journalism was met with such unmitigated hostility that eventually the *Territorial Enterprise* became a magazine, the once-glorious paper metamorphosing into the bland *Virginia City News*.

That was all I knew about the current sociology of the place when I drove into town. I wasn't there five minutes before I understood what had so amused the Fiends about the novel idea of a Mark Twain Museum in Virginia City—every other business on the main drag seemed to be the Mark Twain something-or-other.

The tourist activity was concentrated here—on C Street. The place was said to draw half a million visitors a year, and I could believe it. It wasn't yet ten o'clock and already the ancient boardwalks were straining under the weight of hordes in shorts and sandals. I took a spin around to get the feel of the place. Offhand, I'd have to say it felt like the rest of Nevada. Sardis claims the fact that prostitution is legal there says it all, in a metaphorical sense. As for me, I think of it as the only state where a good meal has nothing to do with the food, which is universally indigestible—it's one in a restaurant with no slot machines.

These were a few of the sights on C Street—the Sundance Saloon, the Pioneer Emporium, the Old Washoe Club ("Virginia City's Oldest and Most Famous Saloon"), the Silver Queen (which houses a fifteen-foot picture of a western belle dressed in a gown made of more than 3,000 real silver dollars), Grant's General Store and Museum, the *Territorial Enterprise* building (housing gift shop and basement museum), Mark Twain's Museum of Memories, the 1869 Territorial Prison War Museum, the Crystal Bar, the Old Sazerac Saloon, the Ponderosa Saloon, the Bucket of Blood Saloon, the Delta Saloon and Cafe, the Wild West Museum, the Nevada Trading Post, and the Virginia City Trading Post. What fun.

Tom Sawyer, I learned, was the proprietor neither of Mark Twain's Museum of Memories (which boasted Mark Twain's old desk) nor of the basement museum of the *Territorial Enterprise* Gift Shop (which boasted another of his old desks). His establishment, it seemed, was called Tom Sawyer's Mark Twain Museum and could be found only by the appropriately enterprising tourist, being situated, as it was, several streets up, at A and Carson. But there was a further problem—according to the locals, it had been closed more often than open lately, Tom having taken to spending most of his time at the Bucket of Blood. Though it was midmorning, I was advised to seek his company there.

And was not disappointed. He seemed so firmly ensconced at his bar stool I practically had to brush off the cobwebs to get a look at his face. A lugubrious visage it was, too. I told him I'd been sent by the Fiends, who'd sworn he was the country's primary authority on Mark Twain outside the Bancroft Library—a white lie, but he needed cheering. It didn't work.

"They lied. They're amateurs at the Bancroft."

He reminded me, in a funny way, of Clemens's own description of himself when he arrived in Virginia City: "I was a rusty-looking city editor, I am free to confess—coatless, slouch hat, blue woolen shirt, pantaloons stuffed into boot-tops, whiskered down to the waist, and the universal navy revolver slung to my belt."

Sawyer had foregone the gun, his beard was hardly more than breast level, and he wore his jeans over his work boots, but otherwise the description came close—particularly the rusty-looking part, and I figured it was no accident.

"Mark Twain," he told the barkeep, who promptly furnished us each a beer. "Twain drank at John Piper's," Tom said, as if in explanation, "but I've got 'em trained here."

"Excuse me?"

"You don't know how the old boy got his name?"

"Sure. From the river sounding for two fathoms."

"Apparently, you don't even know the 'official' version."

"I guess not."

"Let me educate you, my boy. He claimed the name was used first by a Captain Isaiah Sellers, who employed it as a *nom de plume* to write river news for the New Orleans *Times-Picayune*. Clemens said after he died he 'laid violent hands upon it without asking permission of the proprietor's remains.'"

"I had no idea."

"It's a tall tale, anyhow. Point One: Sellers did write river news for the *Picayune*, but he never used the pseudonym. Point Two: He was still alive when our man first used it."

"Oh. Well, why do you think he said that?"

"That wife of his, probably. She might have found the real story too embarrassing. Why, he was known as Mark in this town before he ever used the name in print. Think about it. He liked to use river talk, didn't he?"

"Um-hm."

"And he liked his beer, didn't he? So wouldn't it seem natural he'd stand a friend to a brew now and then? Over at John Piper's, they'd chalk down drinks on the wall like running a tab."

"I get it—he'd say 'Mark Twain' when he meant 'put two drinks on my tab.'"

"I'm surprised the Fiends didn't mention it. How are they, anyway? Still going strong?"

"They sent you their best."

At that, he did seem to cheer up a little. He spoke dreamily into his beer: "I used to think of them as my gang. We almost named ourselves Tom Sawyer's Gang, as a matter of fact. But some of the fellows thought that was too childish. They missed the whole point, of course. Remember what Howells said about Twain?"

"Plenty, I should imagine."

"He said, 'He was a youth to the end of his days, the heart of a boy with the head of a sage; the heart of a good boy, or a bad boy, but always a wilful boy, and wilfulest to show himself out at every time as just the boy he was.'" He was getting morose again. "I thought I could live like that."

"As a boy?"

"I guess everyone's got to grow up sometime."

"You sound like a man in a mid-life crisis."

"I'm nearly fifty, Paul."

I remembered what Huck had said about Pap, and Sawyer read my thoughts. "'He was most fifty, and he looked it,'" he quoted. He sighed and stared into his glass. Seeing it was empty, he sighed again. "Would you like to see the museum? I guess that's what you're here for."

"I wouldn't want you to open it just for me."

"I'd be delighted, actually." It was funny, in a way, to hear the scholar's words coming out of the mouth of someone who looked like a miner from the flush times. I remembered how much Huck had hated "them blamed clothes that just smothers me," the ones he'd had to wear while living with the Widow Douglas. "It's not every day I meet someone who can appreciate it. Except for the kids. The kids always like it. I like to think maybe some of them will stop watching television long enough to read a good book as a result of seeing it."

"Any particular good book?"

"You know it."

He said his car was out of commission, so we took my rented one up to A Street, and, incidentally, on an extended tour of the town. Once off of C Street, we were in a different town—an astonishingly charming one, made up of Victorian mansions and old clapboard houses. In some windows hung tatters; in others lace curtains. Many of the houses (the ones with the nice curtains) had been lovingly restored. "I've always loved this place," said Tom, "warts and all. If you stay off C Street, it's almost like he's here. You can almost believe—"

He didn't complete the sentence. "Believe what?" I asked.

"You can identify with him. You walk the streets he walked, do the things he did. It's as close as you can get to him."

"You must have a wonderful life here." Obviously, he didn't or he wouldn't be spending his days at the Bucket of Blood, but I hadn't forgotten how to dangle reportorial bait.

"In a way," he said grimly. "In a way it's perfect. But Tom needs his Becky."

"You never found her?"

"Oh, I found her all right. I knew I would too. When she walked into the museum, I recognized her on sight."

"But she didn't recognize you?"

"That," he said, "would be putting it mildly. I guess it was all a mistake." He emitted another of his miserable sighs.

We pulled up in front of a perfectly lovely house with a wrap-around veranda, the sort of house, if it hadn't had an old yellow car parked out front, you could easily have imagined in St. Petersburg, Missouri, home town of Tom and Huck. Crossing the threshold was like stepping into Disneyland. The living room was McDougal's cave, in which Tom Sawyer and Becky Thatcher had wandered for three days and three nights.

Near the center of the room were two wax figures of Tom and Becky, wearing their straw hats and holding aloft their candles. Fearsome stalagmites grew out of the black-painted floor, portentous stalactites hung from above. Horribly detailed and loathsome bats, suspended on nearly invisible wires, threatened them on all sides. A papier-maché waterfall gushed out of one of the walls. Off to the left was Injun Joe's Cup, a stone with a shallow hollow in it placed on the stump of a broken-off stalagmite, to catch the drop of water that fell every three minutes. On the far wall, lit subtly, was a cross made with candle smoke, marking the spot where the hapless half-breed had hidden the treasure.

Tom had taken a bit of artistic license; in the book, all of those elements—the cup, the waterfall, and the cross—were miles apart, but who cared? The effect, as the real Tom might have said, was ever so splendid. "It's wonderful," I said, and meant it.

"Isn't it? If this doesn't get them, I don't know what will. You know when you walk down C Street, how you poke your head into all those ostensible museums and yawn and mosey on? I factored that in, you see. I wanted my museum to be irresistible."

"There's just one thing that puzzles me—where do you collect your admission fee?"

"I don't. This museum is a loving memorial to Mark Twain and I will *not* charge money for it."

"Talk about your 'irresistible.'"

"Follow the arrows."

I noticed, for the first time, that he'd painted white arrows on the floor leading to what looked like a grotto in the cave, but was actually a door. Walking through the cave, I was brushed here and there by a batwing, but lightly, just enough for a *frisson.* The latter-day Tom had thought of everything. "Did you build this yourself? Surely not—it would have taken years."

"It did—and of course I built it myself. I put myself through Cal doing carpentry, and I do it, if I say so myself, with the precision of the librarian I am. I restored the house first—shored up the foundation, rewired, put in new plumbing—everything. I did every bit of it myself. Then I built this museum from scratch—except for the wax figures, of course. They cost me a bundle. I based all the scenes on the original illustrations when I could, sometimes combining them. Like the cave here—does it look at all familiar?"

"I feel like I've been here before."

"As a boy, you probably had a book with the True Williams drawings in it. I took the scene from several of them, and had Tom and Becky copied too."

We stepped through the cave grotto into a small hall. "Right," said Tom, and we turned into what used to be a small bedroom, and was now the Mississippi River. On the far bank grew a thicket of trees. We stood on the very edge of the near one, an embankment of real red clay. Tom had used blue paper or plastic—something that shimmered and moved—for the river, and had suspended Huck's raft from the ceiling, so that it seemed really to be floating. Jim was standing, Huck sitting, behind them the wigwam, with two pairs of feet sticking out. Huck looked so cute you wanted to hug him.

"They did a nice job on Huck, didn't they? This one's a combination of two of the E. W. Kemble illustrations, one with just Huck and Jim, like this, and one of the king and the duke asleep in the wigwam. Here I had Huck made very true to the original drawing, which is one of the most appealing of him, but I had Jim made a little more noble. Unfortunately, you can't touch them, because you'll mess up the river."

"I wondered about that in the cave—aren't you afraid people will damage the work?"

"Oh, they do all the time—I can't tell you how many times I've had to replace Injun Joe's cup. But I want them to feel like they're really there, not in some cheapjack tourist museum. This is my home, you see. I consider the visitors my guests. I *use* these rooms. I have two rooms for what most people consider normal use—a bedroom and a library, plus a kitchen—but sometime every day, I come to the cave, and I come to the river, and I spend time with Tom and Huck. They're very real to me."

"I can believe it."

We stepped out into the hall again, and I saw a door labeled Boys and Girls. "I know, I know," said Tom. "It sounds awful—like 'little girls' room'—but Twain said *Tom Sawyer* was for boys and girls, and as far as I'm concerned, my museum is. I don't care how it sounds. Come and look."

He opened the bathroom door to show a claw-foot tub, old-fashioned basin, and genuine water-closet, complete with chain. "Tom and Huck didn't have indoor plumbing, of course, but I didn't want the boys and girls to have to go to an outhouse."

"You've thought of everything."

"Wait'll you see this."

We went into a bedroom with an actual bed off to the right, behind it a heavy china cabinet. Tom sat on the floor, one arm flung up triumphantly. Aunt Polly stood over him, hands clasped, a chair overturned between them. The floor was littered with broken crockery. And flying through the window was a yellow cat. I hadn't the least idea what the tableau was supposed to represent.

"I had only four rooms," said Tom the imposter, "and when you see the last, you'll realize what it had to be. This one I debated. The obvious choice would have been Tom whitewashing the fence. But this one is so much more fun, don't you think?"

"I don't think I remember this scene."

"Funny. Lots of people don't. And I think it's one of the grandest. Don't you remember when Becky gets sick and Tom's afraid she'll die, so he goes into a romantic decline?"

"Vaguely, maybe."

"Well, Aunt Polly tries every kind of quack cure on him, and then she finally hits on Pain-Killer, 'simply fire in a liquid form.' Tom liked it so much he gave it to his aunt's cat, Peter, who 'delivered a war-whoop and set off round and round the room, banging against furniture, upsetting flower pots, and making general havoc. Next he rose on his hind feet and pranced around, in a frenzy of enjoyment, with his head over his shoulder and his voice proclaiming his unappeasable happiness. Then he went tearing around the house again spreading chaos and destruction in his path. Aunt Polly entered in time to see him throw a few double somersaults, deliver a final mighty hurrah, and sail through the open window, carrying the rest of the flower-pots with him.'"

"My God. Do you give that speech every time some kid asks about the tableau?"

"They love it. It's something a kid can relate to, as they say back home."

"I guess it is."

"Come on. Time for the pièce de résistance."

We crossed the hall to the only room that had a door on it—a rude plank one with the bolt padlocked. "In a way this one was the hardest," said Tom, "because there wasn't a drawing to go by—only of this door—and little bits here and there. But the description is the richest of any of the scenes I used for the tableaux. Can you guess what it is?"

I had a feeling it could be only one thing. "Jim's dungeon?"

"What else?" He unlocked the padlock and opened the door. The thing was nation gaudy, in the lexicon of the other Tom.

A wax figure of Jim was sitting on the bed, playing his Jew's harp to charm the animals Tom had insisted upon. True to the book, he had a ten-foot chain on his leg, attached to the leg of the bed. You could just barely see that the leg had been sawed in two, but in case you missed it, there was a scattering of sawdust on the floor. "I thought," I said, "they ate the sawdust."

Tom smiled delightedly. "They must have left a crumb or two."

On the floor were several of the accoutrements of prison-breaking—the picks with which Tom and Huck dug Jim out, the saw they made from a case-knife, the fox-fire they used to dig by (made of real bits of wood and translucent orange paper, with a lightbulb underneath), and a couple of tin plates with "messages" scratched on the bottom.

On a low, crudely constructed table sat Uncle Silas's brass warming pan with a crust on it—Tom and Huck's "witch-pie." I was sure the new Tom wouldn't have done things halfway, but exactly as his namesake would have. Just to make sure, I asked: "Tell me—is there anything under that crust?"

Tom practically preened himself. "Of course. A real rope ladder I made out of a sheet."

Next to the witch-pie were finely wrought and carefully painted spiders, caterpillars, and bugs. Hunkering under the table were a couple of real-looking frogs. The shirt the boys stole from Uncle Silas for Jim to keep his journal on hung on the wall, covered with hen-scratchings. It looked as if Tom had used the prescribed ink. "Real blood?" I asked.

"My own."

"As I recall, Jim used the blood he got when the rats bit him."

Tom laughed. He seemed to have forgotten his lost love. "I couldn't find any likely-looking rats. Had to resort to a Swiss Army knife." He held out his arm so I could see the scar.

"I hope you didn't get an infection."

"Oh, I did. I had to get a tetanus shot." The man did his adopted name proud.

I continued my inspection. Off in a corner was a potted plant, to represent the mullen that Jim had been instructed to call "Pitchiola" and to water with his tears.

But the real centerpiece—Tom's crowning achievement—was Jim himself, in bed with his menagerie and his grindstone. (Technically, the rope ladder should have been there too, but, as Tom had wanted to show the witch-pie in its intact magnificence, he'd apparently decided the ladder couldn't be in two places at once; and anyway, there would hardly have been room for it.)

"Go on," urged Tom. "Go up close and look. Touch the rats if you like."

One rat cavorted on Jim's lap, another on his shoulder; a third lay tamely on his straw tick, apparently soothed by the sorrowful notes of the "juiceharp." Touching one as ordered, I found it authentically furry. Garter-snakes, painstakingly painted, each with buttons tied to its tail to "let on" they were rattlesnakes, wriggled contentedly all over Jim and his bed. One even hung from the grindstone. Casually scattered at the foot of the bed were pens made from a brass candlestick and a pewter spoon, an old nail, and an iron bolt.

Jim's coat of arms was elaborately rendered on the grindstone—a runaway slave, complete with bundle, on a bar sinister; a dog couchant, and under his foot, a chain embattled; Tom and Huck's names scratched sideways, as gules for supporters; and at the bottom, Jim's motto, "Maggiore fretta, minore atto," which, according to the original Tom, meant "the more haste, the less speed."

Underneath the coat of arms were the four "mournful inscriptions" Tom had prescribed:

1. *Here a captive heart busted.*

2. *Here a poor prisoner, forsook by the world and friends, fretted out his sorrowful life.*

3. *Here a lonely heart broke, and a worn spirit went to its rest, after thirty-seven years of solitary captivity.*

4. *Here, homeless and friendless, after thirty-seven years of bitter captivity, perished a noble stranger, natural son of Louis XIV.*

"I'll bet," I said, "you did the grindstone yourself."

"It wouldn't have been regulation otherwise. I used the nail for a chisel and the iron bolt for a hammer, exactly as Jim did."

"Was it fun?"

"To tell you the truth, it was the most fun of making the whole museum. I made the pens too. Huck wasn't kidding—'it was most pesky tedious hard work and slow.'" He paused. "And I loved every minute of it."

"Tom, I've got to hand it to you. This whole thing is a real act of love."

"Wait a minute—you still haven't seen it all. Open the closet door."

As I did, a light went on, revealing another wax figure of Huck, posed like Kemble's final drawing, Huck tipping his straw hat with his right hand, his left over his heart, a sweet, boyish smile on his face. Over the figure's head was a banner: "The End, Yours Truly Huck Finn."

I burst out laughing—and delighted laughter too. However misguided, the museum really was an act of love, and this last little touch, so obviously meant to please, was genuinely charming. I thought this new Tom, twisted psyche and all (I didn't know about his conscience), might be possessed of a sound heart.

"And now," he said, "to business. Could you use a drink?"

"Mark Twain," I said.

CHAPTER 12

Tom's library, to me, was more pleasing than Pamela Temby's. All walls held floor-to-ceiling books, the furniture consisted of two old-fashioned over-stuffed chairs and a desk that looked like an original from the *Territorial Enterprise,* and there was a fireplace.

The "business" Tom spoke of was mostly drinking beer (Twain's beverage during his Virginia City tenure), but also consisted of showing me his collection, which was at least as extensive as Pamela Temby's. "I bought a lot of these things when I moved here," he said, "intending to display them in the museum. But when I saw what the town was like, I didn't think they'd really be appreciated. Besides, then I got the idea for the tableaux, and I couldn't be stopped."

"It's almost a Tom Sawyer museum," I said. "Even Jim's dungeon was really Tom's creation."

"That was my original idea. But I knew I had to do the raft scene. When you think about it, it's really the most eloquent evocation of boyhood in all of Twain."

"'Life is mighty free and easy and comfortable on a raft,'" I quoted.

Moroseness seized him suddenly. "Yeah. If only you could live it on one. I find I'm spending more and more of my time in the raft room."

"What was your previous favorite?"

"Oh, 'A General Good Time.' By a long shot."

"Which one is that?"

"That's the caption True Williams gave the sketch showing Peter and the Pain-Killer." His speech was becoming ever slower and sadder, his face the visage of a condemned man.

I thought I understood some of his problems and in a way, they weren't that different from mine—I might not spend my time hand-chiseling grindstones, but I still had my old baseball glove from junior high, and, if Sardis were to be believed, quite a few boyish little notions. I genuinely wanted to cheer Tom up. It was entirely coincidental that the line of questioning I chose to do it happened to be slightly on the self-serving side. "Tell me, Tom, what's the greater pleasure—the museum or collecting?"

He smiled sadly. "It's almost a toss-up. They're both my life." He looked down at his beer. "Unfortunately, the sum total of it."

"Are you still collecting?"

"Oh, avidly. I've bought two letters in the last month."

"Something I've always wondered—what do collectors get out of it?"

"I will never get to meet Mark Twain, but as close as I can come is having an original manuscript or letter."

The sadness melted as he warmed to his subject. He spoke passionately, emphasizing every word. "If you really respect someone—feel you have an intellectual rapport with him—that can give you something the history books never will. When I hold one of his letters, and read it, I feel as if I know what motivated him—there's a chemical reaction that takes place. It's electric."

"I think I can understand that—I've spent some time in the Bancroft Library."

He seemed not to have heard me. "It's hard to explain to somebody who's never experienced it, but if Mark Twain is truly your hero, whatever's written about him, you can't wait to get your hands on, and once you have an opportunity to peer into his mind, it's almost like being able to listen in on the phone. When you have the opportunity to own a really witty letter, it's a certain feeling—a very exciting feeling. You think, 'What a brilliant person! What a mind!'

"You know one of the things wrong with the current generation? They don't have the same hero structure we had." He drifted off somewhere. "The Lone Ranger . . . Mickey Mantle . . . Look at Reagan. That's why people like him—he's a role model. In a pathetic sort of way. When we can't find the heroes we need today, we have to look backwards until we do find them. Mark Twain was one of those great people that come around so very infrequently—a guy who was wildly successful, but he was so real, and the more you look into it, the better you feel. I could see myself sitting around with him in one of those old men's clubs, just swapping stories. That could be something that could be the highlight of your life.

"Here was a man who went out West to seek his fortune and he didn't make it, but he went on to find a much richer vein than any Comstock Lode—in his own mind. He was a *character.*" He sat back in his chair, having spent his passion. He spoke quietly. "If I were an author, I'd want to be like him—a real character. I guess that's what it's all about."

"I think you're a thoroughgoing character. Anybody would."

He looked sad again. "Do you? I don't know—I'm just a librarian."

"I've heard there's a very choice manuscript on the market."

"Have you?" His voice was listless.

"I think the seller was using the name Sarah Williams—has she contacted you, by any chance?"

"No." He seemed to have virtually no interest in the subject.

"Did you ever run into a woman named Beverly Alexander?"

"I don't think so."

"Isami Nakamura?"

He shook his head, apparently not even curious about who these women were. He seemed utterly to have run out of steam, and I left him to his melancholy, wondering vaguely what had set it off. Perhaps he'd been struck by the same thought I'd had: If the shade of Mark Twain somehow materialized to swap stories, Tom wouldn't have any to offer, having never lived life at all.

"How'd it go?" asked Crusher.

"You really missed something."

"Are you kidding? I flew all over the state."

"I just met a man who's devoted his whole life to hero worship. I mean, this guy hasn't got a single thing going for him, and he's just starting to realize it."

"Well, if it's made him happy—"

"He's the saddest sack I ever saw. He's kind of having an overdue mid-life crisis. Apparently, he finally realized he was lonely, fell in love with the first woman he met, and of course she didn't want him. Who would? He's one-dimensional."

"You trying to tell me something?"

"Well, look, there's nothing wrong with flying, but the actual world, by definition, is that thing down there."

"You don't think I'm a down-to-earth guy?"

"Well, sure, but—"

"I've got my head in the clouds."

"Oh, head, that's nothing. But all ten fingers and all ten toes? Shoulders, liver, pancreas—don't you think that's a little extreme?"

"You didn't mention heart. But, come to think of it, my last girlfriend did. I'll tell you something, Paul—I haven't been too lucky in love lately."

"You should get out more—and I don't mean out in the ozone. I guarantee you if you'd gone with me today, you'd have had an enriching adventure."

"But I did have one."

"Yes, but it wouldn't make good chitchat over a late-night brandy."

"I don't drink—it interferes with the flying."

"The point is, you need some material to charm the ladies with. Look, do me a favor. Next time we go somewhere, stay on the ground with me. Just come along and enjoy whatever happens and then the next time you go on a date, tell her all about it."

"By God, I'll do it! I've noticed they kind of doze off when I get on the theory of aeronautics."

"Great. How about tomorrow? I need to go to L.A. to see a movie producer about a priceless missing manuscript."

"L.A.? But I could fly out over the ocean, maybe circle back, swing over Lake Arrowhead—"

"Do you want to get laid or not?"

"You really think it'll fly?"

"Trust me."

One thing about a cat—when you get home from a hard day of interviewing eccentrics, he'll be there to greet you. "Hi, Paul," said Spot, "it's been hell without you."

"I missed you too, old buddy. Did Sardis call?"

"Can't say, really. I've been busy thinking about the phenomenal versus the noumenal. If the phone rang, I didn't hear it."

Spot's English isn't so good, so usually I have to keep up both ends of the conversation, but this has its advantages. I find he never says stuff like, "How should I know, jerk? Why don't you check your machine?"

Unfortunately, no matter how tactful he is, we're so close I always know what he's thinking. "Okay, okay," I said, "I'll check the damned machine."

I meant to, I really did. I think it's wrong to tell an animal you'll do something, and then go back on your word. But the fit was on me—I felt like storming Sardis's apartment.

Would you believe that damned Steve was still there? Apparently, they'd been together all night and all day. No wonder he was standing behind her, first on one leg, then the other, obviously terrified. Sardis, on the other hand, was serene as an alpine lake. "Paul! Come in. Steve's just leaving."

I stomped past the happy couple and into the kitchen, so I wouldn't have to watch her kiss him good-bye. By the time she'd finished necking, I'd managed to locate a beer and opened it. She came over for a kiss, but I politely declined. "Forget it."

"Forget what?"

"Forget everything. If you're going to be so childish over one lousy mistake, I don't think we have anything to say to each other."

"Well, I think we do."

"What, for instance?"

"'Thanks for the beer, Sardis,' 'Sure, Paul, any time—mind if I have one too?' 'Gosh, I'd be glad to get you one.'"

I got her the damned beer.

"Exactly what," she said, "have I done that's so childish?"

"Oh, just seeing another guy to get back at me, that's all."

"You think you're the center of the universe, don't you? Did it ever occur to you that maybe I do what I do for reasons that don't involve you? Steve happens to be an old boyfriend who just moved back to town. I went out with him for old time's sake and fell in love with him again. Okay?"

"You can't tell me it had nothing to do with the fact that I stood you up."

"As a matter of fact, it had everything to do with it. I wouldn't have been free otherwise."

"Oh, hell, I wish I'd never moved in here."

She laughed. Can you believe it? Laughed. Sadistically. "Oh, for heaven's sake, I can't keep this up. Steve's not an old boyfriend. He's a very sweet designer I used to work with at Pandorf. We're doing a project together, as you would have found out if you'd let me introduce you last night. But, listen, I'm not mad at you—even for that. I think maybe I overreacted about getting stood up. I'm sorry about that. Really."

"Oh, it's okay. I'm sorry I did it."

"Here's the thing—are you really so insecure that you thought I'd dump you just like that?"

"I guess I must be."

"Listen, I'm not going anywhere. Honest. I'm yours. All yours, okay?"

"I guess so."

"What do you mean you guess so, dammit? What can I do to make you feel secure?"

"I do feel secure, all right? That's not the problem."

"Kiss me, then."

I did, but it was only *pro forma*. I didn't really feel like kissing her. There was something about being made secure when I'd gotten all revved up to be hurt that was a little unsettling. Sardis used to say I had lover's block instead of writer's block, but I thought I was over it. Maybe you never got over it. Maybe it just came up from time to time and you had to put up with it and wait till it went away again. Okay then, I'd wait. Why not? I was secure; I had my Becky. No problem.

"How was your day?" I said.

"Okay. I might make a lot of money on this thing with Steve. How was yours?"

"Let's go in the living room and I'll tell you about it."

Unlike Crusher, she was crazed with jealousy at not having met Tom Sawyer, boy grown-up. Like most artists, Sardis loved screwballs, but that wasn't all—she was intrigued by the intricate detail of the museum. "Do me a favor," she said. "Next time you have an adventure that good, take me along, will you?"

"What are you doing tomorrow?"

"Painting. Why?"

"Too bad. Detection waits for no man."

"Maybe I could paint next Thursday."

"Could you? That would be great."

"Tell. I'm on the edge of my chair."

"Crusher and I are flying down to L.A. to beard Herb Wolf. I could really use you to play Sarah Williams."

"You tricked me!"

"No, I didn't. You walked right into it. Besides, I've been thinking about something. I need you on this case, and Booker's paying me enough to hire you as an operative."

"How official-sounding."

"How about thirty-five bucks an hour?"

"Oh, Paul, you sweet man. I can't let you do that—you'd be down to twenty for the hours we work together."

"That's okay. I'm making enough."

"Thirty-seven and a half. I'll split fifty-fifty."

"No, thirty-five. I insist."

"Thirty." She kissed me.

"Not a chance." Time had passed and I was a new man. I found I was able to kiss quite enthusiastically.

CHAPTER 13

Mr. Wolf was in, taking calls from his swimming pool, if there were anything to stereotypes. He would be charmed to see Miss Williams, in fact she was the person he wanted to see most in the world—she should come over instantly, he was completely at her service. He lived in Pasadena.

Pasadena! Not Beverly Hills, not Bel Air, not Malibu, not Laurel Canyon. But Pasadena—star of all the great film *noir* classics—or did it only seem that way? Surely it was real; I remembered it too vividly—first the midnight drive to the mansion, usually in a blinding rain. Then the eccentric old men, rich old ladies, gorgeous young women, most of them homicidal but some in danger, all after the same rare coin or something. Pasadena was an ideal place, when you thought about it, to be tracking down so romantic a thing as a missing manuscript. Especially if you brought an arsenal with you.

Nonsense, said Crusher, who'd lived off and on in L.A. The homicidal or old-money element had dwindled, as we ought to have deduced from the fact that such a parvenu as Wolf even lived there. There were plenty of blacks and Asians there now, lots of condos, and only rarely a rare coin.

Nonetheless, the street we ended up on was clearly a vestige of better times. The houses, though not the palatial estates I remembered from the movies, were old and gracious—some quite fine. Wolf's was a marvelous example of the Craftsman style. I could see now why he didn't live in Bel Air. Obviously he was a man of exquisite taste—the sort of truly cultivated gentleman who'd appreciate a genuine Mark Twain manuscript.

Clearly, he hadn't solved the servant problem, though. His butler wore white shoes, plaid pants, white patent leather belt, and yellow polo shirt stretched over rampant belly. The man's style of greeting bordered on the rude: "Yeah?"

"Sarah Williams," said Sardis, "to see Mr. Wolf."

"Who're the bozos?"

"The bozos?"

"I think he means us," I said.

"Oh, the bozos. Of course. My business associates—Paul McDonald, Crusher Wilcox. Would you mind telling Mr. Wolf we're here?"

"Come in."

As he graciously stood aside, I saw him do a most peculiar thing—speak into a walkie-talkie. "Pinkie," he said, "bring the dog." I had a sudden strange feeling it might be better to interview Mr. Wolf by phone, but before I could mention it, I heard the dog—directly above us at the top of the stairs.

She was a sleek young Doberman who looked as if she'd be very nice once she got to know you. Pinkie, on the other hand, was holding an Uzi, and wouldn't have looked that friendly empty-handed. His nickname, I figured, came from his skin, which appeared to have been inherited from a long line of Irish drunks, and reddened up further by the owner's excesses. He said, "You okay, Mr. Wolf?"

"Yeah. Suah," said the newly elevated butler. "Miss Williams brought friends, that's all. Upstairs, gentlemen, please. Miss Williams, you behind them."

I was mightily disappointed, having hoped to get a better look at the house—I thought it was a Greene and Greene, and I'd never been in one.

"Pinkie, babysit the boys. I'm takin' Miss Williams in here." I glanced in as he opened the door and saw that it was a bedroom. Was the guy a rapist? How had we gotten into this, anyhow? "Come, Lassie," he said, and the Doberman joined him and Sardis.

Pinkie took us into a sort of study across the hall. Good. At least Sardis was close. Neither Wolf nor Pinkie closed any doors. Crusher and I were permitted to hear every word, see every action going on in the other room. The only thing we weren't allowed to do was leave. Pinkie faced us sentry-style, gun at the ready.

"Sit down," said Wolf to Sardis. "Lassie, sit," he said to the dog. Sardis sat on the bed, Wolf in a chair, Lassie at Sardis's knee, close and menacing.

"Nice dog," said Sardis. "Nice doggie-woggie." She put out a hand, as if to pet.

"Stop!" said Wolf. "She won't give a warning growl. She'll just attack. Now tell me—what sort of rare book dealer has a 'business associate' named Crusher?"

Sardis gave a nervous little laugh. "Oh. I can see how you—I never thought—"

Wolf's voice was menacing. "Exactly what are you people trying to pull?"

"Frankly," said Sardis, now sobered, "I don't blame you for being put off when I showed up with two strange men, one of them named Crusher. But I assure you he's a very gentle person. I think it was originally 'Bus-crusher' from some sort of driving miscalculation. He's a pilot now, you see. And is only here because he flew Paul and me down." She shrugged and gave him big innocent eyes. "Honest. We're not trying to pull anything. We're trying to sell you a manuscript."

"Yeah? Where is it?"

"Surely you didn't think I'd bring it."

"Why wouldn't I think that? Seeing as how you said you would. Average honest businesswoman says she'll bring her product, she brings it. How else am I going to know if I want to buy it? But you don't bring the product. Ergo, you don't have it. And you aren't average, and you aren't honest. So, listen—what are you trying to pull?"

"Mr. Wolf, I'm quite sure I didn't say I'd bring the manuscript."

"You've got a short memory, babe. You said it ten days ago—last time we talked. You said if my bid was the highest, you'd get back to me—with the manuscript, so I could examine it. Then you suddenly show up ready to deal this morning—only you've got nothing to deal." He was getting louder with every word, and obviously hotter under the collar. He ended up with "Pinkie! Crusher."

Pinkie moved so fast I hardly saw him, just heard the thwack of the gun across Crusher's chest and saw him reel back. Pinkie took his seat again, silently.

"Miss Williams," said Wolf, "what's your scam?"

"I walked in here in perfect good faith and now you're holding my friends and me prisoner. If you think we're some kind of criminals, why don't you call the police?"

"Pinkie! The other one."

This time both Crusher and I were ready. As Pinkie raised the gun to hit me, Crusher blocked him. I threw him a punch to the stomach and gave him a head in the chest.

He fell backward, Crusher grabbing the gun. But Pinkie wasn't giving in. He held onto the gun, kicking—kicking me over, in fact. As I hit the floor, I looked up to see Wolf coming in the door, Lassie and Sardis at his heels. He spoke fiercely, in German, and suddenly the dog was standing over me snarling. Wolf crossed to Crusher and Pinkie, who were still mixing it up, both holding on to the gun as if to a lifeline. "Crusher! Please observe what my dog is doing. She is trained to kill, and I will give the command unless you let go of the gun—now!"

No sooner did Crusher observe what the dog was doing than Pinkie got the advantage and seized the gun away from him, so I never got to find out whether Crusher would have let me be chewed alive while he proved his manhood. I was just as glad—I figured if it had been me, I would have thought I could have got the gun in time to shoot it, thus saving in the nick of time my much-masticated but still breathing friend. Things looked a lot more immediate when you were the one under imminent fang-attack.

Anyway, Pinkie had the gun, now trained on Crusher. The dog was still babysitting me in her own gentle way. I personally would have said that things looked pretty hopeless, but such a thought apparently never entered the head of the fair Sardis. She leaped upon Wolf's exposed ventral side, locking her legs around him more or less at crotch level, and seizing his head in a great, generous hug. I couldn't see, but I think she must have been pulling one ear with each hand, judging by Wolf's reaction. He had his arms free, but Sardis had him two ways—her heels digging at his crotch, her hands doing God knows what with his ears. He needed both arms to be effective against either hold, and most of his energy just to keep from falling backward.

Pinkie was in a bind. There was no point shooting anyone but Sardis, but he couldn't do that without endangering Wolf. As for Lassie, she couldn't save her master without relaxing her guard on me. Wolf had effectively rendered both bodyguards useless. We were all as immobile as Tom Sawyer's tableaux—all but Sardis and Wolf, that is. Sardis was kicking and squeezing—and trying to get into position to bite. As for Wolf, he was flailing and staggering blindly, which he continued to do until he managed to trip over Lassie, who leaped yelping out of the way, leaving me to catch the full weight of two falling human beings, one of whom was a flesh-and-blood tree trunk.

I got the wind knocked out of me and didn't see what happened next, but as Crusher told it, Pinkie got nervous about all this. So nervous, in fact, he couldn't keep his focus on Crusher, ending up like a spectator at Wimbledon (eyes right, eyes left), which made him vulnerable once more. Crusher simply waited till Pinkie cast one of his incautious glances our way, and rushed him, this time knocking the gun to the floor. Unfortunately, it slid across the room so that neither man could get it, nor could anyone from our party. Lassie, at loose ends for a while, was moved by some sort of doggie logic to resume guard duty—this time on the gun. Crusher and Pinkie, locked together now, rolled over to our side, hitting our pile. As I was still on the bottom of it and still trying to get my breath back, this affected me hardly at all except to cause me to curse my fate. It seemed to have as little effect on Wolf, who lay on me like a leviathan. Sardis, however, popped up as if stuck with a hatpin, looked quickly about the room, found what she was looking for, and called the police. Or at least was in the act of doing so when Wolf heard what she was saying, rolled off me at last, and ripped the phone from the wall.

Before either Sardis or I could move, he spoke again to the dog, who came back, teeth bared. Picking up the gun, Wolf bellowed, "Were you calling the goddam police?"

"You heard me."

"Pinkie! Let him go."

Pinkie and Crusher unhanded each other. Now things looked like this: I was still on the floor, with Sardis standing over me, Lassie subduing us both. Pinkie and Crusher, slightly disheveled, stood to our left. All four humans (Lassie faced the other way) stared at Wolf, who now held the weapon.

Slowly and deliberately, he put it on the chair next to him. "Lassie," he said, "come." As friendly as if she'd just played a rousing round of Frisbee, the dog wriggled over to him, stump shimmying as if it counted. The atmosphere in the room had changed radically. We were no longer six beings bent on bloodshed, but five quiet humans watching a dog drive itself crazy trying to wag a tail it didn't have. And frankly, five of us—if you counted Lassie—were a bit on the baffled side.

"I think," said Wolf, "I might have overreacted. I'm very sorry, Miss Williams. Gentlemen. Will you stay for lunch?"

I was the one who recovered first. "Excuse me," I said, "but did you just ask us to stay for lunch? Does this mean you've finally worked up an appetite threatening and assaulting us?"

Wolf patted his ballast. "I always have an appetite." He looked up. "It means I'm sorry, okay? Pinkie, get us some sherry, will you?"

When the bodyguard had left, no doubt to claim his own sorely needed nip as well, Wolf said, "Look, Miss Williams, you call up about a manuscript, I offer to buy it, I don't hear from you for almost two weeks, then all of a sudden you're here without the manuscript, but with two guys. Count 'em. Two—one real big and the other named Crusher. What was I supposed to think?"

"You thought we were some sort of criminals?"

"You're gettin' warm."

"What changed your mind?"

"You called the cops." He shrugged. "What do you think?"

I said, "Do you usually greet your guests with an attack dog and a semiautomatic weapon?"

"I got things to protect. Listen. We got warm duck salad for lunch. Made with a selection of tender young lettuces. We got Sonoma-Cutrer Chardonnay, maybe some raspberries. What do you say?"

We said yes, of course.

Wolf said, "Sit down, sit down," and we sat. Pinkie brought the sherry and served it as stylishly as the most elegant butler. "When Cynthia gets back, tell her we'll be three more for lunch." Wolf turned back to the three of us, catching me, for one, gulping rather than sipping. "There's a reason I asked you to stay. I want to know who you are and what you're up to."

Sardis looked stunned. "Why, exactly as billed, Mr. Wolf."

"Herb." (The way he said it, it was almost "Hoib.")

"Paul and I are business associates, dealing in rare manuscripts. And Crusher is our friend who was nice enough to fly us down for the day."

"Just how are you and Paul associated?"

"Frankly," I said, "sometimes Sarah's work takes her to the homes of people she doesn't know. She never knows what kind of dog they'll have, for instance. So when she gets nervous, I come along."

"I don't get your game. I offered you almost a million for the manuscript. So I figure if you have it, you'd have brought it. But you didn't, so you haven't got it—like I said before. So what are you doing here? Even to you literary types, a manuscript's not like a puppy—you haven't got to make sure it gets a good home or anything."

I said, "Herb, I'll make a deal with you. We'll give you a couple of answers if you'll give us a couple."

"Done. Why're you here?"

"We get to go first. Do you know a woman named Isami Nakamura?"

"No. Why're you here?"

"Well, actually, we're—uh—"

"Hold it!" He started laughing, lustily, the watermelon he seemed to have swallowed rippling and rocking more like a waterbed. "Hold it, I got it." But he couldn't speak for three or four more sherries—mine, not his. Finally, he said: "You're *looking* for the manuscript, aren't you? You think I've got it."

"Do you?"

"No. My turn again. Why the hell did you think that?"

"Because your name was found in the home of the previous owner—who we think sometimes used the name Sarah Williams." I paused. "But who was strangled to death a few days ago."

"You gotta be kidding."

I shook my head, looking very grave.

"Who was she?"

"Beverly Alexander."

"Who the hell's that?" Good. He'd denied knowing her without my having to ask him about her—I'd saved a question.

"A flight attendant for a small airline called Trans-America."

"Never heard of it. How the hell did she get my name?" He was shaking his head with every evidence of genuine wonderment.

"We were wondering that too."

"It's my turn," said Sardis. "Do you know a Linda McCormick? At the Bancroft Library?"

"The Bancroft Library." He was looking pensive, trying to remember. "Yeah. Sure. The Bancroft Library. She's the gal I talked to."

"About what?"

"My turn, remember? Listen, I'll stop this whole stupid charade and tell you everything I know, if you'll just answer one thing straight: Who the hell are you guys and what are you up to?"

Sardis spoke quickly. "I'm an artist. I mean, I paint." She shrugged, and I knew the pain behind the simple gesture. "But one doesn't make a living from that. So I work part-time for a manuscript dealer—a very important dealer in another state. What we're doing here, frankly, is we're looking for a manuscript we lost."

"It was stolen?"

"I'm afraid so." (At least that part was true.)

Wolf turned to Crusher. "What's your story?"

"I work for Union American National."

"Wait a minute! Donald Wilcox, right? You're a vice-president."

"Have we met somewhere?"

"No, but my brother works with you. Dan Wolf. Know him?"

Crusher nodded.

"He tells stories about you all the time. You're a pilot, right?"

"I think we mentioned that."

"How about you, Paul? Private dick, right?"

"Close."

"Oh, hell, never mind. This *is* a pleasure. Donald Wilcox! Dan says you'd rather fly than eat or sleep."

Crusher looked at me reproachfully.

"Well, all right, then! All right! Now that I know you're legit, I've got a real treat in store for you—and I don't mean the duck salad. But I almost forgot. Just one thing. Do any of you have an I.D.?" Crusher and I pulled out our driver's licenses.

"Sarah," I said, as if I were the hired dick speaking for the client, "wishes to remain incognito." Wolf nodded absently—all he really wanted to know was whether Crusher's first name was really Donald.

"Okay," I said, assuming control now that I was officially the dick on the case, "let's pool our information. Herb, you said you talked to Linda McCormick at the Bancroft Library. May I ask what about?"

"Mark Twain, of course. The Bancroft is the highest authority, and that's where I always go—straight to the top. I wanted the Huck Finn manuscript, so I called them to find out where it was. Linda said part of it was lost, and the rest was in the Buffalo Library, which probably wouldn't sell it no matter what I offered. I said everybody had their price, and I'd send her a case of champagne when I got it."

"However," I said, "they wouldn't sell, I take it."

"They got their price—everybody does. But they weren't ready to negotiate. So I put the word out I wanted something really special—not anything *ordinary*—but something really *hot* in the Mark Twain line."

"Put the word out to whom?"

"I got agents—lots of them. They work through dealers, I guess. Whoever."

Suddenly I had a brainstorm. "How about Rick Debay?"

"Who's he? A dealer?"

I nodded.

"Never heard of him. But if he's big enough, somebody probably talked to him—I told 'em to make blanket inquiries."

"What did you have in mind, exactly? I mean, after you couldn't get Huck?"

"I didn't know, to tell you the truth. But—you're not going to believe this—I wasn't surprised when that 'lost' manuscript turned up. Not at all."

"You weren't?"

"I'll tell you something, Paul. You do what I do, you find out a lot of things—one of them's that everyone's got his price and another's this: an awful lot of 'lost' things aren't missing. They're somewhere. And they turn up eventually, if you know how to ask. You know what I mean?"

"Not exactly. I don't even know what you do. I thought you were a movie producer."

"Oh, that. That's like Sarah working for that dealer. Sure, I make movies—a man's got to live, right? But that's not what I *do*."

"Do you mind if I ask what exactly it is that you do?"

"Not at all. I'm gonna show you. And I'll tell you something you're not gonna believe. You're not ever going to be the same again."

CHAPTER 14

Wolf grew ever more expansive under the influence of the sherries, of which we had quite a few before his wife had picked their daughter up from gymnastics. (All but Crusher, that is—he was driving.) When at last we staggered down the handsome stairway, he waxed positively sentimental: "You know, you're probably three of the only people who've ever been in this house that can really appreciate it."

"It's wonderful," said Sardis. "A Greene and Greene, isn't it?"

"See? You know your stuff. I restored it from a junkpile."

It looked like a museum and to my mind was about as comfortable. Some say the work of the brothers Greene is the ultimate expression of the American Craftsman movement in architecture, and Wolf's house was a spectacular example—absolutely top of the line. The cavernous living room showed off a lot of handsome dark wood and what looked like the original stained-glass lanterns for which the Greenes were so highly renowned.

Along one wall were tiny-paned casement windows, the

dark wood of the lattice pattern barely letting any light in. Underneath was a built-in window seat. On a far wall was a built-in sideboard. The walls were painted a color I could only call avocado.

"You shoulda seen this place," cried Wolf. "The previous owners did it up French Provincial. Can you beat that? But the contractor must have been sick about it. He just covered the walls with canvas and papered over with some flowered stuff. So when we took the paper off, we could see the original colors."

God! Had the brothers chosen the avocado? It blended beautifully with the dark wood—at night the room was probably sensational—but now it made me feel as if I were inside an uncommonly stifling closet. The fireplace, however, was spectacular ("the original Grueby tiles"). In front of it was an arrangement of Stickley furniture the very sight of which could send you howling to a chiropractor—what passed, in the Craftsman tradition, for an armchair (oh, well, it did have arms), a Morris chair, and facing the two chairs a settle boasting all the graceful abandon and hedonistic comfort of a church pew. Wolf could, of course, have filled it with deep pillows, but that wouldn't have been traditional, and of course he hadn't done it. The two pillows it did have, plus the rug and the long scarf on the library table behind the settle, had been painstakingly reproduced from a Stickley catalogue, Wolf told us.

The dining room, on the other hand, was a surprise, the table and chairs a good deal less severe, more graceful even, than the Stickley stuff. "Greene and Greene," noted the proud owner. "Maybe you didn't know they made furniture."

"I'm starting to figure out," said Crusher, "that if they did, you'd know where to find it."

Wolf actually clapped him on the back. "Crusher! That's my boy!"

Cynthia and Samantha were already seated. I'd half expected Cynthia to have a Mayflower pedigree, which would be recited to us, generation by generation, over the duck salad. She'd be blonde and sturdy, I thought, with the kind of foot-long face they grow in Massachusetts. Maiden name Cunningham. Rosy-cheeked and cheerful.

In fact, she looked like a nice girl from the Central Valley—sturdy, rosy, and cheerful, yes, but brown-haired and unmistakably middle class. Samantha's hair was crinkly, almost wiry, like Wolf's, and pulled back in a ponytail. She was thin and graceful, in a kidlike way, but a little awkward too. She must have been about eight, and seemed pleasant enough for a young person.

Wolf's whole manner changed with his wife and child. The bombast disappeared, the seemingly constant need to dominate. He seemed relaxed—tender, Sardis said later, and it came close to being true.

For several courses, we heard quite a lot about Samantha's gymnastics, Samantha's ballet, Samantha's French, Samantha's summer camp, and Samantha's very special private school. Wolf asked her a lot of questions about her progress (excellent, naturally), which she answered obediently and with a minimum of smugness. When he'd finally had his fill of the world's chief wonder, he put a hand on the back of her head, squeezed as one would a melon, and told her she could be excused. She was out of there like a shot, off no doubt to pull the legs off some beetles or Cabbage Patch Kids. I figured a kid with a dad as pushy as this one had to release tension somehow.

"Isn't she something, though?" asked Papa Dearest. Rhetorically, of course. "You know, I come from a good family. Perfectly good family." Pinkie passed around Cuban cigars. "But we didn't have class." He looked at Crusher. "Oh, sure, Dan works over at Union American, but tell me something—has he got any class?"

Crusher looked mightily uncomfortable, but I couldn't tell if he really thought Dan had no class, or was embarrassed for him on his brother's account.

Wolf didn't wait for an answer. "My daughter's got more class in her little finger than the rest of her family put together. Except for Cynthia, I mean. When she was born, I said to myself, 'I might not have class, but my daughter's going to.' She's going to the best schools, eating the best food, staying at the best hotels, riding in the best cars if I have a goddam thing to say about it. And she's going to be surrounded by class. And beauty. And literature. And things no kid her age ever saw before. Cultural stuff, you know what I mean? The best of everything. The greatest. And it's not so she'll grow up to be president or anything like that. I don't care if she never lifts a finger in her life. I just want her to grow up to know she's the greatest, that's all. Look at this house—it's like a museum. Do you see this in Malibu? Ha! And you don't know the half of it."

Cynthia smiled, a little tightly I thought. "Excuse me, will you?" I got the impression this stuff wasn't exactly new to her.

"You know what's upstairs?"

We shook our heads.

"Another museum. This house, it's a museum in itself, but I got another one—a sweet little gem of a museum. Kind of a museum within a museum, you get me?"

Oh, no. Dear God, not another museum. I'd had enough wax tableaux for a decade.

"You want to know what I do? I'll show you what I do. I'm gonna show you something fewer than a hundred people have ever seen—I'm gonna show you Herb Wolf's Museum of the Greatest. You ready for this?"

It looked like a ballroom, and also a little like a rummage sale. Odd things were hung on the walls. Others were displayed on specially built pedestals. There were photographs, but no paintings. You couldn't say there wasn't art, though. Some of the objects were undoubtedly art—priceless art. And some were old clothes. Like a pair of shoes on a white pedestal.

Our host began the tour with these: "Know whose shoes those were? Ty Cobb's."

"Gosh," said Sardis, obviously trying to figure out what the point was.

"I couldn't get Black Betsy—or at least I haven't got her yet. Know what that is, Miss Williams? That's Babe Ruth's bat, which is currently—temporarily, I like to think—in the Baseball Hall of Fame. But I, Herb Wolf, have Ty Cobb's shoes. Ty Cobb, you see, was the greatest average hitter of all time."

"But—"

"I'm getting to why the shoes. He was an ornery guy, you know what I mean? He used to sharpen his spikes, so they'd hurt when he slid into base and hit somebody. See that?" He turned over one of the shoes.

"Up there—look. That's Frank Lloyd Wright's cape." Next to the cape was a picture of the architect wearing it.

"Here's one of the best pieces I have—just look at it. Recognize it?" It was a stunning piece of Aztec jewelry. "Montezuma's. Not any old Indian's—Montezuma's."

I said: "May I examine it?"

"Sure." He handed it over as casually as if it were a cufflink. I had the same feeling, holding it, that I'd had with the manuscript. Tom Sawyer was right—it was something electric. Or was I nuts? But I couldn't help it, I felt it.

"Recognize it?" asked Wolf.

"It certainly looks like something I've seen before."

"Maybe you get the idea why I keep Pinkie. There's a couple of governments want that thing—and they aren't the only ones. Some of this other stuff's the same—not as famous, maybe, passed from collector to collector, some of it absolutely unknown to the general public—but priceless. Beyond price. You gotta be real discreet buying this kind of stuff. Some of it you have to negotiate, maybe years, with people's estates and heirs, and different museums and things. And sometimes servants, museum guards, people like that—do you get my drift? Everybody has a price."

Crusher stared up at a crummy-looking old jacket. "What's that? It looks like a flight jacket."

"Yeah. It's Amelia Earhart's. See her picture? It's the first one she ever had—made out of patent leather, of all things. It looked too new so she slept in it for three nights to bang it up. She paid twenty dollars for it. I'm not gonna mention what it cost me. See this here? It's de Lesseps's transit—the one he used on the Suez Canal. Do you believe that? You better, baby. It's genuine. And that thing. Look at it."

I picked it up and fondled it. "Very nice. It looks like a bit of scrimshaw."

"It's scrimshaw, all right. From Moby Dick."

"But Moby Dick didn't—"

"Didn't exist. Sure. Right. But Melville based him on a real whale—the one this came from. He used to hold that scrimshaw while he wrote—used to fondle it just like you're doing now, and think of *him* out there."

"Gee."

"I've got stuff you just won't believe—look—George Washington's wooden teeth, Sarah Bernhardt's wooden leg, Lassie's collar—look at that a minute. Kind of an anomaly, huh? You notice I don't have one thing from movies in here. It doesn't belong in a museum of the greatest; it's not culture. But I got a weakness for dogs, and Lassie was the greatest. I named my own dog after her, didn't I? The dog my only daughter plays with. Not Rin Tin Tin. Lassie. There's more books about her. Look—Buffalo Bill's rifle, Galileo's telescope, Martin Luther King's Bible. But you don't see any paintings, do you? Know why? The Mona Lisa's not for sale. Not yet, anyhow. And you don't see a manuscript. Now, I've got something in the next room's going to knock your eyes out, but it's not a manuscript. I want the greatest, that's why. Only the greatest. I want Huck Finn. The greatest American novel."

"You don't like *Moby Dick?*"

"It's not available. I would kind of like something by Faulkner, though. Or Pamela Temby."

"Pamela Temby?"

"Why not Pamela Temby? The best-selling author of all time? Yeah, Pamela Temby. This is no snob museum. This is a museum of greatness."

"Gosh," said Sardis again.

"When I get *Huckleberry Finn,* it's going in a special room. It's only got three things in it. You ready?"

We went through a heavily secured door into a kind of vault. As advertised, it contained three things, each on its own pedestal. Very beautifully displayed were a small knife, a miniature statue, and a golf ball. The statue looked like a tiny replica of Michelangelo's *David*.

"That's right—that's *David*. You got it. The original *David*. That, Miss Williams and Mr. Wilcox and Mr. MacDonald—that is the model Michelangelo used for *David*." He paused and said "*David*" again; kind of whispered it, as if he couldn't say it enough.

"And the knife?"

"Shakespeare's. Shakespeare's quill knife. Shakespeare's! Do you realize he literally couldn't have written without that thing? I'm on the trail of a manuscript, too, but it has to be the right one. I'll get it—these things take time. But for now I have the knife."

"You'd put Huck in here?"

"Absolutely. I think it's that important."

I pointed to the golf ball. "Sam Snead's?"

His expression, his posture, everything about him, positively personified smug. "Alan Shepard's."

"You can't mean—"

"I do. The one he hit on the moon."

"But—that's impossible."

"It isn't. I won't tell you how I got it, or what I had to go through to get it, or how much I had to pay to get it. But I will tell you it isn't impossible. I've got it. Me. Herb Wolf. Touch it if you like."

I did, and, as with the scrimshaw, experienced no thrill of electricity. Perhaps you had to want to believe.

"Did you happen to notice," asked Sardis on the way home, "that he didn't name it Samantha Wolf's Museum of the Greatest?"

"You could hardly miss it, could you? How much of that stuff do you think is genuine?"

"Hardly any. Why?"

"I think most of it is. The Aztec thing I'm pretty sure about—I think I saw it in a museum a few years ago. And I figure he's a pretty canny guy with pretty good sources. Probably most of it comes with a pretty good provenance.

But some of it's such obvious hokum. I can't believe the guy's so vulnerable."

"Say, Crusher," said Sardis, "what's Dan like?"

"Classy guy. Paul, can I ask you something?"

"Fire away."

"Next time it occurs to you to give me advice on how to improve my love life, would you mind keeping it to yourself?"

I'd forgotten to feed Spot before I left and he was cranky. "Any calls, old buddy?"

"Yes, and it was damned annoying—I was contemplating the mind-body problem, but it was uphill work, what with my stomach growling and the damned phone ringing off the hook."

"Okay, okay. Here's some Kitty Queen."

"Too little too late. I think Booker's the one who's been calling, wondering how you're spending his money."

"What makes you think that?"

"You've noticed you're not getting anywhere, haven't you? Why wouldn't it have occurred to him?"

He was really in a mood. Actually, I was eliminating suspects like crazy. Pamela Temby obviously didn't have the manuscript and neither did Herb Wolf—unless, of course, they'd cleverly deceived me.

He'd even lied about the phone ringing off the hook. As a matter of fact, I'd think a growling stomach would improve one's understanding of the mind-body problem and the phone had obviously been no bother at all—only one teeny-tiny little message.

"This is Clarence Jones," said the caller, "from Fulton, Miss'ippi. I'm wonderin' if you're the gentleman placed the ads in the Tupelo *Journal*."

CHAPTER 15

"Mr. Jones? This is Paul McDonald. I placed the ads you saw. Which one are you calling about?"

"Both of 'em, maybe. But I never caught onto that before."

"I beg your pardon?"

"Mr. McDonald, one of them ads said you might have somethin' that belongs to me that was written by Mr. Mark Twain. Now I'm wonderin'—is it some papers that start out sayin' they was written by Mr. Mark Twain?"

"Well, not exactly, but—"

"It ain't them papers?"

"No, it is. I mean, I think so. They don't start exactly that way, that's all. But close enough."

"I thought I remembered 'em startin' that way."

Need I mention how fast my heart was beating? "Now, hang on, Mr. Jones, I might have your papers. That is, I think I might know where they are, if you'll just bear with me here. What can you tell me about them?"

"Well, I'd be mighty surprised if you did have 'em 'cuz I threw 'em away ten years ago. But, see, the thing was, there was two ads, and the other one mentioned Mr. Lemon. That was the funny part. See, really, it was Mr. Lemon threw 'em away."

"Edwin Lemon. Yes. I advertised about his whereabouts."

"He ain't been around here in the same ten years. Left town right after I brought him the papers. But I never connected it up, see. Your ads got me to thinkin'."

"Mr. Jones, I'm getting mixed up. Maybe we could start at the beginning."

"Well, see, I'm out of work again. I was looking through the classifieds like usual, and I don't have too much to do, so gen'ally I get to readin' all the ads, like the personals and everything—keep thinkin' maybe somebody left me an inheritance or somethin'. You know, maybe I'll see one says, 'Clarence Jones, it will be to your advantage to call such-and-such.' I read 'em just kind of idle-like, daydreamin', you know. Then all of a sudden there it was—'I may have something that belongs to you.' 'Cept without my name on it. But it did have Mr. Mark Twain's name. Mr. Mark Twain's the pride of our family, you know. Great-granddaddy used to work for him, back in Connecticut. Wadn't that the place the Yankee was from that he wrote about?"

My stomach was doing more "sommersets" than Peter the cat after Tom gave him the Pain-Killer. "Your great-grandfather worked for Mark Twain?"

"Yessir, he shore did. Used to tell stories about him when I was a boy. Bad-tempered gentleman, Great-granddaddy said. But he could always make you laugh. First he'd jump all over you, then he'd make jokes-like, to kind of apologize."

"Your great-grandfather actually knew Mark Twain?"

"Worked for him nearly two and a half years—then he closed up the house and went off to Europe to live. Him and his whole fam'ly. Suffered what my great-granddaddy always called 'financial perverses.' That used to make Daddy and them laugh so—but Great-granddaddy always said that was what Mr. Sam said—he called him 'Mr. Sam'—and he wasn't gonna say it no different."

"Mr. Jones, about the papers—did he give them to your great-grandfather?"

"No, sir, I don't b'leeve so. Didn't give him nothin', so far's I know, 'cept headaches and maybe one other thing. See, what happened was, when Great-granddaddy lost his job, he decided to come back to Miss'ippi, where he had fam'ly. My granddaddy was just a boy then. But our fam'ly didn't do so good here. Granddaddy growed up, had one job, then another, then my daddy growed up and got a job over at the college."

"Itawamba Junior College?"

"Yessir. He was a janitor over there, till he lost his job. That was about ten years ago, back when I was still in high school. Well, sir, it was mighty cold that winter and we didn't even have no money for firewood. Mama says, 'Clarence, you go chop up some of that old junk out in the back. It ain't no good nohow. May as well burn it.' Well, see, the reason the stuff was out in the back was the place we were livin' wadn't no better than a shed. We'd lost our house—wadn't ours, really, we were renters—but we couldn't afford to pay the rent, so the church found us this little place. Couldn't even fit all the furniture in. And what we had wadn't worth nothin', anyhow. So what we couldn't get in the house we just put in the backyard. And Mama couldn't see no reason to keep it.

"So I was just choppin' away on this beat-up old desk that we used to use for a chest of drawers and I come upon these papers. I looked down, couldn't b'leeve my eyes 'cuz I knew every inch of that piece of furniture—used to keep my underwear and shirts in it—but there was this kind of secret drawer in it. I pulled the papers out real carefully and see what the first one says, about Mr. Mark Twain, you know, and I start thinkin', maybe when they took that house apart back in Connecticut, they got rid of some old junk—maybe give it to the servants. So I go to try to fin' Daddy and I found him all right—dead drunk on the bed.

"Now, I shoulda' left well enough alone, but I wadn't but seventeen. I wake him up and I say, 'Daddy, Daddy, did Mr. Mark Twain ever give Great-granddaddy anything? Like any old furniture, maybe?' And Daddy says, 'What you wake me up 'bout a thing like that for?' and smacks me 'cross the face.

By now I'm too mad and my pride's too hurt to go on with it, so I figure I'll do somethin' else. I knew Mr. Lemon at the college library 'cuz his mama, Miz Veerelle, used to come around, bring us things, try to help out, you know. Everybody knowed Daddy got too drunk to work and there was all us kids and everything.

"See, I figure if these papers was really Mr. Mark Twain's, then maybe they're worth somethin'—least maybe his fam'ly'd like to have 'em back and maybe they'd give us a little reward or somethin' for 'em."

"Wait a minute, Mr. Jones—didn't you read the papers?"

"Just the first page—the first couple of lines, really."

"Tell me something—you were in high school, right? Didn't you ever read *Huckleberry Finn*?"

"No, sir. I mean I heard of it and everything, but I never have been too much of a reader. When I say I was in high school, I mean I was just *barely* in high school. Worked when I could, but, the truth was, I cut class just as much as I didn't. To tell you the truth, I never did graduate. Wished I had, though. Now I got kids of my own and cain't get a job any more than my daddy could, even though I'm a God-fearin' Christian saved by Jesus Christ our Lord and never touch a drop myself. I seen how much damage liquor can do. But why do you ask about *Huckleberry Finn*?"

"Because that's what those papers were."

"Well, Mr. Lemon didn't tell me that—he shoulda known, shouldn't he?"

"You took the papers to Edwin Lemon?"

"Yessir, I did. Told him all about how my great-granddaddy used to work for Mr. Sam and how I found the papers and I showed 'em to him and asked if he thought they might be worth anything."

"What did he say?"

"Why, he laughed. He took 'em and he looked at 'em, real careful-like, and he said, 'Look at 'em. They aren't even typed. Who'd pay anything for a pile of old papers like these?' And he tossed 'em in the nearest garbage can. You know what else? He made it seem like my great-granddaddy never did really work for Mr. Sam—like they were lying about it—I mean, my great-granddaddy and granddaddy and grandmama. Like they made the whole thing up. I tell you, I kinda' left there with my tail between my legs. Then he left and seemed like he plain disappeared off the face of the earth. And I felt glad, you know that? 'Course that was before I accepted Jesus as my savior. Now I'd pray for him, that he was safe. But when I saw those ads, I thought, 'You s'pose maybe they was worth somethin'? S'pose he fished 'em out of that trashcan and took 'em off and sold 'em? Is that what happened, Mr. McDonald?"

"I think it might be, Mr. Jones, but listen, could we say Paul and Clarence?"

"Sho'. Call me Clarence, Paul. I'm not but twenty-seven anyhow. Hardly anybody calls me 'mister' 'cept the kids in my Sunday School class."

"Listen, here's all I know. Lemon called a university here and said he thought he had the manuscript. He said he was on his way to have it authenticated, but he never showed up. However, the manuscript turned up a few days ago."

"No kiddin'! You got it?"

"Well, not exactly. I've seen it, though."

"Oh, I see." He sounded like a broken man. "You want me to pay to get it back."

"Oh, no—nothing like that. Actually, I was hired to return it to its rightful owner—"

"You a private eye?"

"Something like that. Only I don't really have a license. Anyway, the person who hired me thought I'd be a good enough detective to find the rightful owner—and it looks as if I have."

"I don't have to pay nothin' to get it back?"

"Of course not. The only problem is, I'm afraid it's been lost again."

"Tell me somethin'—is that thing worth anything?"

"Quite a bit, I think. Lots of people seem willing to pay for it, anyway."

"Well, how you go 'bout losin' a thing like that?"

"Well, actually, it was stolen."

"Stolen!"

"Clarence, I think I should tell you something—there's a possibility a woman has been killed for that thing."

"You shittin' me?"

"No. I just want you to know that there's big trouble about it."

"Thing must be worth a lot then—how much?"

"Maybe over a hundred thousand dollars." (I didn't want him to get his hopes up too high.) "But there's also the possibility we won't be able to find it again."

"Say, Paul, who's we? Who hired you to find the rightful owner?"

"I can't tell you that. All I can promise is that I'll let you know what happens when it happens."

"I don't mean to sound un-Christian, but how do I know that? Why should I trust you?"

"Good question. You don't know me from anybody. But, listen, I placed the ad, didn't I?"

"Yeah, but now you say you don't have the thing."

"Well, I did then. And if I get it back, and I can verify your story, I'll return it to you. I promise."

"Who's the woman who got killed?"

"I'm sorry. I can't tell you that—we don't really know if that's why she was killed."

"Your story sounds fishy, you know that?"

"But it wouldn't if I had the manuscript and I said, 'Okay, you're the man I'm looking for, it's yours.' Would it?"

"That ain't what you're sayin'."

"Yes, but you have to believe me—when I placed the ad, I thought it was that simple. The manuscript disappeared after that."

"I don't know. Sounds funny."

"I'll call you later, okay?"

"I guess that's the best we can do."

I was in a literal sweat. I'd probably told him too much, but he'd caught me off guard and I felt sorry for him. On the other hand, I should have been more suspicious—he'd laid it on a little thick about the Sunday School class and all. Still, that was the way the born-again really talked. His story sounded plausible and could easily be verified—certainly the parts about his father working at the junior college and Veerelle Lemon befriending the family—maybe even his great-grandfather's tenure at the Hartford house. But even if he were perfectly innocent and genuinely the rightful owner, he could cause me trouble.

Spurred by Spot's fit of temper, I called Booker to give him a report. He pronounced himself pleased with the way things were going and gave me marching orders—check out Mr. Clarence Jones thoroughly, continue looking for the manuscript, and whatever happened, keep his name out of it no matter what. Normally, I don't take well to orders, but since Booker and I were in complete agreement as to what I needed to do I decided not to throw a tantrum.

I took a shower and went up to Sardis's. She was drying her hair and getting ready for dinner: "How about a little *pasta puttanesca*?"

"Great."

"Okay. You get started on it and I'll be there in a minute." That Sardis. Definitely not the sort of woman to wait on you hand and foot.

"I'd be charmed," I said, "if you'll do something for me."

"You mean call Russell Kittrell? I've already got his phone number."

So I chopped peppers, olives, tomatoes and anchovies while she made herself beautiful, then she came in without a word, picked up the phone, dialed it, and asked for Russell Kittrell. She said, "Oh, hello, Mr. Kittrell, this is Sarah Williams calling." Then, looking puzzled, handed me the phone.

Dial tone.

"He hung up on me."

"He hung up on you? Wait a minute. That's got to mean something."

"Yeah. Like maybe he knows Sarah Williams is dead."

"Which could mean only one thing. I'd better give Booker a supplemental report."

"I'll make the salad."

I finished my sauce, putting off hearing what I knew

Booker would say, and gathering my thoughts about it, but not coming to any decision. Finally, when the sauce was simmering, I made the call and filled Booker in.

"This calls for a look-see," he said. "You in?"

I said, "All right then. I'll *go* to hell."

"Burgling," said Sardis over dinner, "isn't exactly in the same class with vanquishing your deformed conscience. If you want to know the truth, I think your attitude about this whole thing's a lot more like Tom's than Huck's."

It was true. The idea of Booker and me breaking into Kittrell's house after some nebulous hidden treasure reminded me of Tom and Huck storming the haunted house. Of course they had very nearly come a cropper there, and that ought to have sobered me, but I was caught up with the whole boyish adventure. In a way, I was just like the latter-day Tom in Virginia City—in the grip of juvenile fantasies. The truth was, as in the case of Isami's apartment (where, come to think of it, *we* had very nearly come a cropper), I knew Booker was going to do it and I just couldn't stand missing out on it. I probably *would* go to hell—or maybe jail—and it would serve me right.

There was another side to all this, though. I brought it up with Sardis: "If you're so disapproving, why take it so easy? I mean, a teeny little reprimand is all I get, not 'I'm sorry, I cannot love a man who's a criminal. Good-bye now and thanks for the memories.'"

"You trying to get rid of me?"

"Just curious."

Sardis took a gulp of wine and blushed, something she didn't do too often. "I guess," she said, "I kind of like the vicarious thrills."

I thought so. That's what I liked about Sardis. Like Huck, she tried to do the right thing, and succeeded more often than I did, but she had a bit of me in her, and a bit of Tom, too. Not to mention a bit of the Old Nick himself. My kind of woman.

Booker had taken Kittrell's address and promised to phone back when he'd cased the place. Which he did, about eight o'clock. "He's gone out, but there might be an alarm system. No problem, though. Half an hour?"

"I'll be the one with the stocking mask."

"Wear a suit."

Kittrell lived on Telegraph Avenue, in a "charming" place, not the sort that went in for security guards, thank God. I stood in front of it, waiting for Booker, but saw only a thin young woman crossing the street, dressed in a power suit and carrying an attaché case. She kept her eyes straight ahead, in the don't-even-think-about-it way of the modern woman, and never even looked my way as she whispered, "Hi, big boy—want a date?"

"Booker!"

"You're so cute when you're dressed up."

He gave me the attaché case, which was suspiciously light, and pulled his familiar bunch of keys from his purse. The gate on the building was an iron one with bars—but no problem if you were Booker. After a couple of misjudgments, he found the right key and we were in like Finn. As we climbed the stairs to the third floor, he pulled something else out of the purse—a small metal device that fit in the palm of his hand. Two wires coming out of it had prongs on the ends, shaped like 'loids. "Modified continuity tester," he said.

"You be lookout. If anyone comes, we start walking."

As he unlocked the door, an ominous barking began on the other side of the door. Booker grinned. "Watchdog. Good. He won't have the infamous infrared heat detectors. The alarm goes off if they sense body heat, so you can't have them if you have pets."

"The only thing is, I forgot to get my rabies shot."

"Relax, okay? When we get in, throw this, and take a giant step over the threshold. And I mean giant, okay?" He handed me a hot dog and went back to work, slipping the modified ends of the continuity tester between door and jamb, then running it up and down until I heard something like a beep. "Ah. I thought so. Kittrell would have an alarm with a continuous circuit."

He marked the place of contact with a pen, put away the

continuity tester, and pulled out a most peculiar device—a very thin 'loid with a wire soldered to each end of it. He slipped it through the jamb at the marked spot. "Okay, take these." He gave me two cliplike devices. "Put them on when I tell you to."

"I hear someone."

"We'll have to be fast."

The footsteps were getting closer. He opened the door, separating what turned out to be the two pieces of the 'loid, keeping one in contact with the door, the other with the jamb. "Clip them. Fast. Then throw the hot dog and go in." I leaped about three feet into a carpeted hall. Quickly, Booker swiveled his infernal device, followed and closed the door. The footsteps were just outside it. A friendly terrier, having polished off his sausage, was happily wagging its tail.

I could see now that there was about a ten-foot wire connecting the two paper-thin pieces of 'loid, the wire having been coiled in his purse when we were in the hall.

"What," I said, "would you have done without me?"

"Shut up and don't move. Open up the attaché case and hand me what's in it."

"How am I supposed to do that without moving?"

"Dammit, McDonald. Don't move your *feet*."

I handed him the thing inside the case. He held it in one hand, pulled a can of carpet cleaner out of his purse with the other, and started moving the device over the floor, like a Geiger counter. Pretty soon it buzzed. Quickly, Booker sprayed the spot underneath with the carpet cleaner. "There. Keep still a minute more. It's about fifty percent luck getting into these places; if you hadn't jumped far enough—or I hadn't—we would have set that thing off."

"What is it?"

"A sensor. A pressure mat, they call it. Not really state-of-the-art, but not bad. There'll probably be one at the entrance to every room, and under every window. This," he pointed to his instrument, "is a miniature metal detector."

"I get it. You spray the carpet cleaner on the spot, which doesn't exert pressure, therefore doesn't set it off, yet leaves a mark so you know not to step there."

"And not only that, can be easily vacuumed up by the owner—I can't stand destroying valuable property. Look at these Oriental rugs—wouldn't want to hurt those, would we?"

"Wait a minute—why doesn't the dog set off the alarm?"

"Easy. These are probably pet pads—specially made with a sixty-pound tolerance."

His divining rod before him, Booker walked through the hallway, marking two other spots at doorways and doling out the occasional hot dog.

"Okay. You can follow me now. But don't step any place I haven't tested."

"Isn't there an easier way? Like cutting off the building's electricity?"

"These systems usually have an alternate power supply. Now, I could disable the box, but believe me, this is easier. Only tricky part's getting in the door. And I kind of enjoy that. After all, I'm in this for the thrills as much as the money."

"Yeah, well, I just wish I had a Kleenex for my sweaty palms."

Without a word, he produced an expensive-looking handkerchief and handed it over.

"Think those people saw us?"

"From a distance, we look like any two young lawyers waiting for our pal Russ to let us in for drinks."

"What if he's gay?"

"What does that have to do with it?"

"A female visitor would be conspicuous."

"McDonald, you don't get this, do you? A disguise doesn't make you invisible—it makes you look like someone other than you."

"Yeah, well, what about me? I look like my own sweet self."

He shrugged. "So don't wear your suit in the lineup."

"Could we get this show on the road?"

"Follow me."

The living room was full of giant sofas and coffee tables, very contemporary, very decorated, fairly ordinary. But over the fireplace hung a Renoir. It was the focus of the room, which, for all its self-conscious with-it-ness, had been planned to show off the painting. A couple of pieces of furniture looked like very fine antiques. On one of the coffee tables was a collection of very beautiful—very old—glass objects. Everything was meticulously in place, every pillow patted to perfection. Booker wrinkled his nose. "Gorgeous painting, but this place is a museum, not an apartment."

"There's a lot of that going around."

Off the living room was a library, which, so help me, was very nearly a carbon copy of Pamela Temby's. I was certainly getting a glimpse of a subculture, and its denizens, for all their differences, had a lot of the same decorating ideas. Even crazy Tom Sawyer was definitely one of the gang. "Let's hope," said Booker, "he hasn't got a safe." Idly, he opened a large volume lying on a table. Inside was no book at all, but a hollow cavity, and inside that was the Huck Finn manuscript.

"I don't believe it—you don't put a thing like this in a thing like that!"

"I guess he doesn't know—maybe he's never been a professional burglar."

"I just don't get it—this guy is security conscious."

"Listen, let's worry about it later. Do you mind if we get out of here?"

"Let's put it in the attaché case—got your gloves on?"

Even through them, I could feel the tingle I always got when I touched that thing. Quickly, I loaded it up, and quickly we got out of there, using Booker's little invention in reverse.

For some reason, I was more nervous than ever—what if Kittrell caught us coming out? By the time we made it to the sidewalk my palms were so sweaty, my hands so shaky, I dropped the attaché case. It flew open, a gust of wind catching five or six pages and flinging them about. A young woman in jeans leaped from a car double-parked in front of the building and raced after them. She gathered up two or three, I gathered up two or three, and Booker looked sour, no doubt cursing himself for ever teaming up with such a pathetic amateur. Sweetly, the woman returned the pages, not even wrinkled. When she was gone, Booker said, "Where's your car?"

"In a lot. Where's yours?"

"Didn't bring it—you can never find parking in this neighborhood. Let's find a bar."

"Are you crazy?"

"I'm nervous about that car back there. Did you see who else was in it?"

"No. I assumed it was lovers kissing good night."

"That woman was awfully quick."

"Okay. So maybe someone is after us. What's the point of going to a bar?"

"To split up, that's all. We'll go in the men's room, put the manuscript in a manila envelope—I just happen to have one—then one of us stays there with it while the other one gets the car, carrying the attaché case. If that one gets mugged, we've still got the goods."

"Brilliant plan except for one thing—you can't go in any men's room in that outfit."

"Oh, right. Well, you can make the switch—stick the envelope in your shirt, then come out and give me the case. It's better that way, anyway."

We went into the Little City, and I followed orders. Coming out of the men's room, I gave my compatriot the ticket for the parking lot, directions, and the case. While he was gone, I ordered a kir—a suitable drink for a stuffed shirt. In fifteen minutes, Booker picked me up.

"All clear?"

"No problem. Let's go to my house and get that damned thing in the safe where it belongs."

"Booker, listen, I'm running out of ideas. Sure, we've got the manuscript and we might even have the owner, but how're we going to prove Kittrell killed Beverly? Which he must have done."

"What do you mean 'we,' big fellow? You're the detective."

We were in the Broadway Tunnel, on the way to Russian Hill. Someone leaned on his horn, the way kids do in tunnels, and I turned around automatically, getting ready to curse him. The car we'd seen in front of Kittrell's, or one a whole lot like it—a dark-colored Pontiac—was right behind us.

"Listen, I might be getting paranoid, and if I am, it's all your fault. But look in your rear-view mirror."

"Yeah, you're paranoid—it's the way you get in this business. But I'll tell you something—somebody's on our tail."

"I knew this was too easy."

CHAPTER 16

"Actually," said Booker, "it's kind of a novelty. In my entire extensive life of crime, I've never had a tail before."

"Well, what do you think we should do?"

"We could go to the nearest police station, but I'm not really dressed for it. What would you say to a high-speed chase?"

"I think I'd prefer the police station."

"Okay. As a last resort. But first let's try to lose 'em."

It was amazing how calm I was. We were just two guys in a Toyota driving through the Broadway Tunnel. Maybe the other car wasn't really following us at all. No need to get excited yet.

Out of the tunnel, Booker continued driving normally to Van Ness, where he turned right, going north. It was a busy street, with lots of lanes to weave in and out of. We proceeded to do that, going quite a bit faster than was safe, and causing consternation among our fellow drivers. The other car did the same. There could be no doubt it was after us. "Hang onto your hat," said Booker.

"I'm hanging."

He screeched around the corner at Bay, but it was no good. The Pontiac was with us. Right onto Laguna, then another right onto Marina Boulevard. "Oh, God, I don't think I should have done this—we'll never lose 'em here."

"Why don't we just go across the bridge? Then we'll have all of Marin County to disappear in."

"I want them off my tail *now.*"

He turned left on Fillmore, right on Beach, left on Mallorca, right on Alhambra, left on Avila, weaving through the melodiously named streets of the quiet Marina District. But there were hardly any cars around—just us and the Pontiac. The Marina felt entirely too vulnerable. My palms were sweating like drink glasses. "Help," said Booker. "Back to civilization."

"The bridge?"

"You talked me into it."

He got on Chestnut, which would lead to Richardson, then to Doyle Drive and across the Golden Gate Bridge.

But the Pontiac got tough on Richardson. We were in the right lane, they were on our left, and they started pushing. It was dark, but I could see them. They looked like Hell's Angels—big, nasty, wearing leather jackets and helmets. Something was funny about their faces.

Their car pulled up ahead, forcing Booker to turn right onto Lyon, which was less than a block long at that point, dead-ending at the Palace of Fine Arts. There was a possible escape route—onto Bay, but it was one-way the wrong way and a car was coming. The Pontiac kept even with us, so we couldn't turn left. We'd been effectively forced off the road. Booker screeched to a halt at the curb, narrowly missing a utility pole. Automatically, each of us opened his door and started running, me gripping the empty attaché case.

We were on the grounds of the Palace of Fine Arts, one of the oddest buildings in the continental United States. It's neither a palace nor, as the name implies, an art museum, though lately it's housed a science museum. It was designed by Bernard Maybeck, for the Panama-Pacific International Exposition of 1915, to resemble a Roman ruin, and subsequently allowed to crumble into a real ruin. However, a civic-minded philanthropist, with the help of the citizens of the city and state, had seen to its restoration and now it once again only resembled a ruin. There are two parts of it—the skinny, crescent-shaped building that encloses the science museum and a theater, and the gaudy, bubble-shaped open rotunda that serves no purpose whatsoever. The whole thing is painted the faded ochre of Rome, and its grounds include a lovely lagoon, replete with waterfowl.

In the daytime, it's a charming curiosity; at night, especially a summer night when the fog is in, it's rather magnificently spooky. It gave me what Huck would have called the fan-tods.

I'd brought the attaché case because that's where the thugs thought the manuscript was. I had some vague idea of distracting them with it but it wasn't until I'd been running mindlessly awhile, past column after towering, spectral column, that it occurred to me to throw it in the lagoon. I'd better do it soon, though—someone was padding behind me.

Chancing a quick glimpse, I saw it was Booker, barefoot, with his skirt bunched up around his thighs. A lumbering hulk was gaining on him, and so was the woman who'd helped me gather the papers. I kept running, through the rotunda, out the other side, turning towards the lagoon. It was close—good. I looked around again—another good. Booker was in no trouble now; even with his skirt, he was putting distance between himself and his pursuers.

The only trouble was, two more were coming straight at me—obviously they'd driven to the far end of the building and run around it to head us off. One was tall and skinny, the other bulky, and now I saw what was wrong with their faces. They wore stocking masks.

It was now or never. I gave the case a mighty heave into the murky water. Without a second's hesitation, the tall skinny guy went in after it. The bulky one with him was running straight at me, intent on blocking. I was close enough to shore that I was going in if I couldn't withstand the block. I might be able to, of course, or I might be able to sidestep it, but under the circumstances it just wasn't worth taking the chance. "Stop," I shouted. "I've got the manuscript."

The skinny guy was coming up toward land now, holding the case aloft and shaking his head. Something flashed in the bulky one's hand—a knife. He stopped running at me and started to circle.

By now, Booker'd caught up and was standing helplessly, holding his skirt up and looking ridiculous. His two pursuers were with us too, and panting.

"Hand it over," said the woman. Her companion held another knife. The one in the water was advancing like the Creature from the Black Lagoon.

I started to unbutton my vest. "Stop," said the woman. "Put your hands over your head."

All of a sudden I remembered something and started to laugh. "But I can't," I said, gasping.

"Shut up!"

I had a true fit of the giggles—nerves, no doubt. "I can't."

She kicked me in the shin. "Shut up, dammit!"

She started to give me a pat search, and it tickled. I kept laughing. I could easily have grabbed her and held her hostage—the two others weren't going to stab me as long as I held her tight against me—but I'd lost all control.

She made the search superficial, only covering the major pockets, as she'd instantly determined the whereabouts of the manuscript. But I guess she still didn't dare let me unbutton my shirt—there might be a gun in there with it—so she started to do it herself. "Mmmm, Baby," I said. "Don't stop there."

I'd turned silly and there was seemingly no stopping me. But she whacked me across the face and that did it. Now I was mad—as mad as I'd been silly before. And she was just a slight little thing. I grabbed her and held her against me, holding her arms so tight she couldn't even flail about. She kicked me in the shin, and that made me mad enough to kick her back. "Ouch!" she squeaked, as if she hadn't been an outlaw very long and didn't yet know the ropes.

I looked around at her compatriots, very pleased with

myself, but there had been a development. The tableau, in my second's inattention, had completely changed. One of the hulks now had Booker in some sort of nasty neck-hold and his knife at Booker's ear, ready to slice. "Paul," said Booker, "I hate to see you treat a lady like that."

I let her go. "I guess I forgot myself." She kicked me once more, for good measure. The hulk with Booker, hearing his voice, ripped off his wig and flung it on the ground.

"Now give me the manuscript," said the woman. "Try anything funny and your friend's a one-eared jack."

"The cheaper the crook," I said, "the gaudier the patter."

"Give it to me!"

"Okay, okay. Just say what you want—everything's cool." Quickly, I fished the manila envelope from its warm nest against my chest. She took it, stepped back to examine it and said "Good."

Then she took the knife from the lug who wasn't holding Booker, took Booker from the other one, and said, "Okay. Get him."

She meant me, I presumed. The other three closed in. I had no place to run and even if I had, it would have meant painful plastic surgery for my young friend. Anyway, none of the three was holding a knife now. Maybe they'd just knock me around a little.

But what they did, rather more clumsily than I'd have thought of three big galoots, was toss me in the lagoon. I was still lamenting the wreck of my only suit when Booker splashed in a couple of feet away.

He came up cursing. "Damn! My last pair of pantyhose!"

The gang of four and their black Pontiac were long gone by the time we got back to the car. Booker was sulky. It hurt his professional pride when things went wrong. Searching, no doubt, for faults in whoever was handy, he said, "McDonald, will you tell me one thing?"

"Anything."

"What the hell struck you funny back there?"

I started laughing again. "Well, there's this scene in *Roughing It* where Mark Twain gets robbed." I was guffawing so hard I could hardly tell it. "The bad guys say, 'Hand out your money!' So he goes to get it out of his pocket and they say, 'Put up your hands. Don't go for a weapon!' And he does, so they say, 'Are you going to hand over the money or not?' And he goes to his pocket and they say—"

He looked disgusted.

"Well, it's great. It goes on about three pages."

"Terrific."

"I guess I didn't tell it right."

"I guess not. That 'cheaper the crook' line was good, though."

"You don't know that one? From *The Maltese Falcon*? See, the line before it, you know, that evokes it—"

"Never mind, McDonald, okay?"

Hearing me come in, Sardis popped down instantly. "You look like—"

"Don't say it. You should have seen the other guy. Come on and I'll tell you about it while I'm in the shower."

"I've got a better idea. It's kind of the wrong season for it, but I have the feeling you could use a hot brandy."

"Wrong season, hell. You know what Mark Twain didn't say."

"You mean, 'The coldest winter I ever spent was a summer in San Francisco'? But everybody knows he did say it."

"Greatly exaggerated. Like reports of his death."

She had the drinks waiting when I came out of the bathroom, and we sipped them while I ran down the evening's activities for her. She was broody about it. "This thing is getting scary."

"You're telling me. Those guys were *big* mothers."

"It sounds as if the woman was in charge."

"That's what it looked like. But she was very young—twenty-fiveish, probably. And I never saw her before."

"She was the only one who didn't wear a stocking mask?"

"Yes."

"That's odd, don't you think?"

"The whole damn thing's odd."

"Well, who do you think they were?"

"Hired thugs, I guess. The question is, who hired them?"

"Kittrell?"

"It could have been. Your call certainly tipped him that something was up. But how did he know we'd burgle his house the second he went out?"

"When you put it that way, he looks like the least likely suspect."

"Who do you see as the others?"

"Wolf, of course. He could have had somebody waiting at the airport to follow us when we got back to town. Temby could have had us watched. Or Tom Sawyer—he may not have as much money as the others, but if he can afford Mark Twain letters, he can probably scrape up the shekels for a few hired thugs. Then there's Rick Debay." She swirled her brandy. "Or maybe Linda McCormick."

"Linda!"

"Look, she knew about Edwin Lemon, and she's been in contact with Herb Wolf and also with you. She knows a whole lot of the story. Maybe she didn't kill Beverly, but she might damn well have taken it into her head to go after the manuscript."

"But where would Linda get thugs?"

"You don't know anything about her—maybe she's a motorcycle mama in her private life."

"Oh, God. I can't take it. I need oblivion."

Instead I got a knock at the door. If I'd thought I couldn't take it before, I didn't know the half of it: it was Blick.

He said, "Hello, Asshole. Sorry, Miss Kincannon, I didn't see you."

"Come in, scumbag. What's on your mind? If you'll forgive my taking liberties with the language."

"I got kind of an interesting call tonight, McDonald. Mind if I sit down?"

Sardis and I had been lounging on the bed. Obviously a more formal arrangement was called for. I got chairs from the dining room for all three of us. So there we were, sitting in three stiff chairs, in a kind of triangle, up close because the bed took up most of the room, Sardis and me in robes, Blick in a rumpled suit. A revoltingly cozy little scene.

"This young dick answers the phone tonight and it's some

crazy guy, says he's from Mississippi. Says there's been a murder involving a manuscript of some sort. A woman's been killed for it, he says he heard—doesn't know where, only knows the area code—415—so he calls San Francisco because the phone company says that's what '415' is. 'Course it's also Oakland, and also Marin and the Peninsula, but the guy calls us first. Can't blame him, can you?"

I didn't dignify it with an answer.

"Well, the dick thinks it's a nut call, but then the guy mentions a name he knew I knew, and he turns the call over to me. Guess whose name it was, douchebag?"

I was about to say "Pudd'nhead Wilson," but suddenly I was just too damn tired to spar with the ape. Somehow, I had to get him out of my house so I could go to sleep. But how?

"Mine," I said for openers, hoping to convey the spirit of cooperation and good citizenship.

"Bingo. And as it happens, you just happen to be involved in the murder of a San Francisco woman."

"Okay, listen, Howard. I'll come clean. I'm working for the *Chronicle*."

"Yeah, right. Beverly Alexander was going to give you a story."

"Actually, I may have told a teeny little fib about that. This guy called the *Chronicle* first—the one who called you. Said Beverly had something of his—some crazy story about a manuscript."

"A Mark Twain manuscript."

"Well, how likely is it some guy in Mississippi's really lost a Mark Twain manuscript? See, Joey Bernstein's like your young dick—he thinks the guy's a nut case—only he's having lunch with me that day and he tells me the story and I tell him Mark Twain's a lifelong interest of mine. Well, Joey feels sorry for me, see." Here I tried to look sheepish—the idea being that I was so hard-up that my ex-city editor was trying to find a way to throw me a crumb. "So he asks me to check it out. And that's what I was doing at Beverly's that day. I figured it was probably just coincidence she was killed by a burglar, but you never know. So I've been trying to find some connection between her and this guy."

"Clarence Jones."

"Yeah."

"Did you find it?"

"Do you know if she ever used the name Sarah Williams?"

"What for? She wasn't a criminal—she was a flight attendant. What's this about an a.k.a.?"

"I don't know. Clarence said she did, that's all. Said she was using that name to sell his property."

"To whom?"

"He didn't know."

"So how'd he know what name she was using?"

"I don't know. I didn't think it made sense, either."

Blick looked as if he smelled a slaughterhouse. "Why didn't you tell me about it, asshole?"

Now for the *coup de grace*. "Give me a chance, okay, dicknose? I told *him* to tell you. He called me again tonight before he called your office, I guess. I told him we weren't doing a story—frankly, I think he *is* a nut case—and if he had any information about Beverly's murder, he'd better tell you. I was going to call you in the morning to see if he got you. By the way, he wouldn't leave a phone number. I don't even know how to call the guy."

"You should have told me about him, dammit!"

"Yeah, I know—I'm sorry about that, I really am. But when she was killed, I smelled a story. Only it didn't pan out. I didn't have a story, you didn't have a lead—what was the point?"

"I'm a cop and you ain't, dildo. Jeez. You must think I'm as stupid as you are."

"Listen, I'm really sorry, Howard. I honestly thought there wasn't anything there."

Throwing me one last look of utter disgust, he got up, knocking over his chair in the process, stomped to the door, and slammed it on his way out.

"I guess," said Sardis, "he forgot to bring an arrest warrant."

"You think that's it, do you? You don't think it was that

ironclad story I told him? You don't know him—he's stupid enough to believe it. I better call Joey and get him to cover for me."

I did and he said he would, hardly using the word "asshole" many more times than Blick had. Then there was the question of what to do about Clarence Jones. Nothing, I figured, would do nicely. If he was going to get a few embarrassing inquiries, so be it. Obviously he wouldn't believe a word I told him—he hadn't before—and, in truth, the less he knew the safer he was from harassment, anyway. Besides, he already had God on his side. He'd probably be fine.

Now for the oblivion I craved. Sardis had already made us more drinks and turned on the TV. The eleven o'clock news was nearly over and soon we'd be getting a "Taxi" rerun. It must have been a slow news day. Or maybe it wasn't that—Rebecca Thaxton, the reporter who'd been murdered the day Sardis and I moved, had been an employee of the station, after all. At any rate, they were doing a belated follow story on her murder, saying the police hadn't any leads and asking for information. They were really doing it up nicely, adding on a little obituary tribute, talking about all her past triumphs and previous stories, showing film clips. Suddenly, I was looking at Virginia City. I'd have known it anywhere, perched in the middle of nowhere like it is. A pan down C Street so you could see all the schlocky stores and bars, then Rebecca in front of the *Territorial Enterprise* building, talking to the new owners. She'd done that story—the one about the paper's controversial return to frontier journalism.

"Omigod," said Sardis, "what do you bet she had a nickname?"

CHAPTER 17

Becky. Becky Thaxton. How close could you get to Becky Thatcher? Had she been Tom Sawyer's Becky? She had to have been. Her name was Becky, she'd been to Virginia City, and she was unaccountably dead. Of course, I didn't really know that Tom's Becky had actually been named Becky, but there were too many coincidences to overlook.

Sardis must have thought so too. "I'll go with you," she said. "I want to see that museum."

"He might be dangerous. She's dead, you know."

"Four hands are better than two."

"Not up against a gun, they aren't. She was shot, remember. Repeatedly."

"However, the man you describe is one overcome by remorse if I ever heard of one. I don't think he wants to kill anyone else."

I took a deep breath. "Maybe I ought to call Blick."

"Of course you should. I had no idea you'd look at it so rationally."

"Looking at it's one thing. I'll be damned if I'll turn it over to that ape at this point. Anyway, I've still got the problem of protecting Booker."

"When do we leave?"

We left the next morning, on a commercial flight to Reno—somehow, I just didn't have the heart to involve Crusher again. We told Booker what we were doing, just in case anything happened to us. He urged me to take a gun, so I asked him if he had one I could borrow, knowing full well what the answer would be. "Are you crazy? You get one, you find an opportunity to use it. No way someone in my line has any business anywhere around one."

We rented a car and drove straight to the Bucket of Blood. Tom was already falling-down, commode-hugging drunk, but just shy of blind drunk—right away he noticed Sardis was female. "You remin' me of a girl," he mumbled. "Girl I used to know."

"Becky?"

"Rebecca. She couldn' stand 'Becky.'"

"We've come to talk to you about her."

"Nothin' to talk about. She's dead."

"Could I see the museum?" said Sardis. "I'd love to, really."

"My car's still not workin'."

"It's okay. We've got one."

"You really want to see it?"

"I'd love to."

The old yellow car was still parked in front of the place. I wondered why he didn't get it fixed, but figured he was as broken as it was, and couldn't even manage simple household chores.

Sardis let him give us the museum tour, asking lots of questions, behaving more or less like a kid at a carnival, and seemingly having the time of her life. As he talked, the erudite Tom came back, the one who didn't drop final consonants, and could quote from Mark Twain like a Baptist quotes the Bible. He was starting to sober up, and also starting to warm up to Sardis, two very desirable developments, which she was effecting quite consciously. After the final "The End, Yours Truly," he got morose again. "Tom Sawyer," he said, "this is your life."

"The museum, you mean?"

"That's all there is. I haven't even got a cat to share it with."

Sardis said, "Can we talk now?"

"I guess there's no putting it off."

"I'll make you some coffee."

The coffee was essential. We had to get him sober enough to be coherent. But it was awkward while we waited. What do you talk about with a man you suspect of having killed someone?

In this case, his library. Sardis led him through every book and document in there while the damned water boiled. Finally, we were seated comfortably, each drinking coffee. Sardis was doing so well I kept my mouth shut, mainly.

She was gentle but straightforward. "Tom told me all about the woman you met—your 'Becky.' It was Rebecca Thaxton, wasn't it?"

"You a friend of hers?"

"Just a fan."

"Too bad. I wanted to ask you what she was really like. I realize now I didn't even know. For all I know she was married."

"Did she come to the museum?"

"Yes. On that crazy story about the *Enterprise*. Traipsed all through here with film crews. She was just like Tom's Becky—'a lovely little blue-eyed creature with yellow hair plaited into two long tails.'"

Sardis forgot she was investigating a murder. "She had pigtails?"

"No, of course not. She looked exactly like what she was. But she could have had pigtails. It didn't matter. I just fell for her, that's all."

"Because she looked like your idea of Becky?" Sardis had just entered the confusing world of male fantasies and seemed uneasy there.

"She had the right coloring, but lots of women do—anyway, I'd never particularly looked for a blonde. Or for anybody named Becky. All I wanted was someone who'd live here with me and love my hero. I guess I thought if I ever met a woman like that, we'd fall in love."

"But what about the Fiends? Wouldn't that have been the best place to look for a soulmate?"

He looked very sad. "It's funny. I didn't even think about it then—about women, or finding a wife. I just wanted to live in Virginia City and build this museum. But then when I did, it wasn't enough. It's so lonely here. I guess it finally got to me. Made me a little crazy. Because when I saw her, and heard her talk—she asked intelligent questions, you see—she wasn't a real Mark Twain aficionado—didn't know any more about him than Paul here—but she had a healthy interest, and I knew—I just knew—she could love him. So that would have made her perfect for me. I forgot she had to fall for me first."

"I'm getting a little mixed up. You fell for her because you thought she had a minor interest in Mark Twain?"

I winced. Knowing more about male fantasies than Sardis did, I couldn't have brought myself to ask anything so cruel. We might have a lot of dumb reasons for being attracted to women, but I, at any rate, don't like to have them thrown back at me.

But Tom smiled, for the first time. An ironic smile. "Yeah. When I think about it now, I realize that's all it was. That and the name. I think it was mostly the name. I'd gotten—I don't know, a little nuts, that's all. I wanted a woman so bad I thought about it all the time. But she had to be the right woman—she just had to walk in and I'd know it. So the name, you see, made me superstitious."

"You took it as a sign?"

He smiled again. "Straight from heaven. In which I'd never believed until that moment."

"So you asked her to go out."

"Repeatedly. Sent her flowers, everything. She wanted nothing to do with me. But first, I did an incredibly stupid thing—something worthy of my namesake."

Sardis looked almost unbelievably innocent. "And what was that?"

"I tried to impress her. Remember how Tom used to show off in front of Becky's house? Do handsprings and things? I did something like that."

"I don't understand." Neither did I—had he sprained his back or something?

"I showed her something I shouldn't have—something I'd never shown to another living soul."

"I see." Sardis thought for a moment. She turned around, as if to look out the window, but there wasn't one behind her. "Would you like to tell us what it was?"

"It doesn't matter."

"I think we know. It was Huck Finn, wasn't it? The original manuscript."

He looked excited, even hopeful. "They found it! When she died, it must had been in her house."

"Don't you know? You were there, weren't you?"

"Why . . . no." Both face and voice conveyed bewilderment. And then he put two and two together. "You think I killed her, don't you? For stealing my manuscript."

"Now, take it easy, Tom. We're just trying to find out what did happen. Did Rebecca really steal your manuscript?"

He stood up and began to pace, balling up a fist and beating his other palm with it. "I've thought and thought about it—and I just can't see any other explanation. See, I started drinking heavily after the thing with her. I'd go to the Bucket of Blood every morning, just like I guess you already know. One day I came back and it was gone."

"You don't have an alarm system?"

"Somehow I never thought of it up here. I kept everything locked up, sure, but you could get in if you broke a window." He paused. "Which she did. The manuscript—well, it was under Jim's bed in a locked box. She just took the box." He looked shamefaced. "See, there was no reason to look for it there. The collection is in *here*. And no one knew I had it, except for her. She knew exactly where it was."

For the first time in the interview, I spoke up: "So you went to San Francisco and confronted her."

"No! I mean, yes, I went to San Francisco. But she was dead already. I didn't kill her, damn it!"

Sardis said, very softly, "What about Edwin Lemon?"

He was standing with his back towards us, and now he swung around. "Edwin . . . who's that?" But his face said he knew.

"Tom," said Sardis, "you'll feel a lot better if you tell us about it."

He sat back down and stared at us, his face as long as a horse's, all the fight gone out of him. A tear rolled out of each eye and began to make its unhindered way down his craggy face. And then he doubled over sobbing. We sat in silence until he spoke again.

"I guess I knew I'd tell you as soon as I saw you this morning. I can't live like this any more. There's no point in it. All I do is drink until I don't feel so miserable any more, and then I sober up and I feel miserable again. But I've got to know who I'm talking to. Who are you two, anyway?"

"We're trying to find the manuscript and return it to its rightful owner."

"Did Lemon steal it? He said he found it, but I never did believe him."

"He stole it. We're pretty sure he did, anyhow. What was your connection with him?"

"Met him at library conventions. Didn't know him too well, but he seemed interested in Mark Twain. Not that he knew too much about him, but he liked to talk about him. So we kept in touch a little bit, and last time I saw him I told him I was moving out here. I mean next-to-last time. He just turned up one day, very excited, with that manuscript. Said he was taking it to Cal, but wanted me to see it. Frankly, I think he was so damned excited he just wanted to show it to somebody. But he said he thought I might like to buy it. Said he was going to get it authenticated, then sell it at auction. Wanted me to know about it. I would have given my right leg to get that thing. I don't think you could possibly have any idea how much I wanted it. I couldn't stand the idea of him leaving with it, even though he promised I'd be invited to bid.

"So I talked him into sticking around a couple days. This was before I'd built the museum and I had room for a guest.

All I had in mind, I swear to God, was having that thing in my house for a day or two. Well, I took him all around, to Reno and everything—you know the Washoe County Library? Not exactly a tourist attraction, but it ought to be; looks like an indoor garden. He liked that, of course. And we went to Tahoe and all. Then one night when we were drunk and driving back here, I pulled over at a vista point and we got out to look, and he made a pass at me. So I hit him. Well, like I said, we were drunk, and he hit back. Started screaming something about if I wasn't interested, why was I teasing him? I didn't even know he was gay, or I never would have. But I wasn't thinking that then. All I was thinking was this guy had a hell of a nerve accepting my hospitality and then trying to make me, and then yelling at me. He was a little guy, a lot smaller than me. I guess I hit him too hard; I don't know. His head came down on the pavement—and he died."

For a moment, the remorse was gone, and he tried out on Sardis and me the argument he'd undoubtedly used on himself for the last decade: "I didn't mean to kill him. It was an accident." He looked so clear-eyed and hopeful when he said it, you could almost imagine he believed it.

I hoped he would stay in this strange, detached state—it was probably shock—for a little while longer. "What," I said, "did you do with the body?"

"I came home, got a shovel, drove out to the middle of nowhere and buried him that night. Burned all his clothes and papers, but kept the manuscript."

"And his car," said Sardis. "Why'd you keep that?"

The lemon-yellow Datsun! That's what the old wreck outside was. I'd never even noticed, and all this time I'd been putting Sardis's brilliant deductions down to intuition.

"The car?" said Tom. "I don't know. I guess I didn't know what else to do with it. Seemed safer to keep it than let it be found somewhere."

And it certainly had been—for ten years, at any rate.

"I think we ought to go and talk to the sheriff or whatever you have here—do you feel up to it?"

"May as well—can't very well light out for the Territory." He tried to smile as he said it, but it didn't really work.

It was all going to come out now. With Tom Sawyer arrested, there'd be no way to keep a lid on it any longer. Sardis and I would be questioned and we had to keep Booker's name out of it. Fortunately, I'd already laid the groundwork—albeit unwittingly. I hoped Tom wouldn't take it too hard.

"Listen," I said. "We're not exactly working for the owner of the manuscript. Sardis, to tell you the truth, is here as a friend of mine. And I'm working for the San Francisco *Chronicle*. The owner called us and it sounded like a good story, so we started looking into it."

"Oh."

"Sorry."

"No, I'm glad about it. See, I don't know if you believe me or not, but I really didn't kill Rebecca. Oh, God, that's the last thing I would have done!"

"I know you didn't, Tom." Actually, I was telling the truth. He could have killed Lemon in a way that would let him pretend it was just another boyish adventure—I couldn't believe he didn't know the man was gay and hadn't provoked the pass—but I couldn't see him shooting Rebecca Thaxton over and over again. Call me naïve, but I just didn't think he'd done it.

"I want to tell my story to you. I mean, for publication. Everybody's going to think I killed her. I want to make a public declaration that I didn't."

"I don't think your lawyer would allow it."

"I don't have a lawyer."

"You're going to."

"Look, do me a favor. I've already told you the story. You write it up and read it back to me, and if I like it, you can run it. Lawyer be damned."

"I'll think about it."

It was a hell of a dilemma. It wasn't a newspaper's job to protect an accused murderer if he wanted to give an interview against his lawyer's advice. On the other hand, I wasn't really a reporter any more and frankly didn't want to do anything that would hurt this man. But since I had to pretend to be a reporter to protect Booker, I couldn't see a way out.

"Let's do it now," I said, "before we go."

Tom produced a typewriter and I wrote a story, a sidebar to what would be the main one about Tom's arrest—someone else could do that one. I wrote about Tom Sawyer's life, his passion for Mark Twain, his museum, his chance meeting with Rebecca Thaxton, and my two visits with him. I told how he'd shown Rebecca the manuscript, and how he'd not felt his life was worth living after it was stolen. I omitted any reference to his romantic pursuit of Rebecca.

It wasn't the story he wanted told, but I couldn't help it—I didn't mind writing a yarn that was more or less neutral in tone, but I was damned if I were going to help him lead with his jaw. Finally, he agreed to it. I told him I was going to tip the *Chronicle* about his arrest as soon as Sardis and I had been questioned, but I'd hold the sidebar until Tom talked to his lawyer. I'd get the *Chron* to send a Reno stringer over in a day or two to make sure he still wanted us to run it.

"I'll want to," he said. "It kind of makes me sound like a character, doesn't it?"

CHAPTER 18

"Joey? You know that manuscript story? It's breaking."

"Yeah?"

"They just arrested a guy named Tom Sawyer."

"McDonald, remember what a deadline is? I got no time for practical jokes."

"If anybody asks, I'm working for you, okay?"

"I thought I already said okay."

"Well, just in case—here's what happened. I went to see this guy and he confessed to a ten-year-old murder. That's when he got the manuscript. Kind of made himself the heir. So naturally I heard his confession, I had to turn him in. But I needed an excuse for being there in the first place, so I just said I was working for you."

"Feel free, pal. Any old time. Especially if you get caught robbing a bank or something—just say Joey sent you."

"Listen, I'm telling you—this is a monster. We're talking the original manuscript of *Huckleberry Finn*."

"So you said before. Did it turn up yet? Then we got a story."

"Joey, will you listen? This guy killed another guy for it and hid it for ten years. It was stolen from him shortly after he showed it to the one person besides him who ever saw it."

"Who was that?"

"I thought you'd never ask."

"Jeez, McDonald, don't tell me it was you. There's a limit to how much I can cover for you."

"Not me. Rebecca Thaxton."

"Suddenly I get the impression this is actually a news tip."

"You'll want to call up to Virginia City. That's in Storey County, Nevada. And don't say I never did you any favors."

"Hey, wait, McDonald—you want to write it?"

"Hell, no—I'm out of that slimy business."

"How about a sidebar?"

"How much?"

"Two hundred."

"Come on. I get upwards of that for one of my novels."

"I'll get back to you, okay? Let me assess this thing."

"Okay. Just remember—the whole thing started with a *Chronicle* investigation. When Clarence Jones called."

"Oh, yeah, the Mississippi guy. The only thing is, he'll deny it—due to the fact that he *didn't* call."

"So what? He can't get hurt. And I can."

"Don't tempt me, McDonald."

"You know you love me."

"I hate to ask this, but are you involved in something shady?"

"Of course not—merely protecting my sources."

"I thought you were out of this slimy business."

"Technically, yes, but I've got ink in my veins."

"I'll be in touch."

Fortunately, I knew someone at Rebecca Thaxton's station—Susanna Flores, producer of a show called "Bay Currents." She hadn't worked directly with Rebecca, but I thought she could help me get what I needed.

Susanna's office was several floors up, and the Embarcadero Freeway was just outside her window—maybe forty feet away at eye level. It always made me slightly dizzy just to visit her, but she was one of my favorite women in San Francisco—short, round, very soft, as smart as six or eight people combined and a fan of mine from my reporting days. She gave me a nice kiss, sat me down, and asked what she could do for me.

"Did you know Rebecca Thaxton?"

"A little bit. Since we weren't on the same show our paths didn't cross much. But I thought she was lovely."

"Me too. I think her murder had something to do with a thing I'm working on."

"Working on how?" Susanna might look soft, but she was still a journalist. She had a way of getting right down to things.

"Unfortunately, that's the dicey part. I'm sort of working for the *Chronicle*."

"Oh."

"But not really. Someone hired me to find something. But I needed a cover story so I said I was working for the *Chronicle*. And then I sort of got roped into doing a free-lance piece that I haven't decided whether to sell them or not. But I probably will, so it will look to everyone as if I really am working for them."

She looked puzzled.

"But I'm really not."

"So you think it would be okay to ask me a few questions concerning Rebecca, because you're not really in competition with us for the story."

"Uh-huh. Besides the piece I may sell, which your guys couldn't get anyway, because I already got it exclusively, I won't do anything else on this. Honest."

"If I can help you, do you think it might lead to solving Rebecca's murder?"

"I most certainly hope so."

"Oh, what the hell—what do you want?"

"A look at her Rolodex."

"The police probably took that."

"Maybe someone copied it first or something—you could make an argument that it's the station's property."

"I'll be right back."

She came back smiling, bearing the thing itself. "Her boss hid it."

"My God—didn't he want the case solved?"

"Oh, he eventually gave the cops a list of the names in it. I don't think it helped, though. You'll notice they didn't solve it."

"Haven't yet." And I started going through it, starting with "A" for Alexander. But Beverly was no more there than Isami, Herb Wolf, Russell Kittrell, or Linda McCormick. Rick Debay was, though, and so was Pamela Temby.

Rebecca had probably interviewed Temby, but I didn't want to risk asking. And, much as I liked Susanna, I certainly wasn't going to give her any ideas about Rick Debay. The Tom Sawyer story—with its mention of the manuscript—would probably already be coming over the wire.

It was after five now, and I didn't know how to get Rick Debay at home. Come to think of it, I wouldn't have known what to ask him. But I had to move fast. Once the story broke, I wouldn't be investigating alone. There was still one suspect I hadn't met—the best one we had—and I'd thought of a way to approach him. I dialed Russ Kittrell.

The voice that answered was so cultured I figured it must be Kittrell's butler.

"Mr. Kittrell, please."

"This is he."

"This is a Mark Twain fan. I'm sorry you lost your manuscript."

"Who are you?"

"I think I might be able to get it back for you."

"Are you the chap who was here the other night, by any chance?"

"Let's just say I heard about it through the grapevine. Would you like to talk about it?"

"As a matter of fact, I rather think I would. Where are you?"

"Your neighborhood."

"Very well. Tosca. How shall I recognize you?"

"I'll be the large bearded one in the corduroy sportcoat."

"I see." He sounded as if that was exactly how he thought a thug would look. "Very well, then. Ten minutes?"

"Splendid."

I don't normally say things like "splendid," not aloud, anyway, but somehow it seemed appropriate. Tosca did not. First of all, I was disappointed not to be asked up to the manor house, and second, I thought he could at least have suggested the lobby of the Clift, even though it was downtown. Tosca was an old North Beach hangout with opera on the jukebox—dark and red and comfortable, rather Italian even, but not really elegant. I guess I just didn't measure up.

Twelve minutes later, I strolled through. The man who hailed me so perfectly matched the telephone voice it was preposterous. He was in his late fifties, I thought, aristocratically thin with iron-gray hair. He could have posed for a brandy ad. Up close, though, the mouth had impatient little lines around it; the eyes looked narrow and snakelike.

I extended my hand. "I'm Joe Harper; the man who called."

"Very cute; like Sarah Williams."

"Oh, yes. Miss Williams. I believe you did business with her?"

"I did. Are you a friend of hers?"

"Not at all."

He looked exasperated. "Then who are you, Mr. Harper?"

"I can't tell you that exactly, but I will tell you I'm afraid I lied on the phone. I don't know where the manuscript is, and wouldn't be inclined to sell it back to you if I did. First of all, it isn't mine and it wasn't Miss Williams's. I represent the real owner. However, in order to get it back for him, I need information."

"And why should I give you any?"

"Because I might be able to help you. I can't get the manuscript for you, but I might be able to get your money back."

"Really? You'd do that for mere information?"

"Yes."

A waitress came and we each ordered an Irish coffee. Odd drink for the time of day, but the setting was right for it.

"The only thing," I said, "is, first I have to know who you gave it to."

He laughed. Laughed long and hard and damned nastily, I thought.

"It's kind of embarrassing," I said, "but I don't get it."

"Tell me more, Mr. Harper. You amuse me."

"Maybe I could just juggle for you or something."

He ignored the sarcasm. "Please. Tell me."

"Very well. At one point it came into my hands—I'm not going to say how, but it did. It was stolen from me and, I believe, sold to you. It's since been stolen from you. In the meantime I've been hired by the original owner to get it back."

"What were you doing with it in the first place—when it so mysteriously 'came into your hands'?"

"I was asked to find out whether it was genuine."

"You're a Clemens scholar, then?"

"Not really. Are you?"

"As a matter of fact I am. I daresay I have one of the largest collections in the world. And I have lots of other things. Things, as a matter of fact, are more or less my life. Things, and music, and literature, and travel. And occasionally women, but to tell you the truth, I prefer things. I have no work, Mr. Harper. Do you?"

"Of course. Until now, I would have said everyone does."

"I've tried work, you see, but it never appealed to me. I prefer to experience beauty. And certain other things."

"Seamy sex, maybe?" The king-of-culture act was pissing me off.

He gave me an acknowledging eyebrow lift. "Sometimes. In my younger days. But it's laughter I meant. Some would say my life, full as it is, is austere as well. You think that yourself, don't you?"

"I don't know enough about it."

"You think I'm spiritually dead—a desiccated husk of a human being with no heart and probably no soul."

"Aren't you being a little paranoid?"

"Not really. Everone thinks that. My ex-wives; my children; all the nice ladies who ask me to parties to amuse their guests with my ready, if biting, wit."

"Actually, I don't know about your soul, but I haven't seen the wit yet."

"As a matter of fact you won't. For the moment, you are the wedding guest and I am the ancient mariner. I don't talk seriously to many people—I rarely want to—but you're a perfect stranger and not, unless I'm one, a fool. I'm feeling melancholy tonight—and so I shall talk to you."

"Why melancholy?"

"Because that manuscript brought me the first real happiness I've had in twenty years. Since I bought a certain painting."

I was pretty sure I knew the one he meant.

"I loved it so much I kept it on my library table, to read whenever I took a notion. It made me *happy*, Mr. Harper; it made me laugh."

"So would a $16.95 edition of it."

"If only I had had the sense to put it in the safe."

"Why didn't you? I mean, I know you're a collector, but if you wanted to read Huck, why did it have to be the original? I'd think a serious collector would be careful to touch the pages as little as possible."

"Most would, and ordinarily so would I. But I picked up the first page of that thing and something strange happened. I realized that, touching the pages he touched, I felt close to the author—with whom I identify quite strongly. He, too, was a pathetic and bitter old fool in the end."

"You're not quite that."

"It's what I'm becoming. Don't you agree?"

I merely raised an eyebrow. I agreed so heartily I was starting to feel sorry for the pompous ass.

"But he wasn't merely that. He left something for us."

"Oh, no. Don't tell me you're a frustrated writer."

He seemed taken aback. "What made you say that?"

"Just a thought."

"The manuscript inspired me, you see. I could feel something happening within myself—"

"How long have you been writing?"

"I've been wanting to all my life, I guess." He shrugged. "There just hasn't been time for it. But it was about to happen. I could feel it."

"And then you lost the manuscript. No wonder you laughed when I said I could get your money back. That's not the point, is it?"

"It's not, but that isn't why I laughed. I laughed because you'd be hard put to get it back."

"Why is that?"

"I didn't pay a penny for the thing."

"No?"

"Shall I tell you the whole story? I'd like to, I think."

"By all means."

"Splendid. Shall we have another drink?"

"By all means."

Somehow I had a feeling the story Kittrell was about to tell wouldn't be the whole one—he'd at least leave out Beverly's murder if he'd done it. But I didn't doubt it would be interesting, and probably inventive.

"As you surmised," he said, "I was offered the manuscript by the woman who called herself Sarah Williams. She phoned and asked me to bid. I did, naturally. She eventually got back to me and asked if I wanted to raise my bid, saying my offer had been topped. I said I thought it was time to see the manuscript. And so she brought me some pages from it."

"You met her?"

"Of course."

"What was she like?"

"Blonde. Pretty. Early thirties. Not dumb. She was very well turned out, and very plausible—reminded me of the sort of woman who works for Sotheby Parke Bernet. At any rate, it wasn't she but the pages that caught my eye. I could say I satisfied myself that they were genuine, but that would be oddly understating the case. In fact, I was convinced of it before I even began my comparisons. As I told you, I'm a very sophisticated collector. The people at the Bancroft Library have pestered me for years to see my collection, which, truth to tell, is rather famous in some circles. For reasons of my own I declined."

I didn't ask what reasons—the man was not only rich and elitist, it was obvious he considered himself the sole member of his particular elite.

"This will undoubtedly mean nothing to you—you may even take me for a superstitious fool—but the minute I touched those pages I knew they were genuine."

I shrugged. "Some kinds of magic really exist."

"I beg your pardon; I'm not talking about magic. Trust me, Mr. Harper, when I tell you I know quite a lot about Mark Twain documents."

"I trust you."

"I knew that I had to have that manuscript. But it wouldn't have been good business to say so. I told her I'd think it over. I asked about the provenance, of course, but she declined to tell me. I used her hesitation to pretend my own hesitation, if you follow."

"I do."

"She refused to give me a phone number, but I knew I'd be hearing from her again. And of course I did. At that time I raised my bid."

"May I ask what it was?"

"As a matter of fact, I don't see why not. It was $950,000. I'd have gone to a million if I'd thought it really necessary, but I never pay more than I have to. My offer seemed quite fair, frankly. I'm not sure the thing is really worth more than half a million, but you see, I had to have it."

"In the end, I guess that's how the value of anything is determined."

"Indeed. But after making my offer I didn't hear from her for quite a few days. And when I did, it was by letter. Or note, actually—a note in my mailbox. It asked for $100,000 in cash and the rest in bearer bonds. It gave me two days to get the money together and set a date and time to be at a certain bank. There, it said, I would find the manuscript in a safe-deposit box. I would be free to examine it to my satisfaction, and I would leave the money there. The key to the box was included in the envelope with the note."

"It seems an odd way of making the transfer."

"I thought so at the time, and to tell the truth I didn't much care for it. I didn't know the woman and didn't know where to find her if something went wrong. But I wanted the manuscript, Mr. Harper. If I were going to get it, I'd have to play by her rules. Therefore, I arrived at the bank in good faith, money in hand. But the manuscript wasn't there."

"Really!"

"Only half of it was. And there was another key and another note. The note said to leave half the money—half the cash and half the bearer bonds—and to go to a second bank where I would find the other half of the manuscript and leave the rest of the money. Need I tell you, Mr. Harper, how furious I was?"

It was a good thing he had, because the thing seemed reasonable enough to me. The rich, I remembered, simply aren't like the rest of us. "I can imagine," I said.

"Really! Men don't play games like that—certainly not businessmen. But I was dealing with a woman and apparently one who didn't know the first thing about integrity. She had brought my good faith into question. I saw what she intended, of course—to make sure the money was there before she put the rest of the manuscript in the second box. Really!" he said again. "Why not simply meet with me and make the exchange?"

I thought I had an idea, but I kept my mouth shut; I didn't want him to lose the thread.

"As a matter of fact, I determined to make her do that. I took the half-manuscript, kept the money, and left a note suggesting she meet me at the second bank if she still wanted to make the deal."

"Wasn't that risky?"

"Not at all. I had half the manuscript and all the money."

"I see your point." I could also see what a manipulative bastard he was; I'd known people like him before, and I hadn't much cared for them either. However, they always seemed to do well in business. A shame he hadn't opted for a career as a robber baron—but I guessed he didn't need the money enough to make it worth the effort.

"I drove to the second bank and opened the second box, just in case I'd misjudged her and it was actually there. It wasn't, of course. However, there was one little surprise—two, actually. Another key and another note, directing me to a third bank. And then I understood what she was really doing. The manuscript was already there. If she hadn't found the money in the first box, she'd have time to remove it from the third one while I was on a wild-goose chase to the second. But she'd made a very big mistake in her choice of banks. It wouldn't be entirely inaccurate to say I more or less own the third one. In a manner of speaking. It took only a simple phone call to have the manuscript removed."

"But that's got to be illegal!"

He shrugged.

"Do banks even keep keys to people's boxes?"

"Certainly not—but they have locksmiths on the payroll. Some people don't pay their rent, you know."

"So you stiffed her."

"I'm afraid it came to that. Of course, I still had to go to the bank and pick up my package. She could have waited for me there and demanded her money if she chose. I would hardly have made a scene, merely administered a severe tongue-blistering. However," he said, spreading his hands, "she chose not to. And so, as it turned out, yes. I stiffed her." He looked utterly delighted with himself.

"I guess," I said, "that's how the rich get richer."

"Of course." Canary feathers fairly fell out of his mouth. "However." He sighed. "Apparently, Miss Williams is not without resources. As you heard, somehow or other, she's apparently reclaimed her property. Or perhaps some other interested party has jumped into the fray."

"Did anyone know you had the manuscript?"

"Of course not. Only the pseudonymous Miss Williams. Who, I'm forced to conclude, is a practicing member of the criminal class."

"A shame the sorts of people who prey on honest businessmen."

CHAPTER 19

Afterward, I went to Little Joe's for some food to get rid of the cloying taste of the Irish coffee—not to mention the taste of Kittrell. There were two ways of assessing him—either he was a crook, or he'd told that preposterous story to cover up the fact that he was a murderer. Perhaps he didn't have $950,000 lying around but he'd wanted the manuscript as much as he said he did. And he simply killed Beverly Alexander to get it. Had he killed Rebecca Thaxton too? Were she and Beverly playing the game together?

His story made no sense at all. But if it was a lie, it must mean he'd burglarized my house as well, and I couldn't see a man like him stooping to burglary—actually I could see him stooping, I just didn't think he could pull it off.

There was one thing that argued his story was true—the fact that he'd told it to me. When I left him, he'd looked at me steely-eyed and said: "You're wondering, I suppose, why I told you all this."

"I thought you were the ancient mariner."

"And you're quite as anonymous as the wedding guest.

The fact is, I don't know who you are, Mr. Harper, or how you really fit into this."

"I told you."

"Of course. But rather sketchily, wouldn't you say? I just want you to know that I'd be happy to leave the door open for negotiations. If you should find the manuscript and that original owner of yours wants to sell, I still have my $950,000. And if he doesn't, I feel sure I could make it an even million. Do you understand me?"

"Perfectly." I wanted to be polite, but I couldn't control my voice. It was as cold and hard and nasty as a knifeblade.

Odd, considering I'd never before been offered a million dollars. I intended to find the manuscript and there was a good chance I would—I had once, already—but I wasn't even tempted. It was worth at least that much never to have to see the Kittrell again.

On the way home, I picked up the early edition of the *Chronicle*, for the story on Tom Sawyer's arrest. It should have been on page one, but a quick perusal showed it hadn't made the paper at all. I phoned Joey the second I got home, not even playing my messages first.

He said: "They're not talking."

"Who's not?"

"Nobody in Nevada, so far as I can see. I sent my best man on it—"

"Debbie's not a man."

"Picky, picky. Anyway, if Debbie couldn't pry their jaws open, no one could. They won't hold out long, though. Someone tipped Debbie they're trying to find the body—what's left of it—and get it identified. In fact, if you want the truth, they think your Tom might be a crock."

"I can see that."

"But she says they're excited as hell and it'll be like Niagara Falls as soon as they're sure they've got a story to give her. Nobody in Storey County ever had their name in a big-city newspaper before."

"That's not the half of it. The networks are going to be on this thing like sand on a beach."

"Okay, okay, McDonald. Three-fifty for the sidebar—if it's worth a damn."

"It's Tom Sawyer's life story, that's all. I could sell it to a magazine for at least seven-fifty."

"Five hundred."

I sighed. It was a bird in the hand. "Done. Just give me Debbie's number in Nevada, okay?"

"What for?"

"I miss her. I want to talk to her."

"You can't kid me, McDonald. You miss reporting."

"Yeah. Like I miss my teenage acne."

What I needed Debbie for was to talk to Tom once she got the story and could get permission—to see if he was still willing, after he talked to a lawyer, to let us run the sidebar. But I wasn't about to tell that to Joey. Even Debbie told me I'd gone soft. But she also promised to phone as soon as she got the go-ahead; she was a little on the soft side herself.

That taken care of, I listened to my messages—Booker had called to say his dad and Isami were back from the Sandwich Islands, and it was music to my ears. If there was one person I needed to talk to, it was Isami.

But it was nearly ten, I'd just driven back from the city, and Spot wanted to discuss the sound of one paw clapping. Since the story hadn't run, I figured I could risk waiting till morning, but it would have to be very early morning. When Isami went to work, she went to New York, and I didn't want to take a chance on missing her.

I arrived at eight A.M., an uncivilized hour by most standards, but Isami couldn't have been nicer. Wrapped in a light-blue robe and rubbing sleep from her eyes, she assured me she wasn't going to work that day—hence not going to New York—and that I'd be very welcome at eleven A.M. or so. I could have gone out for breakfast like a normal person, but maybe she was lying. For all I knew, she'd been Beverly's partner and was giving me what used to be called the slip. So for the next three hours I sat in the Toyota.

By eleven I felt like a human pretzel—a very sleepy one at that, rather desperately in need of a bathroom. And hardly prepared to meet Booker's dad. But apparently he wasn't going to work that day either. He probably felt he had to stick around to make sure his sweetie didn't get bullied by the mysterious stranger.

Isami Wommy had changed into jeans and a pink shirt. Kessler senior was wearing khakis and a polo shirt. They'd been drinking coffee in the kitchen and I would have been a lot happier if they'd asked me to join them there, but they led me into the living room. Which I promptly left to visit the bathroom.

When I returned they were together on the sofa, holding hands, Dad Kessler looking ready to do battle. I sat in a chair across the room, feeling outflanked.

"As I mentioned before," I said, "I work for the *Chronicle.*"

"That's funny," said Kessler. "I called there and they didn't know you."

"You must have talked to someone new. I haven't been on salary there in quite a while—I'm free-lancing now."

"Could I see your press card, please?"

"Free-lancers don't get them, but if you'd like to call the city editor, he'll vouch for me."

"I already talked to him."

"I beg your pardon? You talked to Joey Bernstein?"

"Is that who answers when you get City Desk?"

"Not often. Usually, it's a copyperson."

"Mr. McDonald, watch my lips. They don't know you there."

"But they do. All you have to do is talk to the right person."

Isami appealed to him with helpless almond eyes. "Shall I try them, Jack?"

"Oh, hell, I'll do it."

When he was gone, I tried small talk. "Had you known Beverly long?"

"Jack told me not to comment unless he was present."

Oh, comment, comment, comment! Why did perfectly normal people talk like second-rate politicians around reporters? After an interminable time in which neither of us commented even on the weather, Jack came back.

"Well?"

"Bernstein's in a meeting. I think you'd better go."

Forseeing this might happen, I'd worked up a contingency plan. "Actually, I'm here as a private citizen as much as a reporter. Miss Nakamura indicated this morning she'd be glad to talk to me and if you don't mind, I'd like her to tell me if she wants me to leave."

She stared at Kessler, stricken. She was obviously a girl who couldn't say no, and he'd told her to. Or else she was a good actress.

"My house was burglarized after I came here, and I want to know why."

The almond eyes went almost round. "But I was burglarized too."

Good. I had her attention. "Several times, I hear."

"Three." She spoke in a whisper, as if she still hadn't taken it in.

"McDonald," said Kessler, "why don't you get to the point?"

"Frankly, I do think the burglaries have something in common. I really am working on this damned thing for the *Chronicle*—as you'd know if you'd paid a little more attention to getting information and a little less to trying to be a hero—but I'm also damned mad about the burglary. Your roommate got killed in a burglary, Miss Nakamura. Maybe I would have been killed too, if I'd been home. I don't feel safe in my own house any more and I'm trying to get to the bottom of this."

"With all respect, Mr. McDonald," said Kessler, "that's a job for the police, isn't it?" He was soft-spoken and ingratiating now, apparently trying out some of that psychology he taught.

But I'd given Isami something she could identify with. She said, "Why do you think I can help you?"

"All I want is a list of your roommate's friends."

"But I hardly knew her. We had different schedules and didn't see each other more than a couple of times a week. I only knew her boyfriend. Ex-boyfriend."

"Well, that's a start. What's his name?"

"Rick something. Duboce? I'm not sure."

There it was—the missing link. "Debay, by any chance?"

"Yes, of course. Rick Debay. Do you know him?"

"We've met once or twice. How well did you know him?"

"I never saw him more than four or five times. But then he broke up with Beverly a few weeks before she died."

"He broke up with her? I mean, it wasn't the other way around?"

"No. He dumped her. She was very depressed about it—until a week or so before . . ." She started to cry. "And then, that last week, she seemed so happy again. I thought she had a new boyfriend. Oh, poor Beverly!" She fell sobbing into Kessler's arms. He smoothed her hair and cooed for about half a century, obviously in an advanced state of rapture. He might be a psych professor, but he seemed to have forgotten about Oedipus.

Oh, hell, I might as well break it up. "Miss Nakamura," I said.

"Can't you see she's under stress?" The prof forgot himself and yelled.

"I can see," I said, "that she's very sad because her roommate died. I think it would help her to talk about it."

"What are you, a psychologist?"

"Mr. Kessler, with all due respect to you, I don't think you have to be one to see that."

"As a matter of fact, I happen to be a psychologist and I can assure you she doesn't need this."

"Frankly, I don't think she needs a daddy, either. She seems a perfectly capable adult to me, and you seem determined to infantilize her for your own gratification. She may be under stress and I can verify that I am, but you seem to be having the time of your life, Jack."

"Who do you think you are?" He stood up, not quite putting up his dukes, but flinging his arms about at any rate.

I lazed back in my chair, nonthreatening as anything. I spoke in the soft, phony manner of a shrink from central casting. "I'm a very nice man and so are you, Jack. Just two nice guys, talking in a sunny living room. Everything's going to be okay, now . . . there's really nothing to . . ."

"Don't you condescend to me, you asshole." He doubled up a fist. Isami, who hadn't caught on that I was baiting him, jumped up and started petting him, convinced, I guess, that he was going off the deep end. "Papa Bear," she said, "sit down, okay? Be Isami Wommy's nice Papa, pretty please?"

Naturally, under the circumstances, that sent him out of his tree. Looking as if it took every bit of his self-control not to turn her over his knee, he kicked over a magazine stand and sat down heavily, turning gradually purple.

I hoped I could finish the interview before he recovered, but he was sulking so energetically it was hard to concentrate. "Miss Nakamura, to your knowledge had Beverly ever been involved in anything illegal?"

"Oh, no. She was from a very good family."

"Did she know any of these people, to your knowledge? Russell Kittrell, Herb Wolf, Pamela Temby?"

"Of course. Everyone knows Pamela Temby."

"Did she know her personally?"

"Not that I know of. But she could have—her family is very influential."

"How about Linda McCormick?"

"I don't think so."

"One last thing—have you seen Rick Debay since Beverly died?"

"Of course not. Oh, wait, yes, I have. At Beverly's funeral." The tears were starting to come back.

"Did you happen to tell him I was here—asking for Beverly?"

"No, I—but I did! We were talking about the investigation and I mentioned you came while Inspector Blick was here, and I thought . . ."—she flushed—"it was mysterious. I mean, the inspector thought . . ."

"It's okay. Blick and I just kid. We're like brothers, really. Nice to have met you, Jack."

CHAPTER 20

I tried to call Booker, but he wasn't home—or more likely, since he was a night worker, wasn't answering. The time had come for a pow-wow, so I left a message inviting him to dinner. Cooking, I thought, would stimulate thought. Next I invited Sardis. And, finally, I went shopping—I was going to make a meal that would have knocked Huck and Tom's socks off.

Just thinking about all the thinking I was soon going to be doing made me so tired I took a nap. I was awakened by a wildly ringing phone—Debbie Hofer calling to say she'd finally got the story and not only that, she'd seen Tom and he still wanted my sidebar to run. I called the *Chronicle* and dictated it. After that, I made the first apple pie of my life. Also, the first biscuits, and decidedly the first fried okra. I rounded out the menu with fried chicken and corn on the cob, though these were not the most challenging parts of the meal—the average three-star chef could probably have done as well.

As it happens, I was not struck by inspiration during my labors. I was quite struck, however, by the unappreciative noises made by my guests. In fact, I nearly struck them. "Gosh," said Sardis, "calorie city."

"*Arrr!*" said Booker. "Okra!"

"Try it, damn it. It tastes like fried oysters."

"Oysters should be eaten raw with a little lemon juice, not fried."

Two pathetic victims of the rampant food fad. But good home cooking will out those California-cuisine snobs ended up pigging out as if they'd never heard of baby vegetables and underdone fish. If Sardis and I had just met, that meal would have won her over for sure, but now she knew me too well.

We washed it all down with a number of beers and in between compliments on my culinary prowess, I brought them up to date. All roads, I said, led to Rick Debay. I figured it this way: Rebecca Thaxton, sensing a story in the manuscript, had researched it by calling a rare-book dealer listed in the phone book as specializing in Mark Twain. Or maybe she'd already known Rick Debay. At any rate, I was sure the fact that his number was in her Rolodex meant she'd consulted him about it. Seeing a great opportunity, Debay had stolen the manuscript, and Beverly Alexander, whom he'd lately dumped, had gotten over her broken heart when he phoned and offered to cut her in if she'd help him sell it.

"Wait a minute," said Sardis. "Why'd he need her? He was already in the best possible position to sell it himself."

"Easy. He's a 'reliable' dealer; he didn't want it to get around he was dealing in stolen property. And there was one other thing. He knew Tom would confront Rebecca about the theft, so he killed her before Tom had a chance. Because if Rebecca found out it was stolen, she'd let the cops know whom she'd told about it and the theft would be easily traced. But even after killing Rebecca, he wasn't completely safe. There was always the possibility that Tom, putting two and two together, would go to the cops—Rick, of course, couldn't know Tom had his own murder to cover up. And if the cops started nosing around, they'd probably do what I did. Go to UC, go to Rick, go to the big collectors, and if anyone had a shred of honesty—Temby, Wolf, or Kittrell, say—he or she would tell the cops Rick had offered it and they'd have him cold."

"But he didn't mind sacrificing Beverly," said Booker. "He didn't mind killing her."

"I hate to think," said Sardis, "what their relationship must have been like."

"I figure he killed her after she made the deal with Kittrell. That's what that charade with the three banks was all about. He wasn't about to take a chance on Kittrell finding out who he was really dealing with."

"Whom," said Booker. "But wait a minute—aren't you leaving something out? He didn't really kill Beverly to keep her quiet, did he? He did it in a rage, when he found out she'd lost the manuscript."

"I think it's safe to say he was going to kill her anyway."

"Thanks, Paul, but it doesn't help, you know." He looked absolutely miserable.

Quickly, I started talking again. "God knows what possessed him to go to her funeral—guilt, maybe. At any rate, he had a stroke of luck—Isami happened to tell him about my coming to the house—she knew my name and the fact that I lived in Oakland, so she must have told him both those things. He came over to have a look, saw me leaving for Mississippi after carefully putting the key under the mat, came in and helped himself. Then he went through the ersatz sale with Kittrell. But Kittrell stiffed him and he had to get the thing back. He went to Kittrell's apartment, intending to burglarize it, but we beat him to it, and then all he had to do was take the booty away from us."

"What about those two heavies he had with him? And the girl? Last thing you need for a burglary." Booker's contempt was so strong it gave me new insight into his profession—he didn't just like burgling, he liked being a really great burglar. It had reached the point that this was the only identity he had.

Hoping to soothe him, I said, "Debay was an amateur. Maybe they were hired pros."

"Maybe. Anyway, I take it you figure Debay's got the manuscript now."

"Uh-huh."

"Then we'll have to take it away from him."

"It's not that simple, Booker. The manuscript's evidence in a murder case. The cops need to find it in Debay's possession."

"McDonald, that thing's got our fingerprints on it."

"I'm pretty sure," I said, "the cops will give you immunity on this one. Your testimony could swing the whole case."

"Oh, bullshit. They'll probably find the gun he used to kill Rebecca. That's all they need and you know it."

"How are they going to know where to look for it?"

"Didn't you tell me the whole Tom Sawyer thing's going to come out in the paper?"

I looked at my watch. "It's after nine. The first edition's probably already on the stands."

"They're going to pull it together from that. Once they know about the manuscript, Rick Debay's name in Rebecca's Rolodex is going to seem a lot more important to them. Damn! And they're probably going to do it tomorrow too. I've had four beers, McDonald—I can't work tonight. You did this on purpose, didn't you? Invited me over here and put me out of commission so you could tie things up your way. You're going to throw me to the dogs, aren't you?"

"Of course not. They're going to question me, sure, but I'll do everything I can to keep your name out of it."

"What do you mean, everything you can? Are you going to finger me or not?"

"I'm certainly not going to 'finger' you, as you so colorfully put it." I may have spoken a little testily, but he was overreacting and it was making me mad.

"Maybe they *will* give me immunity, but I'm going to be a known felon, do you realize that?"

"Well, maybe it's about time you went straight, anyway."

He stood up abruptly. "I've got to get out of here."

I hadn't expected that. Hurt, I blurted, "You can't go—I made apple pie." He slammed the door on "pie."

I felt the way I often do in relationships with women—I was in the middle of a fight and I didn't know why.

Sardis gave me a wry look. "I guess he feels trapped."

"Oh, Jesus, this is *murder*—doesn't anyone get it? Debay killed two women. What am I supposed to do—stand by with my trap shut and *hope* he gets nailed? God, I hope Booker doesn't do anything stupid tonight."

"You mean like hit Rick's shop? He won't. He hasn't cased it and he's half-drunk. And as he's fond of mentioning, he's a pro."

"Honest to God, I had no idea he'd get so upset. Do you see anything I could have done differently?"

She thought about it a minute. "I think you did the right thing. You've given him good service on what he asked you to do and both of you have known all along the thing was evidence in a murder case. In fact, if anything, maybe you should have opted out right at the beginning—when it turned out Beverly had been killed."

"I couldn't do that without betraying Booker."

"Listen, once Tom Sawyer confessed to killing Lemon, it was out of your hands. You had to turn Tom in, and that set in motion the chain of events that Booker's upset about. Friendship's one thing, but as you happened to mention, this is murder we're dealing with. If Booker suffers, it's the consequence of his own actions, not anything you've done."

"I feel really bad about it."

"How about I give you a back rub? Then maybe we could try some of that pie."

Sardis is really a terrific woman—I had to smile at her good intentions, but a back rub wasn't what I needed. "Thanks," I said, "but I think I need to be alone. Would that be okay?"

She smiled back and rose to go. "Sure." She hesitated. "Actually—"

"What?"

"Well, I don't know if I should say this, but there's maybe one other thing—"

"That I should have done, you mean?"

"Shouldn't have."

"Oh, never mind. I know what it is. I had a valuable object in my house and I let it get stolen. I should have given you the damn key in the first place."

"Oh, Paul, don't beat yourself up about it. I knew I

shouldn't have—" She was interrupted by the phone ringing. Sure that it was Booker calling to say he was sorry, all was forgiven, I reached for it. Giving a little wave, Sardis let herself out.

"Paul McDonald," said a female voice, "I am appalled."

"Excuse me?"

"This is Pamela Temby, and I've just gotten back from the city, where I happened to pick up tomorrow's *Chronicle*—someone interviewed me last week, you see, and while I hate to appear overanxious, I suppose you know how it is. But I certainly got more than I bargained for! I need to see you instantly."

"You know something about all this?"

"That's far from the point, darling. I have the manuscript."

Her voice was slightly slurred, but I didn't see how she could have had a drunken delusion about a thing as important as that. If she needed to see me, she was welcome to. I was at Miniseries Manor in ten minutes.

This time Temby was wearing the caftan I'd missed before—the imaginary one I'd thought appropriate for a romance writer. But I'd had in mind something a little more flowing. Temby's, in turquoise silk, skimmed lightly over her opulent attributes. She showed me into her library ("So cozy, don't you think?") and offered strong drink.

Accepting a brandy, I settled into a chair as far away from her as I could get. Even so, I couldn't shut out the fact that she was showing quite a lot of distracting cleavage. She brought out the manuscript. "See? I was telling the truth. When I saw your story, I realized this thing had something to do with that poor girl's death—that nice Rebecca Thaxton. I quite liked her, didn't you?" She shuddered. "And suddenly I couldn't bear to have it in the house any more. I thought perhaps you'd know what to do with it."

"First you send those goons to steal it from me, and now you want to give it back?"

She laughed tipsily. "Goons indeed! What a fine way to describe my daughter and her little friends."

"Your daughter!" Oh, shit, the tall skinny one. No wonder they'd worn stocking masks, and no wonder the only one dressed like a woman had seemed to be the leader. She was the only one who could speak—if the others did, the intimidation the whole thing depended on wouldn't have worked. No wonder they'd seemed to strain a bit when they threw us into the lagoon and no wonder they'd reacted so violently to my sexist remarks—I'd thought they were just big galoots protecting their girlfriend.

"Rosamund looks quite impressive in her leathers, doesn't she? I assure you, however, that stealing the manuscript wasn't my idea. My daughter, you see, has a rather unnatural attachment to me."

"It certainly seems to cut two ways."

"I beg your pardon?"

"On the one hand, she performs criminal acts for you; on the other she rebels to the point of becoming a—'diesel dyke,' I believe, is the phrase she used."

Temby laughed again. "Did she? She does try to be shocking, but she just wants to be noticed, poor girl. Her father deserted us when she was quite young, and I was forced to turn to my pen for a living. I'm afraid I didn't have as much time for her as we both would have wished—and of course her father had none, not being around. I had other husbands, later on, but by that time she was so rebellious none of them ever really took to her. And so attached to me. They were jealous, you see. Actually, I sometimes wonder if she's really gay at heart—I think perhaps she's just using that to keep from having to fall in love with a man and leave me."

"She could move out by herself—or with another woman."

"But she doesn't, you see—that's the point. Anyway, none of her girlfriends ever seem to last. Remember little Sukie? She left almost as soon as she came. I rather think it had something to do with you."

"How's that?"

"Rosamund began watching you then—not very efficiently, I think. Just now and then, whenever the urge hit her. She followed you. I don't think Sukie liked that."

"I don't think I do either. What on earth was she trying to prove?"

She shrugged her well-padded, subtly seductive shoulders. "I think she had some preposterous idea of being able to get her mother's dearest wish for her—and in the end she did."

"You knew about this?"

She looked at me sad-eyed, like a naughty child. "Darling, don't be upset. Would you like another brandy?" She poured one without waiting for an answer. "Of course I didn't know about it. She only told me when she gave me the manuscript. Oh, Paul, she did it so beautifully!" Her face was aglow with parental pride. "She wrapped it up in several bigger boxes, so I wouldn't guess, all in wonderful gold paper, and fresh flowers tied to every single one."

"But did she tell you how she got it? She strong-armed me."

Once again she shrugged. She was quite something when she did that. "Well, darling, you're terribly attractive, but after all I hardly knew you. And it was such a *devoted* thing she did. How could a mother be mad?"

"I guess I'm just being silly. And it was silly of me to swallow that story about some unnamed vandal letting the air out of my tires too. She did it so she could take me home, thereby finding out where I live."

"Oh, my dear—and you a mystery writer. Rethink that one."

"It wasn't Rosamund?"

"Certainly not. Most people would have called AAA, not have to be driven home to get a contraption. Anyway, she could just have followed you. She must be very good at it, since you never noticed her before she wanted you to."

"I saw her at least fifteen minutes before she wanted me to."

"Alicia let the air out of your tires. Rosamund's friend. You see, when Rosamund dropped her for Sukie, she was very hurt. She mistook your car for Sukie's. Rosamund was rather touched by it, actually. When Sukie left, she took Alicia back and Alicia was only too glad to play Robin Hood with her."

I almost gagged at the comparison.

"She's rather large—I expect you saw her that night.

Rosamund seems to like a woman with a certain amount of heft." She gave me a coy look. "What about you, Paul?"

"Me." I felt my neck go hot. "Actually, Pamela, Sardis and I—I mean Sarah and I—are kind of engaged."

"Oh? Rosamund says you're just neighbors."

"To tell you the truth, I'd prefer it if we talked about the manuscript and the reason you invited me over."

"Sweetheart, we are talking about why I invited you here. I want to make love to you."

She walked over to my chair and sank down to the floor at my feet. Firmness was clearly called for. "Pamela, it's a lovely idea, but I'm afraid I have other commitments—"

"Tonight?"

"In life. To Sarah."

"Whose real name is Sardis Kincannon."

"Exactly. There's no reason to keep it secret, anyway. I'm really the one who's working on the manuscript problem. She was kind enough to pose as the seller—Sarah Williams—the day we came to see you. We were trying to find out if you had it."

She put a hand on my knee and looked up at my face. "And what's your interest in all this? Rosamund told me how you got it. If I'd been the one who had it, would you have burglarized me?"

"Look, it was stolen from me in the first place."

"By Rosamund. I'm quite well aware of that."

"I mean before Rosamund stole it. I was merely retrieving my property."

"*Your* property? Darling, aren't you forgetting I'm a *Chronicle* reader? It belonged to some poor man killed by that crazy person a decade ago."

"Pamela, listen, it's too complicated to go into. Why exactly did you want to see me about it?"

"I thought that, since my daughter took it from you, I might give it back to you."

"However, there was something about the newspaper story that made you come to that decision."

"Well, of course. It's evidence in a murder case. I can't very well stand in the way of justice, can I? Besides, the police might come looking for it, and it would be rather embarrassing to be found with it. Anyway, if I were, I'd just have to tell them where Rosamund got it—which would get you in trouble in the end. I thought perhaps I could trust you to do the right thing."

"You mean turn it in to the cops?"

She shrugged again; I wished she wouldn't do that. She reminded me of Simone Signoret in her heyday. "Whatever," she said. "I just want to be rid of it."

I stood up. "I'll gladly take it off your hands."

She was still on the floor, and now she raised herself to a kneeling position, her face almost directly in front of my crotch. She reached up to unzip my pants. I tried to step back, but only ended up flopping down in the chair I'd just vacated.

I felt oddly panicked. "Pamela, listen, we can't, really—"

She sat down in my lap and whispered, "Yes we can, darling." She explored my ear with her tongue.

I tried to stand up, but she was too heavy—I couldn't do it without dumping her on the floor. If brute strength wouldn't work, I'd have to try intimidation. I shouted, "I've got to go, Pamela."

Her face was two inches from mine and her eyes were amused. "You don't want to go without the manuscript, do you?"

I didn't answer.

"All you have to do is fuck me."

CHAPTER 21

All my life I've stayed out of fights by writing angry letters—to companies that cut my credit off, women who treat me badly, bosses of rude clerks, and airlines that overbook. A stupid, childish thing to do, but harmless if you don't mail them. Until a couple of years ago, I mailed them. I'd pull the paper out of the typewriter, frantically address an envelope, ransack my desk for a stamp, and dash down to the mailbox before I changed my mind. I knew it was a dumb thing to do but some inner demon that intermittently got the upper hand over my better judgment made sure I did it before I lost momentum.

That was how I ended up on the library floor with Pamela Temby. I did not make love to her—I did exactly as she asked. Fucked her. Fucked the bejesus out of her. I did it partly to get the manuscript and partly because she was licking my ear and I was going out of my mind with lust and partly because I realized I couldn't stand her. And partly because I was furious about the vampirish way she kept her daughter under her thumb, and partly because I was jealous of her. And absolutely because I went out of my mind for a while. Under the circumstances one could hardly call it rape, but there was an aggressive element in it that was scary and sickening. Afterward, I felt disoriented, as if I'd waked up in a strange place and couldn't remember how I got there.

Pamela was aglow with delight, to all appearances—or possibly it was just the pride of possession and the effects of half a bottle of brandy. But why shouldn't she be delighted? She'd most thoroughly had her way with me. Who'd done what to whom in a physical sense was hardly the point; I felt as much assaulted as assaulter.

It was a little after one when I got home, and Sardis's lights were still on. I thought about going up—I wanted to see her, to tell her what had happened, but I didn't; I knew that was the last place I was going to get any comfort.

Spot was curled up on the dining room table, in the middle of the dirty dishes. The candles I'd lit for dinner were still burning. The matches I'd lit them with were on the floor, along with a napkin, knife, and fork, knocked off by Spot—it was plain dumb luck he hadn't knocked one of the candles over as well. Kicking myself for being so careless—among other things—I started clearing the table, mechanically walking back and forth between the dining room and the kitchen. It suited my mood of disorientation. I was still wandering aimlessly, almost contentedly, when Sardis arrived, unable to sleep and wanting apple pie. She came in chattering guiltily: "Look, I know you want to be alone, but I heard you leave and come back and then I heard you walking around, so I knew you weren't asleep and I thought I could just take the pie back upstairs—I won't stay, really."

"It's okay. I'm glad you came down. Help yourself, I'm just clearing the table."

"What's that?"

It was the box in which Pamela Temby had put the manuscript—an old one of hers, apparently. She'd typed the title on a neat square of white paper and pasted it on: "*Platinum*, by Pamela Temby." Sardis first examined it, then opened it without waiting for an answer. Seeing the contents, she gave me a quizzical look: "I have a feeling hereon hangs a tale."

"How about wine instead of pie? I could use some."

"Okay."

I wiped the now-cleared table, opened a bottle of wine, and got glasses. "That was Temby who called when you left," I said, "telling me she had it. She'd seen the first edition with my story in it, and said she wanted it out of her house."

"So you just went over and she gave it to you? That was it?" There was a slight edge to her voice that made me think she had a pretty good inkling what had happened.

I said, "Not exactly."

"I don't think I want to hear this."

"I'm not sure I want to talk about it." The truth was, I did. And Sardis was the very person I wanted to tell it to; I wanted her to say, 'There, there, dear, it's all right, anyone might have done it.' But she wouldn't. I knew it, but I couldn't stop myself; I threw out some bait: "It was pretty awful."

Sardis fidgeted. "I don't know. Maybe you ought to tell me."

It was now or never. "She made me fuck her for it."

"Oh, Paul! Don't tell me you actually did it."

"Wait a minute. You knew I was going to say that."

"I figured she made a pass at you and *something* happened. I didn't imagine you'd be stupid enough to believe you really did it for the manuscript. That is the most absurd self-deception I've ever heard in my life. You know very well you did it because she's beautiful and she was there and you felt like it. I mean, that's bad enough, considering—considering how I'd feel about it, for instance—but to claim she *made* you fuck her. Give me a break!"

Oh, God. Now it was happening for the second time that night. I was in a fight I didn't understand. Sure, Sardis was bound to be mad, but who knew how she was going to come at it? "Well, she presented it that baldly, to tell you the truth. And she was sitting on my lap and kissing my ear at the time."

"Sitting on your lap! She had to be invited there, didn't

she? Don't tell me she just dropped down out of the heavens onto your knees."

"It was kind of like that, to tell you the truth. First she tried to unzip my pants, and then when I tried to get away I fell down and she pounced."

"Unzip your pants! What kind of woman is she?"

"A perfectly terrible woman. That's what I'm trying to tell you. Do you think I enjoyed it?"

"Oh, my God, I can't stand this!"

She got out of there faster than Booker had. Hearing her feet flying up the stairs, as if she couldn't get far enough, fast enough, I could have cut my tongue out. What the hell did I think I'd been doing, to tell her a thing like that? And yet I was angry at her as well as myself. If we didn't talk about the thing, it was going to remain between us, ugly and festering. Now that she knew about it, that is; which thought brought the guilt back on my head.

I got the manuscript and brought it into the dining room. Tomorrow I'd have to give it up once and for all. I wanted to hold it while I thought about what to do, which had suddenly become the one thing it was tolerable to think about at all.

Rick didn't have it, so the cops weren't going to find it at his place. But I was sure Rick was guilty. Maybe the cops would figure it out and maybe they wouldn't. Oh, hell. I'd come this far; I owed it to Booker to give it one last shot. Slowly, as I fingered the pages of Huck Finn, a plan formed in my head. It was a crazy idea, but it might work. Or maybe I'd think it was stupid in the morning and call the cops. But there was a problem with that, and his name was Booker. On the other hand, was friendship really worth facing down a murderer?

Feeling confused, depressed, and more than a little drunk, I went to bed. At seven I woke up confused, depressed, and hung over. I had coffee and felt no better. I stared at the manuscript and scratched my head. Finally, I went out for a long walk.

After about an hour, my hangover was gone, but I still hadn't come to any decision. However, as I turned onto my street, I saw a sight that made up my mind for me—Howard Blick parked in front of my house. He must have read the paper and come to harass me. Well, goddammit, I wasn't going to sit still for it. If I went to the police, it would be on my own damn terms. I walked back to College Avenue, found a pay phone, called the San Francisco cops, and asked for Blick. On being invited to leave a message, I said: "This is Paul McDonald. I have important information for him, and I thought, since I'm in the neighborhood, I'd drop by. I'm going out of town, but I'll try to call him from the airport."

"Could you hang on a minute, please?"

"Sure."

A minute later: "Inspector Blick went down to get a cup of coffee. He's in the building for sure."

"Okay, I'll be right over."

I waited five minutes, to give Blick time to get out of the neighborhood, then returned for a page from the manuscript, my pocket tape recorder, and my car.

My plan was simple. Using the page as proof I actually had it, I'd offer to sell Debay the manuscript, for resale to Kittrell or sale to one of the others, the deal being a sixty-forty split in my favor. Naturally, he'd want to know why I should get the lion's share and I'd say the extra ten percent was my fee for failing to tell the police he'd killed Beverly Alexander and Rebecca Thaxton. I figured he'd make the deal and try to kill me later—he wouldn't want to do it in his shop, and wouldn't dare do it till he had the entire manuscript. Meanwhile, I'd have our conversation on tape, a tape I'd be perfectly charmed to present to my good friend Inspector Blick.

It was nearly nine now, and the worst of rush hour was over. I was at Debay's shop in less than an hour. I parked at the Union Square Garage and strolled casually toward a morning confrontation with a murderer. The casualness was a front.

In the distance, I saw an ambulance parked in the street, very near Debay's store. As I got closer, it seemed as if it were right in front, but it pulled away before I could be sure.

Jenny Swensen was crying at the cash register. Though

she was the sort who probably cried watching sitcoms, I doubted she did it at work that often. "Jenny, what is it?"

She looked horrified. "Omigod! It's you."

"Did I make that bad an impression?"

"You lied about what you were doing."

"Jenny, did something happen to Rick? Is that what's wrong?"

She pointed at a ladder across the room. "He fell."

"Hurt bad?"

"I don't know. I just don't know." She seemed about to drown in despair. "I don't know what I'm going to do."

"Could I get you anything? A cup of coffee?"

"Just leave, please."

"I wanted to talk to Rick." I went over to the ladder she'd pointed to. "How did he happen to fall?"

"He just fell, that's all. Can't you leave me alone?"

"He must have climbed these ladders a hundred times a week."

"What are you saying?"

"Jenny, did you see my story this morning?"

"What story?"

The *Chronicle* was lying on the counter. She knew perfectly well what story, and I'd begun to think it was damned coincidental Debay had had a serious accident the day it ran.

"The one about Rebecca Thaxton."

She came out from behind the cash register, moving deliberately. "Yes. I saw it."

"Rebecca came in and asked Rick about the manuscript, didn't she? And you overheard them."

She moved fast, unshelving a book and heaving it at me almost before I had time to duck. It missed me, but the second one didn't. It caught me at the corner of the right eye, and I clutched at the ladder to steady myself. But it was too far away, and I reached too eagerly. I went down, dropping the manila envelope in which I'd stashed the manuscript page. Jenny dashed for the back room.

"Paul!" It was Sardis's voice, but I was too groggy to realize she wasn't supposed to be there. She bent down next to me.

Jenny said, "Don't move. Either one of you." She was walking towards us, pointing a gun—the same gun, I figured, that she'd used to kill Rebecca Thaxton. "Who's this?"

Sardis stood up and faced her. "Sardis Kincannon."

"Are you with him?"

"Yes."

"You're with me now. Paul, don't try to follow us. This is what I believe is called a hostage situation."

"You won't get far without money."

"That's my problem." Her white skin was stretched taut across her face.

"I have something you need." I reached for the envelope.

"Keep your hands still."

"Jenny, listen. I've got the Huck Finn manuscript. I'm willing to trade it for Sardis. The only problem is, it's at home."

"Go to hell."

"I was just going to show you a page. It's in the envelope. Let me show you, okay?"

She didn't speak, just stared, mesmerized. I thought I saw a flicker of hope pass over the tragedy mask she called a face, but it might have been a trick of the light. I pulled out the page and held it up. When she didn't react, I started to get up.

"Stop. Where do you live?"

"Oakland."

"Do you have a car?"

"In the garage."

"Okay, let's go. I'm going to keep the gun in my coat pocket. Miss Kincannon and I will link arms. Get up. Walk in front."

The walk was an agony. Surely she wouldn't shoot Sardis on the street. Surely all I had to do was knock her down, and that would be that. I'd have caught a murderer before breakfast, and everybody'd be happy. But she was about as desperate as it was possible to get, and I didn't think she was all that well wrapped to begin with. Maybe she'd shoot

Sardis and then herself before I could stop her. It wasn't the sort of thing you took chances about.

I drove and she sat in the back with Sardis. No one said a word until we were on the bridge, but the silence was getting to me, so I tried a little light conversation. "What I can't understand is why you needed Beverly Alexander."

"Why I needed her?" Jenny sounded surprised. "I'm a public figure. I could hardly call Pamela Temby and offer her a stolen manuscript. Beverly was my front." She seemed glad of a chance to talk. I suppose she was nearly as tense as we were.

"How did you get her into it?"

"Nothing could have been less of a problem. Beverly loved money as much as she hated Rick after he dumped her. That's why she wanted him, you know. For the money. Rick really does quite well for himself."

"I should have thought of that—I'd have realized he probably wouldn't kill two people for money."

"At any rate, Beverly was the single least principled person I knew. So naturally I thought of her."

"Who stole the manuscript? You or her?"

"From Tom Sawyer, or from you? I did. In both cases."

"You must have been with Rick at Beverly's funeral—that's how you found out about me. It's funny—Isami didn't mention it."

"No one notices me. I'm just mousy Jenny Swensen, the perfect murderer when you think about it. Because I'm so ridiculously inconspicuous." I glanced in the rear-view mirror, but couldn't see whether her face was as bitter as her voice.

"So you knew I was the person you'd stolen the manuscript from the first time I walked into the shop. It must have taken a lot of nerve to have lunch with me."

"Not at all. I enjoyed it. I had the advantage, you see. I lied to you about everything you asked, and you didn't suspect me for a moment, did you? Authors simply don't commit burglary."

"Or murder, usually."

"The stupid bitch lost the manuscript!"

"What about Rebecca?"

"Poor Rebecca, who never did anything to anybody. Lovely, pretty, likable, popular, rich little Rebecca whose life was charmed. I didn't have a damned thing against Rebecca."

I remembered what I'd thought the night I heard the news report: *Why destroy her face?*

"But once I started shooting I couldn't stop."

I didn't like the way the conversation was going. If earlier she'd been crying tears of remorse about Rick, she seemed to have put such wimpy emotions behind her. She was talking about killing as if she liked it.

"Goddammit, why couldn't I have had even a little bit of what she had?"

"You know, Jenny," said Sardis, "Paul's an author too."

"A journalist. They get paid regular salaries."

"He only free-lances for the *Chronicle*. For pennies. His real job is writing books. He knows what you've been through."

"And Sardis is an artist," I said. "That's a tough life, too. We know what it's like. Really."

Jenny didn't answer, and I can't imagine what she'd have said if she had. We must have been a pathetic sight, two potential murder victims trying to save each other's lives by convincing our captor we weren't worth envying.

"How," she said at last, "did you get the manuscript back from Kittrell?"

"The same way you got it from me."

"But . . . authors don't commit burglary."

I shrugged.

"Wait a minute—did you take it from Beverly?"

"Of course not. Why would I have gone back to the scene of the crime?"

"You already had it, though. How the hell did you get it?"

"From a news source."

"A news source! That thing's worth a million dollars."

"He's a very principled burglar. Wanted it returned to the rightful owner."

"The rightful owner's dead. What were you going to do with it?"

"Edwin Lemon's dead. As it happens, *he* stole it from a man named Clarence Jones. Who happens to be even poorer than you."

Jenny didn't say another word the rest of the way to Rockridge. I don't think she could stand the idea of someone being more deprived than she was.

"Where's the manuscript?"

Not "nice place" or anything. Just "Where's the manuscript?"

"Under the cat." Spot was on the table again, asleep on what would seem the most uncomfortable thing in the house. Jenny had the gun between two of Sardis's ribs. The two of them walked like Siamese twins into the dining room, me a few steps ahead like a Moslem husband. I removed Spot, revealing Temby's title.

"*Platinum*? What in God's name are you trying to pull?"

I thought it ironic that if *Platinum* really were in the box (and were still unpublished) it would be worth at least as much as Huck—maybe more. I said: "Be patient," and took the lid off.

Jenny let out her breath in relief, but she was still suspicious. "What's it doing in that box?"

"It's kind of a long story."

"Tell it. And put the page back—the one you brought to the bookstore."

I laid the page on top of the pile. "After I took the manuscript from Kittrell, Temby took it from me, but I got it back. That's the short version."

"You stole it from her?"

"She gave it back." Though I tried not to, I sneaked a glance at Sardis and saw that she was smirking. I thought it was nice the gun in her ribs hadn't hurt her sense of humor.

Disappointment flitted briefly on Jenny's face, as she saw a possible market go down the drain.

"Listen to me. I'm not going to kill you unless I have to. There's no reason to now. There was no point shooting Rick. I'd have been arrested almost immediately. My only chance was to try to kill him and make it look like an accident. After

I knocked him off the ladder, I hit him with the gun a few times, but the store was open and I was afraid someone might come in. Usually we don't have many customers that early, but I panicked and didn't do the job right. I'm horribly afraid he's going to live. Do you know what that means? As soon as he regains consciousness, he's going to name his attacker."

"I don't understand," said Sardis. "Why did you want to kill Rick?"

"Because of the newspaper story, you stupid bitch. He was going to read it and put two and two together. He knew I heard Rebecca Thaxton's story when she came in the shop. Eventually, he was going to put that together with Beverly's death. Now, listen to me—I'm trying to save your lives, don't you understand?" Her voice was very shrill. More softly, she said, "My only chance is to get out of the country fast. It doesn't matter that you can identify me, because Rick can too. So what I need now is time. All you have to do is cooperate, all right?"

We both nodded. I wasn't sure I believed her, but it didn't matter—she was certainly going to kill us if we didn't.

"Paul, do you have an extension cord?"

"Several. In a drawer in the kitchen."

"Let's go get them."

We did the diffident twin wives routine again, into the kitchen and back. Jenny said: "Sardis. Tie Paul to that chair. Use square knots, like you learned in Girl Scouts."

Sardis's first attempt was transparently halfhearted. Jenny made her do the job over, but Sardis wasn't strong enough to get the wire tight enough to bite into my wrists and ankles. I still had a little slack. As she was putting on the finishing touches, Jenny bent down and raised her gun.

"Look out!" I called, but not fast enough. Jenny slugged her, then slugged her again. Sardis moaned and closed her eyes. Jenny put the gun on the table, and pulled Sardis's body up into another of the dining-room chairs. Working quickly—hands shaking—she started to tie Sardis with the two remaining extension cords. Sardis's head lolled and her mouth opened. Why the hell had she come to Debay's store that morning anyway?

But I knew why; she was worried about me. I'd gotten her into this and, whatever Jenny said, we had no assurance she wasn't going to shoot us once she had us trussed like pigs. In frustration, I hit my chair against the table. The jolt knocked over a glass of red wine—Sardis's unfinished glass from the night before. A purple splat hit the manuscript.

Horrified, Jenny retrieved her gun with one hand, reached for the wine glass with the other. With one quick stroke, Sardis knocked the gun out of her hand, sending it flying toward the kitchen. Then she was out of the chair, both hands around Jenny's waist, trying to get her down. I didn't know if she'd really been out, or had been acting, but she'd gotten two nasty blows on the head and her strength probably wouldn't last long.

She fell over backward, pulling Jenny down on top of her. On the floor, near the two writhing bodies, I saw the knife and fork Spot had knocked off the night before, along with the matches. I'd forgotten them when Sardis came in. Could I somehow use the fork as a weapon? I had a better idea. With my head, I knocked the manuscript box onto the floor, the momentum taking me with it. I was lying on my right side—and hurting from neck to knees. Sardis and Jenny were rolling back toward the living room. I maneuvered myself to the matches, picked them up, dropped them, found them again. I opened the book, pulled one out, and tried to strike it. Damn! Forgot to turn the book over. My hands were shaking so much I dropped it again.

Jenny was on top of Sardis, but Sardis had a hank of her hair in each hand, pulling hard. Their fighting grunts sounded oddly masculine. I closed my eyes to concentrate better on the task at hand. I got the book, struck a match, and threw it at the box. It went out before it landed. I twisted a little closer and struck another match. I did it again, and again, and kept on doing it. Finally one landed inside the box, where it could catch the dry pages at the bottom of the pile. Mark Twain's manuscript crackled and whooshed into flames.

Jenny tore herself from Sardis and ran for the fire. Simultaneously, Spot, cowering in a corner, was startled by the whoosh into a mad, aimless race on a collision course with Jenny. She tried to swerve, but he was moving too fast. She tripped and fell hard, her hair only inches from the flames. Sardis, kneeling for leverage, pushed the ugly, heavy coffee table on top of her and streaked into the dining room. Jenny started to wriggle out from under the table, and Spot, still under her, fought for his life, clawing at her belly and caterwauling.

Sardis whisked last night's half-empty wine bottle from the table and brought it down with a nasty thunk on Jenny's head. A purple geyser exploded from the open end, sending Rorschach splashes all over the walls. Jenny collapsed, a black bullet speeding finally out from under her towards safety under the bed. Sardis looked around wildly.

"By the kitchen door," I shouted, but already she'd seen the gun and gone to retrieve it. Jenny still lay in a mangled heap.

"For God's sake," I shouted, "put out the fire."

But there was no need. It was starting to die down of its own accord, having consumed every scrap of the manuscript. Wet pages and all. The floor would be scorched, but it wasn't going to catch.

Jenny made no move to get up. She lay under the table and sobbed till the police came.

CHAPTER 22

I cooked for Sardis and pampered her for a few days while the headache went away—petted her, as Huck would say. She said she hadn't been knocked out at all, just play-acting and waiting for an opportunity. As for Rick Debay, he had been hit repeatedly, but he spent only a few days in the hospital. Bludgeoning obviously wasn't Jenny's strong point.

Jenny had acted fast when the story ran—sent her children to their grandparents and made reservations on a flight to Mexico for that afternoon. If Sardis and I hadn't turned up, she'd probably have gotten away. Her arrest rocked the literary world. Joey Bernstein and several magazines offered big bucks for my personal account of the adventure, but I didn't have the heart for it. Also, I was feeling fat after Booker paid up—to make amends for getting mad at me, he even threw in an extra thousand dollars.

Sardis and I resolved our difficulties regarding Pamela Temby as well. Or maybe they resolved themselves as a result of our becoming comrades in arms. She'd waked up feeling depressed and mad at herself, and had taken her tea into the living room to brood. She'd seen me leave for my walk, seen Blick arrive, seen me return and spot him, seen him leave, seen me return and leave, and, in a flash of intuition, had guessed where I was going. She was terrified, and, thinking I was going to be killed, forgot about the fight. She threw on some clothes and drove to Debay's, intending to call the cops if she saw me in there alone with him. But seeing nothing, she came in, walking into my confrontation with Jenny. And things worked out, in a curious way.

I'm still mad about letting Pamela Temby push my buttons, though. I think that's what made it easy for Sardis to forgive me. There's nothing like a little remorse to soften the other guy up. All that petting I did while I was nursing her back to health probably didn't hurt, either. I was with her day and night for a while there, going out only for groceries and one other errand—to get a key to my apartment made for her. Solemnly, she presented me with one to her apartment. Or semi-solemnly, anyway. She said, "With or without this key, I thee bed." I couldn't tell if it was a commitment or some kind of joke.

A few days after Jenny's arrest, when I felt I could handle it, I called Veerelle Lemon and told her I was sorry about her son.

She said, "I've known for a long time he was dead." Her voice said she'd never really accepted it.

"Mrs. Lemon, do you know a man named Clarence Jones?"

"Clarence? Known him since he was born. His mama kept that family together through some of the worst times you ever saw. His daddy worked over at the college a while, but I don't b'leeve he drew a sober breath the last thirty years of his life."

"What kind of man is Clarence?"

"Decent boy. Real decent. Never got too much education, so he kind of has trouble staying in work, but it's not because he doesn't try hard. Nice wife and two kids. Churchgoing family too."

"Do you know if his great-grandfather ever worked for Mark Twain?"

"I never heard that one."

"If Clarence said it, would you be inclined to believe it?"

"I've never known him to lie."

"Did he know your son Edwin?"

"Oh, my Lord, I think I see what you're gettin' at—Edwin took the manuscript from him! That's how he got it in the first place."

"Well, he might have, but I don't know if we'll ever be sure. Did he know Edwin?"

"Why yes, his family knew my family."

"Do you know anyone who might have known Clarence's great-grandfather?"

"You could ask the pastor over at Clarence's church. He'd probably know. And I'm sure he'll vouch for Clarence as well. But can I ask you something? Why are you askin'? I thought that manuscript burned up."

"Well, I was hired to find the rightful owner and I'm still working on it. That's all."

I rounded up a few old-timers who remembered Clarence's great-grandfather's tales about Mr. Mark Twain and then I tried to check his employment through Linda McCormick, but she couldn't find any record of it. Everyone I talked to in Tupelo vouched for Clarence's good character, so I decided to go with oral tradition.

I phoned Russell Kittrell. "This is Paul McDonald."

"A.k.a. Joe Harper. I saw you getting interviewed on the news."

"Good. Then you know I'm a reporter."

"Only too well."

"I need to talk to you."

He sighed. "I guess you better come over."

An invitation to the inner sanctum—his estimation of me must have risen. It was pleasant sitting in that room with the Renoir, sipping Kittrell's excellent wine and committing blackmail. "You know I could be very dangerous to you."

"Are you going to be?"

"I've already done a little homework. I know which bank you 'own,' as I think you put it. The story'd make a very nice follow-up to this whole Huck Finn thing. You're a prominent man—I could see it on page one."

"Somehow I get the idea you aren't quite committed to it."

"I think there might be mitigating circumstances. On the face of it, one would think only a criminal or a sociopath would do what you did. But we've all done things we regret; maybe you're basically a decent person who doesn't deserve to be ruined for one mistake. I was hoping you'd let me in on another side of your character."

"Actually, I have a very generous side. I often like to give grants to struggling artists, musicians"—he waved a hand expansively—"even authors."

"Large grants?"

"Oh, fairly large."

"I was thinking somewhere in the neighborhood of $750,000."

His aristocratic eyebrows shot up. "Were you now?"

"It's less than you would have paid for the manuscript—that is, if you'd been an honest man—and seems quite a bargain when you consider it allows you to keep your reputation, the remainder of your fortune, and your bank free of a nasty investigation."

"It's only your word against mine, you know."

"Nonsense. 'Sarah Williams' at that point was Jenny Swensen. She might be in jail but she can still talk. She'd be only too happy to tell the world how you stiffed her. It would make you look small, Kittrell. Petty and mean. The very things I'm asking you to prove you're not."

"Five hundred thousand."

"Done." I handed him a piece of paper. "Send a cashier's check for that amount to Clarence Jones at this address. Have it there in a week or the story runs."

"Wait a minute. Who the hell is Clarence Jones?"

"A very deserving person, actually. He's a Mark Twain scholar who's conducted a number of interviews with people who knew Clemens intimately. On your tax return you could just say he's the sole grantee of the Russell Kittrell Foundation for Oral History."

"Surely you're not serious."

"I'd send that check Express Mail if I were you. If it's not there a week from today, you're front-page news."

Next I made a call to Tupelo. "Hello, Clarence? Paul McDonald. I guess you heard about the manuscript burning up and everything."

"Hey, Paul! I saw you on TV—tol' all my friends, 'I know that guy.'"

"Well, listen, I'm sorry I couldn't save the book for you, but there's some insurance money coming to you."

"Insurance? You mean that thing was *insured?*"

"In a manner of speaking. You ought to be getting a check within the week."

"Hoo boy, insurance money! You know, I still haven't found a job. Say, how much is it, anyway?"

"Well, I think it'll tide you over awhile."

"Oh, come on, how much?"

"Remember I said the manuscript might be worth more than a hundred thousand dollars? Well, I think the insurance will come to at least that."

"No!"

"I'm pretty sure of it."

"A hundred thousand dollars! Sara Sue—hey, Sara Sue, you hear that?"

He forgot I was on the line, but I heard from him again three days later. "Paul? Is that you? This is Clarence here."

"Oh, hi, Clarence. Did your check come?"

"It shore did. I couldn't b'leeve it. Why didn't you tell me it was gon' be so much money?"

"I wanted you to be surprised."

"Well, I shore was. Two hundred and fifty big ones! Who'da ever thought Clarence and Sara Sue Jones were gon' be so rich?"

"How much did you say?"

"You know how much. You knew all the time. Two hundred and fifty smackeroonies! Wooooeeeeee!"

"Congratulations, Clarence. Don't spend it all in one place."

"Well, I got to tithe, of course. And after that, I'm gon' see me a lawyer, set up foundations for the kids' education and everything. Maybe invest a little, buy Sara Sue a new weddin' ring. She had to pawn her old one, you know."

"That's great, Clarence. Good luck to you."

It should have been a very uplifting phone call, a real boost to the sagging spirit, a happy ending to a tawdry tale of human greed and degradation. Why did it have to remind me that some people are no damn good? I'll tell you why: because some people are no damn good.

The End, Yours Truly Paul McDonald